THE CURE

Michael Mills

This novel is entirely a work of fiction. The names characters and incidents portrayed in it are the work of the author's imagination. Any resemblance to actual persons, living or dead, events or localities is entirely coincidental.

There are numerous quotations throughout the text, most of which, I believe, have some association with, and are pertinent to the particulat section in which they appear. With each one I have made every effort to corroborate the original source. If, however, I have inadvertently misquoted within this text I wish to apologize in advance, and would value any correction that may be necessary.

Order this book online at www.trafford.com/06-2826
or email orders@trafford.com

Most Trafford titles are also available at major online book retailers.

Cover illustrators – Simon and Lydia Cheung

Note for Librarians: A cataloguing record for this book is available from Library and Archives Canada at www.collectionscanada.ca/amicus/index-e.html

ISBN: 978-1-4251-1067-3

We at Trafford believe that it is the responsibility of us all, as both individuals and corporations, to make choices that are environmentally and socially sound. You, in turn, are supporting this responsible conduct each time you purchase a Trafford book, or make use of our publishing services. To find out how you are helping, please visit www.trafford.com/responsiblepublishing.html

Our mission is to efficiently provide the world's finest, most comprehensive book publishing service, enabling every author to experience success. To find out how to publish your book, your way, and have it available worldwide, visit us online at www.trafford.com/10510

www.trafford.com

North America & international
toll-free: 1 888 232 4444 (USA & Canada)
phone: 250 383 6864 ♦ fax: 250 383 6804 ♦ email: info@trafford.com

The United Kingdom & Europe
phone: +44 (0)1865 722 113 ♦ local rate: 0845 230 9601
facsimile: +44 (0)1865 722 868 ♦ email: info.uk@trafford.com

10 9 8 7 6 5 4

For Susan, Simon, Anna, Victoria, Mel, Lydia, Jessica and Ashleigh

CHAPTER ONE

I am well aware that many people find me unbearable;
but Everybody *finds me impossible to ignore*
– Sir Archibald McIndoe

I had been lost, deep in thought, hopelessly wrapped up in the world of sickness, pain, suffering and impossible, demanding relatives; not to mention that peculiarly unique, almost antiseptic smell that haunts the corridors of NHS hospitals.

The shrill, high-pitched ringing tone of the car phone instantly shot me back to reality causing me to swerve, narrowly missing an on-coming delivery van in the process.

"Yes!" I barked at the mobile sitting snugly in its cradle on the dashboard.

"Dr Ryan?" The voice was that of a young female who I instantly recognised as a junior house doctor at the hospital. It would have been difficult not to recognise, with its soft, seductive, purring quality, coupled with that cocky air of confidence.

Recently qualified and extremely attractive, she was well aware of her looks and the effect they would have on any normal male between the ages of twenty and ninety.

I had taken an instant dislike to her when she had arrived on the scene a few weeks before. She had come to start her junior house surgeon post in the gynaecology department. To me she appeared arrogant, brash and conceited and I couldn't help feeling that these were most probably her better qualities!

"What is it?"

"Oh, I'm sorry to have woken you," she continued, with an obvious hint of sarcasm, "but my consultant, Miss Hargreaves, has been in theatre for the past hour dealing with an ovarian tumour and has now run into a major problem. The patient is haemorrhaging non-stop and she was wondering if you would be good enough to give us some of your expert advice as she's certain the cause of the bleeding is not surgical."

"The cause never bloody well is surgical with surgeons, is it?" I barked back. "Dr Reynolds, why the hell are you bothering me with this problem? I mean, what is it that drives surgeons to waste a senior hospital consultant's valuable time with such trivia; trivia, which, by the way, they should have bloody well learnt all about when at medical school?

"Your boss is well aware of the procedure here. So please ask her from me why the hell, in the first instance, she cannot contact our on-call specialist trainee registrar, whose sole reason for being on call is to provide the ignorant likes of her with the necessary advice she requires?

"Now, will you kindly stop unnecessarily bothering me and bleep the duty medical registrar," I bellowed, fumbling for the *off* button.

* * *

There are times when I seriously question what I'm doing here and how I got into it all in the first place. Then, as I think back and begin to reminisce, I realise that there is nothing else I would rather have done and no other hospital I would rather have worked in.

After all, Eastwich General had a good reputation within the Region. It had managed to maintain high standards of medical care, despite the severe budgetary restrictions imposed by the Region as a result of the increasingly avaricious financial demands made by the neighbouring teaching hospitals.

Set in a few acres of green belt, on the outskirts of a relatively quiet south coast town, it served a population of a quarter of a million would-be sufferers.

Driving to work late, through a light drizzle, on that early spring morning, I could not help feeling smugly content with my life.

At forty-eight, I had a secure career as the resident consultant haematologist, specialising in blood diseases. I had gained the respect of a number, but I hasten to add not all, of my colleagues and, after many years flirting with bankruptcy, could at last declare myself financially secure.

The only blemish on my humble background was the matrimonial path, which for me had been liberally strewn with banana skins. Suffice to say, I am not an easy person with whom to share domestic life, being prone to periods of sulky melancholia, interspersed with episodes of unpredictable, and outrageously antisocial behaviour. I suppose I am what the popular press refer to as *a loner*. Having spent some years inflicting my particular brand of torture on the female of the species, I had settled for the single life, and bought a modest detached house in the country, a few miles from the hospital.

My leisure time is spent avoiding the gardening, for which I have a particular aversion, and have now employed an extremely garrulous pensioner, who answers to the name of George and manages to do exactly as he pleases with my herbaceous borders, despite my wishes. I have given up trying to change his ways, and allowed him carte blanche with regard to matters green, provided I am allowed to listen to Messrs Beethoven and Bach in peace. This inevitably means that mowing and other noisy gardening pursuits are limited to those periods when I am at work.

By now, one will have gathered that I have been blessed with an argumentative nature that, over the years, has been honed and refined to tackle any injustice that incites my anger. In fact, I am proud of my reputation for taking on all medical and administrative causes I view to be unjust, and I am pleased to recount there are always many such battles to be waged at Eastwich General.

* * *

On arrival at the hospital, my unusually serene mood was soured on finding the barrier to the consultant's car park jammed in the open position, a not too infrequent problem recently. Consequently, the enemy, by which I refer to that ever-increasing army of visitors not entitled to a car park pass, had filled every available space.

Resisting the temptation to block the entrance with my locked car, I opted to park in the road. As a result, I wandered into the haematology department even later and decidedly frosty.

"Administration was on the phone, Dr Ryan," my completely scatty, but wonderfully loyal and efficient secretary Anne greeted me. "Apparently, you were due at a meeting on resource management ten minutes ago but I couldn't find it anywhere in your diary," she said, without lifting her gaze from the pile of recently opened letters stacked neatly in front of her.

"If I had wanted to be a ruddy book-keeper I would have studied accountancy and not medicine. I suppose seeing patients is considered not *you* in the modern health service," I replied. "After all, it costs money to treat patients and I suppose on the global scale that's not exactly good for resource management is it! Where is this congress on high finance being held then?"

"In the board room, where they're always held, as you well know," she replied, returning her attention to the mail.

"Ah! Yes, the *bored* room. How aptly named! Give me twenty minutes, Anne, and then bleep me out will you? There's a dear."

"Really, Dr Ryan, I don't know how you have the gall. Surely they realise by now?"

"Not them my sweet. They couldn't smell a skunk at ten paces. Now, if it was an *adder!*" A poor joke, totally wasted on Anne who rarely paid much attention to anything I had to say much before noon.

I wandered off in the direction of the boardroom. On my way down the corridor, I bumped into Dr Jonathan Frobisher, the physician with an interest in sick kidneys.

A genial chap in his mid-fifties, Johnny was somewhat of an eccentric, given to dressing in flamboyant clothes, always with a colourful bow tie on display. He had five children, the youngest aged three, having started a family relatively late in life.

He was an avid pigeon fancier and spent much of his spare time preparing his feathered friends for racing events. He also had a penchant for small cigars and expensive wine.

"Hello, Johnny you old dog. How're you doing?" I enquired.

"Not bad Andrew. But Jenny's gone missing again." He was obviously concerned, and started to cough.

"One of those itinerant daughters of yours?"

"No. My racing champion," he replied with a wheeze.

"Oh yes, of course. I shouldn't worry, Johnny. She'll come home eventually. She always does. Remember the time she took four days to get in from Caithness? You were convinced she was lost, but when she eventually showed it was obvious from her demeanour that she'd had a little romance along the way. I don't like the sound of that cough though. You ought to get that sorted out."

"I expect it's those cigars. Afraid I cannot leave the damn things alone these days. As a doctor, I suppose it's not exactly setting a good example to the rest of the hospital, especially our juniors. I really must try to cut them down," he said with a look of guilt on his face.

"By the way, did you hear about that poor young woman admitted yesterday via the Accident & Emergency department?"

"Which woman?" I enquired.

"She was a known, insulin-dependent diabetic in her late twenties, who had been under the care of the diabetic department for some years. She required admission to the hospital when her diabetes became unstable. Routine sort of case really. Anyway, following treatment in A&E she revived and was transferred to the ward for overnight observation. She did well, and was even sitting up chatting and laughing with the nurses when they checked her at eight that evening. Then, an hour later, she was found dead in bed. And not a single clue as to a likely cause."

"The coroner's post-mortem should reveal the cause," I said. "Probably a pulmonary embolus, or a stroke due to haemorrhage from a ruptured Berry aneurysm."

"Doesn't matter how much experience you have at this game, every now and then a case like this makes you sit up and wonder what it's all about," he said gloomily.

"Cheer up. Of course, it's all very sad but, as we well know, these things do happen from time to time in our hospitals and in most instances we discover there was not a lot anyone could have done at the time. I mean, I'm afraid it goes with the job," I tried to brighten him up.

Changing the subject, he continued, "Andrew, when you have a spare moment would you be good enough to take a look at a patient of mine on Nightingale ward? Her name is Heggerty and she was admitted last night with a spot of kidney failure. She also has a funny blood picture I don't understand."

"No problem," I replied. "I'll pop up, as soon as I've managed some resources in the jolly old board room."

* * *

I briefly slipped into the gents just off the main corridor to clean my old, badly fading, once bright blue college tie, which had suffered a direct hit with soft egg yolk in my rush to down my breakfast earlier. After all, I did so want to look my best for the committee!

As I gently splashed cold water onto my face, I gazed at the aging and by now slightly wrinkled features staring back at me from the mirror. My first impression was that I wasn't alone, it having been quite some time since I had last taken a close look at the effects of nearly half a century of ageing and dedicated physical neglect on my countenance.

The tie appeared the least of my problems, when I noted the greying hair with the telltale bald patch beginning to appear. What the heck, I thought to myself, it's as good as it'll ever get and there's no sense just staring in the hopes of bringing about some instant miracle. Look on the bright side, I told myself, it's fast becoming the sort of face younger travellers get up for on trains and buses to offer you their seat.

Yes, I mused, as I straightened the tie and flung the paper towel into the waste paper bin on my way out, it was definitely one of those days when my cup was half full and as such I was as ready as I would ever be for the next episode of the Eastwich Inquisition!

* * *

On entering the hushed boardroom, I was greeted by the chairman Dr Boris, *Boring*, Baldwin. Boris was one of those physicians you love to hate. Born with the proverbial silver spoon in his mouth, an only child, he had all the mannerisms of a person who had been thoroughly spoilt in early childhood.

It was common knowledge that even his parents finally sickened of him and packed him off to some minor public school in the Midlands to have education beaten into him. It obviously worked, for he excelled at his studies, forsaking the playing fields for his books.

His passage through medical school had been no less successful and he managed to acquire a number of prizes including the gold medal in medicine. Not one to make friends easily, he chose to keep himself largely to himself. Following pre-registration hospital jobs, he specialised in general medicine, with a particular interest in endocrinology and things hormonal.

It was not long before he became interested in administration, spending more and more of his time in committee work, his clinical interests taking a back seat. Many of his colleagues took a dim view of his flirtation with the other side, deeming him to have crossed the floor of the house in joining the opposition.

"Ah! Good of you to join us, Dr Ryan, even if it *is* a quarter of an hour late." He never missed the opportunity for a bit of sarcasm, and it was no secret that we entertained a healthy dislike for each other.

"Sorry. It's only that on the way here I was captured by terrorists, tortured to within an inch of my proverbials and was extremely lucky to get away with my life. But, thanks for your concern all the same," I whispered to myself.

"What was that, Dr Ryan?"

"I said it was the least I could do, Dr Baldwin. I had thought of seeing some patients but then that is likely to cost the authority money, or should I call it 'resources'? Sorry!"

It never ceases to amaze me how the administration have been allowed to get away with the systematic murder of the English language, replacing it with its very own brand of jargonistic claptrap; not unlike *newspeak* in George Orwell's novel, *Nineteen Eighty Four*. Phrases such as *resource management, on-going revenue consequences*, and *restricted budgetary control* simply fall from their mouths, like droppings from a passing pigeon.

"We were discussing the important issue of drug budgets, Dr Ryan," our esteemed support services manager, Hugh Hudson-Brown, interjected. "I was saying, before I was interrupted, that we are already four percent up on drug expenditure for the same period last year."

"That's truly amazing," I said, "considering that the figures show we have actually seen and treated nine percent more patients during this period. Any ten-year -old would realise that must indicate increased efficiency. Would someone please run out and find me a ten-year-old?" I thought I was entering into the spirit of the occasion wonderfully well.

"Hardly the issue," cut in our humourless chairman. "Some drastic action is needed if we are to achieve our projected fifteen percent saving for the year."

"Oh! Indubitably," I replied. "I suppose it's that new hormone replacement therapy that's all the rage these days." A veritable poisoned arrow, aimed directly at poor old Boris' endocrinological heart.

"I think we should stick to good old aspirin. After all, if it was good enough for our grannies it ought to be good enough for the current generation of sycophantic, menopausal pop-worshippers."

"This is no time for flippancy." Dr Baldwin was taking his position as chairman very seriously. "One obvious area for reduction is in the out-patient prescribing. It would appear the current practice is to dish out at least four weeks drugs to the patients at each visit.

"Surely, seven days' supply would be adequate, and then the patients could get the remainder from their own practitioner. After all, we seem to forget all too easily that the practitioners are the patient's primary carer and, as such, are responsible for the overall care and welfare of their patients." By now, he was looking decidedly smug.

"Why a whole week?" I questioned. "Why not only the one day, or *even* a single bloody dose? Then the poor geriatric sod can get the rest actually on his way home from the hospital, and save us all a fortune," I suggested, I thought helpfully.

"Really, Dr Ryan. This is no place for levity," our principal pharmacist, Douglas Whines, obviously felt wounded, alas not mortally. I couldn't help thinking how odd it is that a surname often fits the personality of the character to whom it relates, not unlike the way many owners have an uncanny way of resembling the appearance of their dogs.

"Risk management is the key to the modern health service, Dr Ryan. You would do well to take heed. We simply cannot go on squandering money unnecessarily. There are certain areas simply crying out for attention when it comes to major savings and one of them is certainly the drug budget." Dr Baldwin was obviously slipping into hyper-drive, and I decided to propel him into a time warp.

"Oh Yes! You mean areas such as the ever increasing administrative hierarchy, with their plush expensive offices, thick pile carpets, forests of plants, lease lend company cars and self-propagating number of secretaries and personal assistants."

"Really, Dr Ryan.........."

Bleep, bleep. Bleep, bleep.

Saved by the bleep. Wonderful things, bleeps.......... sometimes!

CHAPTER TWO

Physicians are like kings, – they brook no contradiction
– John Webster

I arrived on Nightingale ward in time to witness the usual scene of confusion and mayhem. By the desk stood the captain of the ship, Sister Travers, a phone in one hand and a drug chart in the other.

She was remonstrating with a schizophrenic patient, trying to explain that the noise on the roof was not in fact the Martians landing but the maintenance man repairing the air conditioning unit. Between asides to the patient, she was barking instructions down the phone to some poor relative.

I steered a wide berth, heading for the note trolley in the corner, where I retrieved Mrs Mavis Heggerty's folder and disappeared down the corridor in the direction of the six-bedded unit.

Mrs Heggerty was a plump, pale, middle-aged lady, who looked as if she would burst into tears at the very mention of her name. In fact, she was most pleasant and helpful, answering all my questions with a clarity rarely witnessed in hospital administrators.

It would seem that she had enjoyed perfect health until three weeks before, when she had experienced a severe sore throat and fever. This had passed off uneventfully within a few days. However, over the past week she had become increasingly more tired and breathless.

At first, she had attributed these symptoms to a simple cold.

After fainting at home, however, she realised something more serious was likely. As a result, she presented herself to the casualty department and from there was later admitted to the ward.

The investigations revealed she had some degree of kidney failure, which was considered to have been a possible complication of her recent infection. It was also noted that she was considerably anaemic, more than could have been caused by the kidney problem alone.

On direct questioning, there did not appear to be anything of significance in her history to account for this finding and I decided to check the blood film down the microscope before committing myself to an opinion in her notes.

I left her to get some rest and returned to the laboratory, only to be reminded that it was my turn to finish the anticoagulant clinic.

This clinic is the bane of the haematologist's life, with upwards of eighty to a hundred patients to see, dosing their blood-thinning tablets and answering their numerous questions. Little wonder the haematologist often emerges from the session feeling battered, bruised, and brainwashed.

It was from such a clinic that I returned to the laboratory at around noon. Anne, often the recipient of my whiplash tongue on these occasions, had quite understandably beaten a hasty retreat and disappeared for an early lunch.

"I've finished my round of the ward patients, Dr Ryan." It was my haematology registrar, Dr Schofield, appearing round the corner on his way to the canteen. He was accompanied by a couple of his colleagues.

Dr Paul Gibson was also one of the medical registrars and was working for Dr Jean Drummond in the department of cardio-thoracic medicine. He had not been with us all that long and I did not know him all that well. He seemed bright enough and was always smiling and very polite and, according to my consultant colleagues, had so far proved most hard working and conscientious.

As they appeared, he was deep in conversation with Dr Gillian Reynolds, the gynaecology house-lady, with whom I had clashed on the phone on the way to work that morning. Her smile immediately turned to a deep scowl as she caught sight of me.

"Hello Dr Ryan, how are you doing," Paul butted in.

"Fine thanks, Paul," I replied feeling a little uncomfortable as I felt Gillian's blank stare cutting through me.

It was a relief to turn the other way to answer Dr Schofield. He had been working with me now for eight months and during this time had impressed me as a most conscientious, caring and capable doctor. I had no doubt that one day he would make a fine haematology consultant.

"Oh good, Hugh. Any problems?"

"Not really. The new leukaemic patient seems to be settling down quite well and the others are all quiet. Well, as quiet as it's possible for that lot!"

"Good. I'm popping over to the Blue Boar for a spot of liquid sanity and a sandwich. I don't think I could stomach another session of medical politics in the doctor's dining room; the surgeons grumbling about the *lazy* anaesthetists, and the physicians arguing about the on-call rota. I'll see you on the ward round at two o'clock."

"O.K., see you then," Hugh replied as they disappeared round the corner.

* * *

The bar of the Blue Boar was crowded with local traders and businessmen catching up on events. The air was thick with tobacco smoke, and Frank Sinatra could be heard in every corner.

After much elbowing and shoving, I managed to collect for myself a beef sandwich and a pint of best bitter. As the barman handed me my change I caught sight of Johnny Frobisher in the corner, half hidden behind the current edition of *The Pigeon Post*. Threading my way carefully between the customers, I headed for his table and settled into the seat beside him.

As he glanced at me over the top of his paper, he started to cough; lightly at first, but then quite noisily, and with a nasty, persistent wheeze.

"I saw that lady of yours this morning, Johnny. Not sure what's going on but I'll take a look at her blood film later."

"Thanks, Andrew." He looked a little embarrassed at having been caught with his favourite journal on his lap, instead of the *British Medical Journal* or *Lancet*. "How did resource management go, as if I didn't know?"

"The same as usual. That smug bunch of hypocrites is still trying to steal from the patients' budgets, in order to squander the money on administration. You know, I got the distinct impression that they don't like me. Can't think why!

"*Boring* Boris went through his usual bout of histrionics and verbal diarrhoea. At one stage, I thought he was going to drop in a fit of apoplexy. But then, I suppose that's too much to expect!"

"You know, you really had better watch it, Andrew. According to the rumours, they're really gunning for you these days, for constantly making waves." Johnny seemed genuinely concerned for my welfare, and started to cough once again.

"Well, you can't have a seaside town without waves now, can you?"

"Seriously, Andrew. The group I refer to includes a few consultants as well as administrators, and they have considerable influence with the chief executive. And what's more, they're not above using it if they feel they have the slightest chance of ridding themselves of a troublemaker like you."

"What could he do? Wall me up in the laboratory for the duration? Anyway, they're a pretty spineless bunch of cretins when it comes to action. My goldfish makes more decisions in a day than they come up with in a month."

"You don't have a goldfish!"

"Well, it would if I had one. And don't forget, I'm on good terms with our illustrious leader, David Marshall, ever since I correctly diagnosed his wife as having pernicious anaemia. What an appropriate condition for an administrator's wife.........*pernicious* anaemia!" I giggled.

"All the same, you are not the most subtle of doctors and I do seriously feel you ought to tone it down a little. Your animosity toward the administration is well known. Besides, it's not fair to tar them all with the same brush. One or two of them have been most helpful to us over the years." Johnny was appearing for the defence and beginning to wheeze much more noticeably.

"I view the modern administration as a form of malignancy, slowly spreading its way down every bloody corridor in the hospital and infiltrating its way into rooms that once served a useful function. Once in place, they represent a form of cancer completely resistant to any known type of treatment. I think I'll have another pint. How about you?"

"No thanks. By the way, that young diabetic lady's post-mortem failed to reveal any obvious cause for her sudden death," he said, changing the subject and looking decidedly glum once again.

"Well come on, Johnny, as you well know we cannot always explain certain events in medicine. Occasionally, one experiences the sudden unexplained death of a patient. And sometimes, despite all the wonderful advances and new investigative techniques occurring in medicine, we are still unable to reveal the cause. It's all so sad and depressing, and lives with us as part of the rich tapestry of our profession."

"Oh! I know Andrew. But somehow, I really can't help wondering what could possibly have happened to snuff out such a young life, so suddenly and with such finality. As you rightly say, it's all very depressing," he said, glancing over at me with that sad expression of concern once more covering his face. "I must rush. And don't forget, Andrew, take it easy with the administration."

"Absolutely, my friend !"

* * *

The ward round over, I was sitting at my desk slowly sorting through a set of patient's notes, when there was a gentle tap on the door. Before I could say anything, it opened and my senior laboratory technician, Carol Donnelly, appeared in the doorway.

"May I have a word with you, Dr Ryan?"

"Of course, Carol, come in. What's the problem?"

"I'm not sure how to begin," she said, looking worried. "I hope I'm not wasting your time or jumping to wild conclusions but I am a little anxious regarding a situation that appears to be developing in the laboratory."

"What's up? Administration demanding twice the productivity for half the cost as usual?"

"I'm afraid it's more serious than that," she said, looking a little embarrassed.

"Well, suppose you sit down and tell me all about it," I suggested.

She placed herself in the chair opposite the desk, and started to fidget nervously.

"It's to do with Alan Makepeace and Julie Webber," she began.

Alan was one of our senior technicians. He was a pleasant enough chap in his late twenties, who sported a crew cut hairstyle and a gold earring. He was a good worker with a cheerful disposition. A confirmed bachelor, he fancied himself greatly with the ladies and wasn't backward in coming forward, as the expression goes.

Julie was a most attractive junior, who had only been with us a few months. She was married to a technician from the biochemistry department and seemed blissfully happy.

"Alan never seems to leave Julie alone these days," said Carol. "He appears to have taken her under his wing, and never misses an opportunity to show her some new technique in the laboratory. The others are already beginning to gossip, and it's all proving most embarrassing."

"It's probably innocent enough," I said. "He's always struck me as being very keen and helpful, especially to the juniors."

"I'm afraid I think it's more than that in this case, Dr Ryan. For instance, yesterday I had to get some reagents from the storeroom. I found the door unlocked, and when I opened it I found the two of them in there looking very sheepish indeed."

"Were they in each other's arms, wildly confessing their love for each other?" I enquired, playfully.

"Not exactly. But they did look very surprised and quickly gathered a box of test tubes and rushed past me out of the door without a word."

"I doubt anything serious has happened," I said. "Julie appears a sensible girl and I'm sure wouldn't do anything silly. I think we had better be careful before we go making accusations, don't you?"

"I suppose so. But all the same, perhaps I'll have a quiet word with Julie when the opportunity presents itself, to check she has no problems."

"O.K. Sounds a good idea. I'll leave it with you," I agreed. "Keep me posted. If there's anything I can do let me know."

She disappeared through the door and I returned my attention to the pile of patient notes cluttering my desk.

* * *

The rest of the day passed uneventfully and that evening, as I relaxed at home in my comfortable, leather armchair listening to Beethoven's fourth piano concerto, I recalled my earlier meeting with Mrs Heggerty on Nightingale ward. Something she had said caused a faint stir at the back of my mind.

I reached for the latest offering from *Wine Without Tears* and poured myself a generous glass. What was it she had said? Following her sore throat she had experienced transient, flitting joint pains and had taken some pain-killers prescribed by her general practitioner.

I made a mental note to check this out and then settled back to enjoy the music of Ludwig, with a little help from some rather cheeky, but not insolent, Chateauneuf-du-Pape.

CHAPTER THREE

Physician, heal thyself
– The Gospel according to St. Luke

The following day I was receiving a particularly pushy drug company representative in my room. He was trying hard to persuade me of the relative merits of their new, expensive antibiotic drug. The logo on the sales pamphlet red, *Slug the bug with Bactokill......the new wonder antimicrobial agent, which gets to those bacteria others don't.*

I had a vision of some wizened, old, white-haired man locked up in a back room, where his sole function was to think up idiotic jingles like this! I finally managed to get rid of the rep with a promise to review the literature he left me regarding his *unique* compound.

Anne appeared with some letters to sign and placed the morning mail on the edge of the desk.

"How about a nice cup of tea," I suggested. "I feel really parched this morning. Not to speak of this dreadful headache. I think I must have had Master Beethoven going at too many decibels last night."

"You know very well it has nothing to do with Beethoven, or his bells!" I'm afraid Anne, who has known me far too long, is well aware of my excesses and is not easily fooled on that score.

"Don't forget those bone marrows that need reporting. The radiotherapy department have been on to me this morning, chasing up the results."

"Ah!" I replied, rubbing my forehead gently with the back of my hand. "I'll do them later Anne. I don't think I could focus down the microscope right now," I said, with perfect honesty.

"As soon as I've had my tea I'll pop up to the ward and see how the patients are coming along."

"You really ought to take more care of yourself you know. You simply cannot go on treating life as if it were some game." It was Anne's attempt at mothering me.

"My good woman, as the celebrated American humorist, Tom Lehrer, once said, *Life is rather like a sewer; what you get out of it will depend very largely upon what you put into it!"*

"That's exactly what I mean, even if it is rather a cynical view of God's precious gift."

"Now Anne, you're not going to get all religious on me now, are you? You know very well it only succeeds in sending my blood pressure into orbit," I sighed.

"What I was saying is, that Tom fellow was right. If you keep pouring wine in at one end, you're going to get more than hang-overs at the other.......er! Well, you know what I mean!" She turned to the wall, looking acutely embarrassed at what she had just said but wasn't quick enough to hide her face as she started to blush.

"I think I do, Anne, and you're priceless. Whatever happens don't change. I need you to keep me on the straight and narrow......or, should I say, *marrow*! "

"I suppose you think that's funny?" she recovered, pulling a face at my poor attempt at a joke

"Not really but it was the best I could manage under the circumstances. Now, run along and make me that tea. There's a good secretary. And then I'll treble your wages!"

She disappeared through the door as the phone started to ring. It was the sister on Cresswell ward to tell me that Johnny Frobisher had been admitted overnight with suspected pneumonia.

I thanked her for letting me know, and told her I would be along later. I also warned her to remove his cigars from the bed-side locker.

I then turned my attention to the mail and came across an envelope with a Sydney postmark. Intrigued, I reached for the letter opener, wondering who in Australia could possibly have written to me. All was soon revealed.

The letter was from Frank Jenkins, who had trained with me all those years ago in London. Soon after qualifying, he had tired of life in England and taken himself off to the Antipodes in search of the high life. Here, he settled into a cosy medical practice on the outskirts of Sydney and within a few years was happily married with two children.

A little later, he had been accepted as a clinical assistant in the haematology department at the local hospital. He currently did two sessions a week helping out in their busy outpatient clinics. It was whilst engaged in this capacity that he had stumbled upon an article by me in one of the international journals of haematology. It was to do with the treatment of leukaemia in the elderly; a subject that apparently interested Frank.

The upshot was that, having read the paper, he developed the idea of getting me to deliver a series of lectures on this subject at his hospital. With this in mind, he had succeeded in persuading one of the more generous drug companies to sponsor the event. The package would include free first class travel. So, not only would I get a chance to meet some of my Australian haematology colleagues but I would also grab a few days' holiday, virtually free, into the bargain.

The idea was most appealing and I decided to give the matter some serious thought, when I had more spare time.

* * *

Whilst I was reviewing the mail, Johnny Frobisher was being examined by Jean Drummond, one of the consultants in chest medicine. Jean had achieved considerable success in a largely male dominated specialty and had rightly earned the respect of her colleagues.

She also had a well-earned reputation for her outspoken views on certain issues. One such issue was smoking and it was on this particular subject that she was now lecturing poor Johnny, who was in no shape to offer any resistance to her onslaught.

"If you will persist in using your bronchial tree as a chimney, you can hardly expect me to keep bailing you out every time you have one of these episodes. I have very little sympathy for those guilty of self-inflicted illness, as you well know, particularly when they are doctors who should know better.

"Do you have any idea how much you lot cost the nation every year to keep your chimneys swept? Besides, what sort of an example do you think you are setting the rest of the hospital, not to mention your own juniors? Not a good one and that is a disgraceful thing for a senior hospital consultant to have to admit." She was taking advantage of his indisposition to give him both barrels, as he cowered behind the sheets.

"I'm sorry Jean. I really will make an effort to cut down on the cigars," Johnny hissed.

"Cutting down is simply not good enough and you jolly well know it. This attack is a severe warning to you to cut it out completely, before it cuts you out. There are simply no half measures acceptable at this stage." Jean had him where she wanted him, and she wasn't letting go.

"I'll do as you say Jean. I don't think I could take another episode like this." The message had got through.

* * *

On my return to the office later in the day, after looking in on poor Johnny, Anne handed me a fax that had arrived a little earlier. It was an *urgent* patient referral from the Lansdowne Community Practice, one of the local general practice surgeries.

Over the years, there had not been a lot of love lost between this particular surgery and the hospital in general and me in particular. They were one of the so-called *fund-holding* practices, an idiotic invention, I believe, of some infamous previous Tory government I had long ago chosen to forget.

As far as I was concerned, the implementation of *fund-holding* was totally iniquitous and a glaring example of the government's failure to come to terms with the real issues of the health service and to take their responsibilities regarding its management seriously.

To my mind, it was yet one more classic example of a political fudge; one with no possible hope of success and one that would almost inevitably result in abject failure with the worst possible consequences for the patients.

Under the original system, a particular practice would be funded centrally by the relevant health authority. As such, it had been directly answerable to its health authority, both professionally and financially, regarding the overall management of the practice. In the new system, the fund-holding practice was given its total budget up front, to manage itself and was no longer directly answerable to any higher authority.

This meant that it was responsible for all its own administrative and organisational decisions, without firstly having to seek the permission or agreement of the local or regional health authority to produce the funding. It would seem that, as long as they did not exceed their budget, few questions were asked and there was little with regard to any formal overseeing or monitoring from the government's point of view.

The whole inept business was in fact a slightly more sophisticated way of brushing all the dirt and rubbish under the carpet. So long as everything continued to look fine and in perfect order on the surface, the family practices were left well alone.

Once instituted, the new system effectively allowed these fund-holding practices to purchase all their various services from wherever, and whomever they pleased.

Whilst all this was going on, the patients appeared blissfully unaware of the existence of this invidious system and the apparent lottery into which they had been entered.

In fairness, by far the majority of the fund-holding practices were run by decent, conscientious GP's, whose main interest was in providing the best possible service for their patients. Most of them found the process of fund-holding a great burden. It had been heaped upon them, largely against their will, by an incompetent, ill-advised government that seemed hell-bent on the inevitable destruction of the health service.

This enormous, bureaucratic blunder had greatly increased the burden of administrative paperwork they were expected to wade through on a daily basis. And this, in turn, resulted in their having to spend increasingly more of their precious time away from their patients who, by now it seemed, were to take second place in the National Health priority tables.

To me, *The Cure* to all this on-going, government initiated, wanton waste of health service funds was incredibly simple. In fact, I believe this has often been the case with so many of these so-called major *Government Health Service Reforms,* or *Initiatives,* as they have been so fancifully called recently. One has merely to look back at the history and track record of the service and take note of the enormous number of such sweeping changes that have been instituted over the years, all in the name of improving the service for the voters! Or did I mean patients?

However, despite the enormous cost involved in instituting each of these changes, most of them had subsequently bitten the dust, only to have been replaced by yet more idiotic, ill-conceived, incredibly costly schemes bearing some other senseless, jargonistic, fancy name, specially chosen to hoodwink the poor unsuspecting public! My God! If we ran our household budget on similar lines, we'd probably all be bankrupt by Christmas!

I glanced down at the fax. As usual, I could see little in the content, of what was the briefest of unhelpful notes, to justify an *urgent* referral in this case.

The letter related to a middle-aged housewife, who had incidentally been found to have the mildest of anaemias. Furthermore, on checking the records, it was obvious that, for some time, she had been known to have this mild anaemia and there had been no evidence of it getting any worse. Certainly, as far as I was concerned, there was no indication for an urgent referral in this instance.

Nevertheless, this particular practice was in the habit of flexing its muscles with Eastwich General, with which it had been conducting its own form of personal vendetta for some years. These practices now had the money up front and the NHS Hospital Trusts were compelled to compete for their business.

This was indeed a most unsatisfactory state of affairs and one which, in my opinon, went totally against the principles of the NHS as it was originally conceived. In practice, it was very much a case of the tail wagging the dog. Needless to say, I was distinctly unimpressed.

I had been completely lost in my thoughts when the phone rang, rudely waking me from my dreams and I nonchalantly flicked the fax into the *Routine Appointments* tray, as I lifted the receiver and pressed it to my ear.

CHAPTER FOUR

If you are going to have doctors, you had better have doctors well off
– George Bernard Shaw

Later in the day, after my routine excursion to the Blue Boar for a little light refreshment, I was accosted outside the X-Ray department by Mr Samuel Wetherby. This was somewhat of a surprise, as Sam is one of our orthopaedic surgeons and is rarely to be found within the confines of a nationalised health institution such as Eastwich General, choosing to spend the bulk of his professional time down the road at the local BUPA private hospital.

This, not unnaturally, had infuriated many of his colleagues, as he was plainly not fulfilling his NHS contract, whilst still continuing to draw a decent salary from the government. And all the while, others, usually his juniors, had to cover for him at Eastwich General. It is hardly surprising that a number of his colleagues now refer to him, perhaps a little unkindly but nevertheless accurately, as having specialised in *diseases of the rich*.

A large man, with an ego to match, I give him nine out of ten in the local pomposity ratings. One thing about Sam that you can always rely on is that he never misses a chance to complain about his colleagues and their respective departments, presumably working on the well-known principle that attack is the best means of defence. Today it was my turn and he was obviously raring to go. I thought I'd fire the first shot.

"You look lost, Sam. Do you need directions?"

"Very funny, I'm sure," he sniggered. "Andrew, old chap, why is it that your department always manages to foul up one of my important cases? This morning I had a knee replacement at the other hospital……"

"Which hospital is that?" I enquired, with malice in my voice.

"You know very well which hospital I'm referring to and there's no need to be so sarcastic about it. If it wasn't for the BUPA Samaritan hospital, there would be even greater pressure on the NHS beds at Eastwich. They provide a fine service for our local community and receive little recognition for it.

"Anyway, there we all were in theatre, scrubbed up and ready to start with the patient anaesthetised and on the table, when the anaesthetist calmly announces that haematology has once again failed to provide the necessary blood for the operation. The whole thing had to be cancelled, resulting in a heck of a fuss when the relatives found out." By now poor old Sam had turned a deep crimson and was trembling with anger.

It was my turn and I was ready.

"If your patient was George Carpenter," I said calmly, "Then there was every reason for our failure to supply the necessary blood. According to my blood bank, the patient's blood sample and the request form bore conflicting information.

"As you well know there are very strict rules we must obey when cross-matching blood for transfusion, in order that we do not give the wrong blood to the patient and kill him before you have time to get your bill in!

"Now, I fully understand that, in your case, you are beyond hope when it comes to understanding modern science but I would have thought that even you would have realised that we simply cannot issue blood under these circumstances.

"You would do well to remember that a transfusion of blood is a form of tissue transplant and in many ways no different from any other transplant such as a kidney or heart. As such, it carries many of the same risks and complications if the blood donor and the patient do not match each other sufficiently.

"I happen to know that your secretary was informed of the error in good time for you to have rectified it. As far as I'm concerned it was your responsibility and that's an end of it."

By now, I was becoming decidedly bored with the conversation in general and this surgeon in particular. I cannot help thinking what a dreadful waste of a good medical education it is when a newly qualified doctor decides to become an orthopaedic surgeon.

Sam slipped away mumbling disconsolately to himself. One up to the good guys! I'm not sure why, but there is always something distinctly satisfying about proving a surgeon wrong.

However, I do not blame all surgeons. Some of the blame must lie with the lay public, who will insist on placing these self-opinionated wielders of the scalpel on such a high pedestal; all the greater height from which to fall, in my opinion.

* * *

I managed the rest of the journey back to the department without incident.

On my desk, I found Mrs Heggerty's blood results and blood film. I placed the film on the microscope and peered through the eyepieces, as I began to adjust the focus. There was nothing very remarkable about it at first sight but then, on closer inspection, I noticed an odd feature about the red blood cells.

At last the pieces of the jigsaw were beginning to fit into place. I ordered a couple more tests on the blood sample to confirm my suspicions and then wandered off to the ward to have another word with Mrs Heggerty.

On this occasion, she appeared in much brighter spirits, no doubt as a result of her recent blood transfusion. It took me only a few minutes to obtain the necessary information to clinch the diagnosis.

After recording my findings in her notes, I left her, happy in the knowledge that she wasn't suffering from any serious blood disorder and that she would soon be feeling much better and on her way home.

* * *

"Frobisher you old fake! Whatever are you doing lazing about in that bed?" I thought I'd cheer him up.

"Don't shout, Dr Ryan. We have some seriously ill patients on the ward, as I'm sure you are aware!" The ward sister was making it painfully obvious who was in charge.

"Sorry," I replied, in an exaggerated whisper, with a hand covering my mouth.

Johnny was sitting propped up on four pillows, wheezing away and looking decidedly blue about the gills.

"Who's been a naughty boy then?" I chided him.

"Not you as well! I don't think I could take two lectures in one day. Jean was in a little earlier and has been reading me the riot act about smoking," he said, with his basset-hound expression on full display.

"But I came to cheer you up, my wheezy, little horizontal friend."

"I'm not your *wheezy friend* and I don't need cheering up," he said, testily.

"That's not my impression from where I'm standing. You look decidedly peaky and in need of some light relief. Now, I have some good news for you about that lady of yours with the kidney failure. I have finally discovered the cause of her anaemia, and a very fine piece of detective work it was too, even if I do say so myself," I said in all modesty, a quality for which I am justly renowned.

"It would appear that when she had all those aches and pains a few weeks ago she took a painkiller called *mefenamic acid*, more commonly known as *Ponstan*. Now, this particular analgesic is undoubtedly an excellent drug and in her case kept the pain away. However, on very rare occasions it can fool the body into thinking its own red blood cells belong to someone else. As a result the body makes antibodies against its own red cells and kills them off, like a form of cellular suicide or autodestruct, thus causing the anaemia."

"You mean they can cause a haemolytic anaemia," hissed Johnny.

"Precisely, old man. You know, we'll make a haematologist out of you yet!"

"No thank you. I'd rather do a proper job!" He was feeling down. "What treatment is she going to require?"

"Nothing. She has already stopped the tablets and been transfused. The whole thing should be self-limiting now. I have informed your team and will follow her up in my clinic when she goes home, if you like."

"Thanks very much Andrew. I'm sorry. I didn't mean to fly off the handle," he said, in repentant mode. I think I preferred the aggressive one; more my style.

"Think nothing of it dear chap. All part of the service. Now, how long did Jean think you'd be stuck in this godforsaken place?" I enquired.

"Too damn long," he replied. "She has stuck me on some strong antibiotics and ordered some special physiotherapy. It's more like the third degree, if you ask me. I'd swear that Amazonian nightmare of a physiotherapist came within inches of killing me this morning. I didn't realise how well I was until she started attacking me!"

"Cheer up," I said. "Look on the bright side. I mean, think how many committee meetings you'll miss. I don't suppose there's any chance of *me* catching it is there?"

"I don't think that's funny Andrew. Anyway it won't be your lungs that will give out first; it'll be your liver if I'm any judge." He'd obviously hit rock bottom. I knew the signs too well.

"Now, now," I said, "As I told you before, I only drink to make other people more interesting!"

Changing the subject, I handed him the faxed patient referral I had received earlier from the Lansdowne Practice. "What do you think of that load of rubbish?"

"What's this?" he enquired, reaching for his reading glasses.

"Another of those *urgent* referrals from that infernal, bullying practice up the road."

"What's the problem?" he asked, perusing the page.

"It's from that complete nutcase, Dr Rosa Pauling who, despite having known me for at least fifteen years, still insists on addressing all correspondence to *Consultant Haematologist*. I know a lot of her GP colleagues also do it but why doesn't she use my bloody name, for God's sake?"

"Oh dear, Andrew, 'The perils of Pauling', as you keep saying. The poor lady! Under the circumstances, she probably can't bring herself to mention your name. Conjures up too many bad memories, no doubt. Or perhaps she's fed up hearing that you always refer to her as 'Rose Appalling'! Anyway, what's wrong with the referral?"

"*What's wrong*," I shouted, earning a fierce glare from the sister at the end of the ward. "Look at the bloody results they've had the cheek to enclose with the referral."

"What's wrong with them?" he asked, briefly scanning the figures.

"What is *wrong* is that they're from that infamous bloody private laboratory in Scotland this practice has the gall to use rather than us." I blurted out, turning crimson in the process.

"How would you feel, when you know that your service is infinitely superior to the other and yet they still persist in throwing away NHS money on this crap?" I was getting into first gear and nothing was going to stop me.

"And Scotland of all places! It'll probably be bloody Iceland next. I mean, look at the dates on the report. The sample was taken on the Friday, but was not analysed by their machines until the following Tuesday. Four bloody days! And, to add insult to injury, the report wasn't issued until the following day. What sort of a laboratory would be stupid enough to perform a blood count on a sample that old?

"I mean, it's well known that many of the measurements will start going off within just a few hours from the time the blood is collected. And, to think that they are an officially accredited laboratory. I suppose all that means these days is that the bloody fire escapes are in the right place and there's sufficient room for the technicians to have their tea!" By now I was out of control and poor Johnny was looking very concerned.

"Calm down, Andrew, for God's sake. It won't do you any good getting so irate. We all know about this kind of practice but there's no sense having a heart attack over it. That way, they only get to win. Anyway, there's nothing you can do about it. So you might as well learn to relax and look the other way."

Johnny was making sense but somehow I found it difficult to follow his advice over this issue, about which I felt so strongly.

"That's what they said about Hitler! One of these days, someone is going to die during the time it takes to get some of these results. And then what! I've got copies of results on a six-year-old, who presented early on a Friday morning, with spontaneous bruising all over the body, nose bleeds, mouth ulcers and a high fever.

"Any first year medical student would immediately be thinking of this as very possibly a new case of leukaemia. I mean you don't exactly have to be a Nobel Prize winner in medicine to come up with that as the most likely explanation for these findings! And yet, it would seem, they were happy to wait for the results, which were not produced until late on Monday afternoon to show he did in fact have an eminently curable type of acute leukaemia.

"He was lucky, he made it. But how would you have felt if he was your son and had died of a cerebral haemorrhage over the weekend, due to his dangerously low platelet cell count? Especially knowing that, if the blood had been sent to the local hospital, the child would have been in the ward by the same afternoon, receiving the necessary platelet transfusions. And don't forget, we're talking about a situation where the child had an eighty five percent chance of cure with the currently available treatment! In this day and age, such delays cannot in any way be considered good practice.

"Of course I take it seriously. It's patient's lives we're talking about here. Not some poxy budget or personal vendetta. And no one seems to care enough to do a damn thing about it because it means standing up to the school bully and calling it as you see it. It's typical of the British.

"Why, even the Americans complain in restaurants when there's a problem with the food and something gets done about it. But, not the British though. Oh! No. They will grumble about it non-stop to anyone who cares to listen but would never consider making a formal complaint. Too much bloody trouble. They'd rather opt for the easy life than get involved, believing it will all eventually go away of its own accord. As I said, the world sat back and said the same about Hitler! Well, six years and tens of millions of lives later they realised they'd made the wrong decision!"

Johnny half grinned, as he interrupted his friend in full flow," Now, come on Andrew, there's a hell of a difference between the two situations and you well know it."

"I know, Johnny but you understand how I feel about the situation."

"All right, Andrew but quieten down or you'll have a bloody stroke! Right though you may be, somehow I don't see you changing the system all on your own. But you could well have a fatal coronary if you persist in carrying on like some hyped-up teenager at a pop concert." Johnny handed back the referral letter, frowning at me over the top of his glasses.

"I'm sorry, Johnny. I shouldn't be going on like this with you in your sick bed but somehow I just cannot control myself."

"Well, if I didn't before I certainly do now!" he grinned. "Now, do an ageing renal physician a favour and make an effort to cool it. At least, for the time being. I know you're incapable of long-term commitments in this field of endeavour, but at least try."

"I will," I promised.

"Now, get to hell out of here and let me get on with my reading!"

I glanced at my watch. "Hey! I must dash anyway. I have a meeting with the acute unit manager about the over-spend on the haematology budget. Scintillating stuff! Can't think where all the money's gone! I'll pop back later and throw grapes at you, you hissing old geezer."

"See you," he wheezed, reaching for the *Bird Fancier's Gazette.*

CHAPTER FIVE

He said my bronchial tubes were entrancing,
My epiglottis filled him with glee,
He simply loved my larynx
And went wild about my pharynx,
But he never said he loved me
– Cole Porter

"Dr Ryan," Anne pushed her head around the door early the next morning.

"What is it Anne?" I had already been at my desk for an hour, blissfully unaware that anyone else had even arrived in the department.

"I noticed you were in early and wondered if you would like a cup of coffee?"

"Brilliant idea, my old darling. Any post yet, my little saviour of hangovers past?"

"You're in a particularly good mood today. Not too much Beethoven last night, obviously! Post hasn't arrived yet. But there was a call from that nice lady rep from the company that produces the new leukaemia drug you've been using."

"Oh! You mean Victoria Hall at Cytotec"

"Yes, that's the one. She wondered if you'd call her on this number," she said, handing me a slip of paper with the number written in pencil. "She was just off for a quick meeting with her boss and hadn't time to speak but asked if you could return the call as soon as possible as she has some good news about your proposal for a new trial."

"O.K. I'll phone her when I've checked on the lab."

"She specifically asked if you could phone soon, as she's got another meeting at ten."

"No problem."

She disappeared, as I stared at the number in front of me and reached for the phone that had become hidden under a mess of notes at the back of the desk.

I'd known Victoria for some years now, ever since her company had started to get involved in the development of new drugs for the treatment of leukaemia. She was without doubt one of the most stunningly attractive women I had ever met. In her mid-thirties, she was one of the few women in whose presence I was lost for words.

Although obviously aware of her effect on the male of the species, she never flaunted herself, or took unfair advantage of her femininity, which is more than can be said for most of her contemporaries.

What's more, she worked for a most reputable company, dealing with a tremendous range of drugs that ensured our relationship was maintained and on a sound professional footing.

Unlike the situation with most drug reps, I always enjoyed seeing her. And not only because I consider myself a normal male in every respect and was greatly attracted to her, but because we obviously enjoyed each other's company and were able to communicate on a personal as well as professional level.

"Victoria. It's Andrew Ryan. Anne tells me you have some good news."

"Andrew, thanks for calling back. Yes, I have and it really sounds exciting. As you know, after our last meeting, I put your trial proposal to our research group. Well, typically they took their time mulling the protocol over but at long last I'm pleased to confirm that they really are very interested in this project, and would like me to pop down to finalise the arrangements."

"That's great. When do you want to come?"

"They're keen for me to do this as soon as possible. Then, providing they do not find any obvious problems with your final plans, I can tie up the drug for the trial."

"How about Friday morning? I'm free about eleven."

"Not possible I'm afraid. Got an appointment in London. Then I've got a meeting early afternoon back at head office. How about I pop down early evening? Then perhaps I could take you out to dinner, at the company's expense of course"

"Are you sure the company can run to that? I'm not cheap, you know?"

"We'll have to see won't we. Then we can discuss it all over a decent bottle of wine."

"Now you're talking, like a true drug peddler! See you then."

* * *

Some days in hospital nothing seems to go right. If the patients themselves aren't complaining of long waiting times in clinic, it's their demanding relatives, virtually accusing you of producing the very illness currently afflicting their loved ones, and which you are striving against considerable odds to cure.

You simply cannot win and find yourself wondering what exactly it was that made you choose medicine as a career in the first place. Then, the moment you feel like throwing yourself off the top floor, everything seems to fall into place and you can't imagine what it was that made you question the whole business in the first place.

This day started very much along these lines. Patients failed to arrive for their appointments. Others, who weren't expected, appeared and demanded immediate attention. Vital medical records went missing. Those unsung heroes, the medical records girls, from deep within the bowels of the hospital, insisted that when last seen they had been booked out to my department.

It is hardly surprising that I found myself in the Blue Boar at lunchtime, seeking sanctuary from the evils of medicine. To my utter surprise I caught sight of Johnny Frobisher in the far corner, his head partially hidden behind one of his magazines.

"They let you off the reservation early did they?" I inquired

"Not exactly, Andrew." Johnny looked startled, as he gazed rather sheepishly at me, the familiar cigar clutched in his right hand.

"Oh! Do a runner, did we?"

"Thought I'd slip out for lunch. Didn't think anyone would notice. They all seem so busy and preoccupied with their ward routine."

"And I suppose Jean Drummond prescribed that cigar did she?" I wasn't going to let go. He was one of my few close friends and at certain times such friends need bullying for their own good. "Sort of hair of the dog and all that! Or should I call it 'dog-end'!" Even I didn't think that was funny but somehow it just slipped out.

"Oh! Don't *you* start. Anyway, I really don't believe it makes a bit of difference," he said, sulkily." If anything, the breathing is definitely easier now."

"You know, Johnny, I can't help feeling old Jean's barking up the wrong tree in your case. Not that I don't agree with her over the smoking issue. Dirty, filthy habit if you ask me, which I know you won't. But have you ever noticed any particular pattern to your breathing problems?"

"Not that I can say, no."

"Well, I have an idea. I know it may sound strange but every time I've witnessed you in this state, it appears to follow a period when you've been spending a lot of time with those wretched birds of yours. You know, cleaning out the coup and all that."

Johnny stared at the wall for a while and a faint look of recognition crept over his face. "Are you trying to tell me that you think I've got Bird Fancier's Lung? It really isn't possible," he wheezed, in his most indignant tone.

Bird Fancier's Lung, or *extrinsic allergic alveolitis* as it is known in the trade, is an allergic reaction to the protein present in the droppings of certain types of bird, particularly pigeons and budgerigars. In certain people it can lead to recurrent wheezy chest problems.

"Well, it is possible isn't it? I mean, in your case, you probably got it from those magazines you spend most of the time with your nose in. And I don't suppose you thought to mention it to Jean, did you? I mean, it makes sense doesn't it? Every time you get a bout you come winging your way in here for a few days' free board and keep and everything resolves quickly, regardless of what treatment they give you. Not to mention those cigars you continue to smoke throughout your stay......in the ward toilet! Why, I wouldn't be surprised if it wasn't you who set off the fire alarm the other day!" I was giving him the *Full Monty* on this one.

"Oh! Don't say that Andrew. It couldn't be the case could it? I mean, well they're such an important part of my life. My one and only hobby, in fact. It would be so unfair."

"Well, you could try resuming communications with that lovely wife of yours. I mean, I really don't know how poor Jill puts up with you. I've heard of a man's attention straying to other birds, but this is ridiculous!"

"Oh! Jill understands. She's only too pleased I've got a hobby and it keeps me in the house. Well, nearly. But, I really *can't* have that stupid condition."

"Study the facts, Johnny," I said. "It makes sense. The timing is perfect and you do get better the moment you're removed from the bird environment. It was the same in my case.....only a different species!"

"It does sound logical when you think about it. I suppose I've never really wanted to consider it. I couldn't bear having to give it all up, you see." He was sounding decidedly despondent.

"Who said anything about giving it up," I interrupted. "God knows, you've got enough children scattered about the place. Why not encourage them to do the cleaning out. I'm sure they're bribeable. Everyone has their fee!"

"I'll give it some thought," he said, looking a little brighter. "Suppose I'd better get back before they notice I've skipped."

"See you," I said, as he got to his feet and made to leave. "By the way, don't you think you'd better leave that cigar here?"

* * *

That afternoon, I met John Lindsey in the Radiotherapy/Oncology Department. John, one of our consultant oncologists, has been extremely successful in establishing our local cancer centre. The unit has a fine reputation, thanks largely to John, who is very dedicated to his work and, since his appoinment, has put in some incredibly long hours at the hospital

We have been friends and colleagues for fifteen years, during which time we have run a weekly, combined clinic dealing with patients suffering from Hodgkin's disease and other related disorders. Over the years, the clinic has become a great success, both with staff and patients, and has gone from strength to strength.

John is also interested in research and we often meet up to discuss new ideas, run over recent results, or even merely to sit and grumble about the establishment. On occasions we even act as father confessor to each other, assuming the role of analyst for our various problems.

On this occasion I wanted to discuss our plans to enlarge the combined Oncology/Haematology Ward, in an attempt to improve the facilities for treating our leukaemic patients. Our eventual aim was to set up our own Stem Cell Transplant Unit.

Many of our patients require such transplants as part of

their treatment and at present they have to be transferred to the teaching hospital, some distance away, for this procedure. It is not too surprising that many of the patients find this difficult to tolerate, due to the long separation it imposes on the family that often runs to many weeks.

The establishment of such a unit locally was therefore one of our priorities. However, this was obviously going to require the input of a considerable sum of money, not only to set up the unit, but also in terms of the continuing running costs. *Ongoing revenue consequences*, as Boris *Boring* Baldwin would put it.

Now, although Haematology is the *numero uno* speciality for me, this is not how it is perceived throughout the hospital. Many of my colleagues, particularly the surgeons, fail to realise that we actually see real, live patients and manage their treatment and on-going care. Consequently, they are at a loss to understand how we manage to spend so much of the hospital's money every year.

I think they see us as the people who stick the blood bottles into machines in the laboratory to produce the patient's blood count for them. We're the chaps who match the blood for transfusion for their patients, so that they can extract fat fees from them at the BUPA Samaritan.

In other words they see us as no more than glorified laboratory technicians, doing a strict nine-to-five job and who never get within a mile of live patients. We're the lackeys and must never forget it! Not surprisingly, paranoia runs rife with me at times, and at such times I often seek out John for a sympathetic hearing.

"My, you're looking gloomy," John greeted me. "What's up, problems down at mill?"

"Nothing special. The usual problems. Certain patients insisting I remember there's a Patient's Charter, with waiting times and lists to be adhered to. Where's the bloody Doctor's or Nurse's Charter? That's what I want to know! I can't help feeling this job would be great if it wasn't for the patients!"

"And the relatives, my friend! You can't forget the relatives!"

"Yes and the relatives. How could I ever forget *them*?" I was obviously sounding very sorry for myself.

"Cheer up. It could be worse. You *know* you live for the patients really and you'd be lost without them. You must try to be more optimistic. Whenever you start feeling like this just try to remember that guy who jumped off the top of the skyscraper. Now that's optimism for you!"

"I'm sure I don't know what you mean. Which guy was that?"

"You know, the eternal optimist. The one who, on the way down, as he passed each floor, was heard to say, '*So far so good, so far so good!*'"

"Very funny, John. I know you're right. Only it's a little hard to shake off these feelings some times, particularly when you're feeling so tired."

"Anyway, so why this honoured visit from the Chief of Haematology?" he inquired.

"I wanted to talk to you about our plans for the stem cell unit."

"What's the problem," he asked.

"Well, now we've put in our Business Case for the Trust Board's consideration I think we should prepare for their probable response."

"Such as?"

"Well, we know that the Trust's Capital Programme for the forthcoming year has been agreed. In view of the figures presented, there doesn't seem any way we will get a favourable response from those lay people on the Board. They can't even spell *Haematology*, let alone have any idea what it means."

"I think you're underestimating the poor dears. I mean, it's not directly their fault. It remains a fact of life that their resources are limited and, obviously, as a result, they're in no position to please everyone. If you wait for their agreement you may never achieve your goal. No, what you need is a fund."

"A what?"

"You know. A charitable trust fund. For instance, you could call it *The Eastwich Stem Cell Transplant Unit Fund*, or whatever. You get it registered as an official charity and you're away.

"The folks in this town are stinking rich, mostly made from suspicious activities they'd rather not discuss. Talk about guilt! They'll be falling over themselves to contribute. Anything to ease their consciences. And, what's more, you'll be doing them a favour, relieving those overburdened consciences and helping them to rest easy at night! Sort of a two-way process!"

"Do you really believe it is as easy as that? Come on. I mean, this type of person is probably the very last to start throwing their money around, especially on an NHS Hospital they wouldn't dream of entering. Not when they've got the BUPA Samaritan up the road."

"You'd be surprised, Andrew. Do you know how long it took them to raise the money for the new MRI Scanner for the X-Ray Department? Eighteen months. Admittedly they didn't get the whole sum. But, it was enough to shock the Policy Board into making up the difference. So, what do you need? Say £350,000, possibly £400,000. Well, you raise £250,000 and I guarantee the old Board coughs up the rest. Besides, it'll also be a Cancer Centre development and that makes it an emotive issue, tugging away at their heartstrings. And, all for a damn good cause too!"

"Put that way it certainly does have promise. You know, John, if you believe in us having a previous life, I think in your case you must have been an incredibly successful second-hand car salesman!

"Anyway, thanks for the chat and the advice. It has been most helpful, as usual. I'll have to see what I can do. Must go. I promised Hugh Schofield I'd go round the wards with him. Thanks for the chat.

"You know, John, sometimes I don't believe I'd ever be able to survive in this place without your continuing friendship and support."

"No problem. Fancy a pint after work?"

"Is the Pope a Catholic?"

* * *

Thursday was not particularly eventful from the haematological point of view. The patients behaved themselves and, even more surprisingly, so did their relatives. Everyone in the laboratory seemed content and even Anne could find no fault with her boss. I managed to get on with some research I'd left unfinished a few weeks before and put some ideas on paper regarding the trust fund for the stem cell unit. I worked quite late, eventually slipping away from the hospital at 7.30.

I had a quiet evening watching a nostalgic black and white film on the video, whilst I slowly sipped my way through a particularly lovely Australian Shiraz. Suitably relaxed, I dashed off a letter to my pal Frank Jenkins in Australia, accepting his offer to lecture at his hospital and suggesting a possible date later in the year.

By now, feeling completely at peace with the world, I decided not to stay up to watch the news, as it is always so depressing these days. Instead, I opted for an early night and headed for bed, only to fall fast asleep within minutes, with my open book balanced on my chest, the light on and the bedside radio blaring away.

CHAPTER SIX

A faithful friend is the medicine of life
– Ecclesiastics

There is something about Fridays that always lifts my mood, no matter how I've been the rest of the week. Perhaps it's the thought of the weekend ahead, or merely a feeling of satisfaction at what's been accomplished during the week. Whatever it is, this day was no exception.

I awoke early, with a feeling of peace and semi-contentment. More importantly, as I eased my head from the pillow, there was no semblance of a headache. Not exactly a first for me but encouraging none the less. I even caught myself humming a popular melody during shaving mode. And, to cap it all, not a single cut to be found. Now that definitely *was* a first for the week. I started to wonder whether haematologists cut themselves more often because they know all about the stuff that's trickling down their cheek intermittently, all morning.

I breezed into the car park, taking the prime slot next to the path leading to the back of the hospital. This coveted space is definitely for the early bird who, for the rest of the day, can relax smugly in the knowledge that his colleagues will know that he was in before them. Juvenile perhaps but not without a modicum of truth. I hurried towards the department, pausing only to thank the night telephonists for having left me well alone throughout their shift. They were about to go off duty and looked decidedly weary.

With the coffee machine gurgling in the corner of my room, I sat at the desk thumbing through some papers I'd left lying around the night before. As I glanced up in search of a pen, I caught sight of the photo propped against the computer. It was of my three children and had been taken at Christmas a couple of years before.

Mark looked painfully shy, as indeed he could be at times and somehow vulnerable. He would have been eighteen then, and had recently started at university studying physics.

The girls had more of an air of confidence about them. Emma, now nearly eighteen, was hoping to start a nursing course in London, provided she could obtain the necessary qualifications. She was a real softy and had sworn to protect her dad, whom she saw as eccentric and totally incapable of looking after himself.

At fourteen, Jane was a very confident young lady, doing well at school and with an ambition to succeed in business.

In many ways they were very different. In fact, often when asked how many children I had, I would reply with that well-worn Groucho Marx comment, *'Three. One of each!'* Understandably, they had become quite bored with hearing this on numerous occasions and were convinced I was entering my dotage. *'Repeating yourself is the first sign of senility,'* they had yawned.

I got to see them quite often although now they were older, they tended to use my house mainly as a resting place for their clothes, whilst they were out on the town. They were the greatest joy of my life and, at times, I missed them terribly. They lived with their mother on the other side of town and when Mark was down from university he'd often drive them over when they didn't have some more pressing engagement, such as the local discothèque.

They were very considerate though, often giving me as much as ten minutes warning, only to complain later that there wasn't enough food in the house. For a number of reasons, I hadn't been able to see them for many weeks and I made a mental note to contact them at the weekend.

As I placed the photo back on the desk the phone burst into life, making me jump. It was the switchboard. They had tried my home number first but failing to get me there had realised I must be at work. The night crew obviously hadn't mentioned that they'd seen me before the shifts had swapped over.

"It's Dr Roberts on Manvers ward. She'd like a word with you."

"Thanks. Put her through."

Dr Hilary Roberts was one of the general medical registrars. A most competent doctor, she was hoping eventually to specialise in renal medicine and was currently working for Johnny Frobisher. She was the on-call medical registrar and was calling me from the Oncology/Haematology ward.

"Morning, Hilary. What's the problem?"

"Good morning, Dr Ryan. Sorry to trouble you at this hour but we've had a problem with one of your patients."

"It's no problem. I was in anyway. Which patient?"

"It's Mr Bremner. He's suddenly dropped his blood pressure and is feeling very clammy and unwell."

Mr Bremner was one of my leukaemic patients, having been diagnosed with acute myeloid leukaemia two months before. He'd taken his first course of chemotherapy very well, although he had suffered a serious infection as a result of this heavy treatment. On recovering from this, he was found to be in complete clinical remission.

In other words, as far as all our investigations were concerned, we could not see any evidence of any remaining disease. Although we couldn't consider him cured at this stage it was a very good result and we had recently readmitted him for his second course of treatment.

To some extent this set back could be expected, as the treatment causes very low blood counts for a few weeks and it is during this period that the patient is most susceptible to overwhelming infections or even severe internal bleeding.

"Has he any fever or localising signs?"

"No, but he has had a couple of bad episodes of uncontrollable shaking and I've got the impression he's probably brewing an infection."

"I agree. Sounds like he's probably developing septicaemia. Most probably Gram negative too. Is his renal function O.K.?" In these circumstances I was particularly concerned about keeping his kidneys working normally, since they are particularly prone to failure with these infections.

"Yes, the creatinine's in the normal range at 110 and the output's good."

"O.K. Hilary. You'd better do the usual screen. Blood cultures, MSU, chest X-ray. You know the score. Then I'd start him on i/v antibiotics. Better use the big guns, and give him Gentamycin 4.5 mg/kg stat dose with blood levels pre-dose tomorrow, and Tazocin 4.5 gms t.d.s. Got that?"

"Fine, Dr Ryan. I'll get that going right away."

"Thanks, Hilary. Tell sister I'll be along later to see how things are going. Oh, and in the meantime would you mind letting my registrar, Hugh Schofield, know what's happened, when he comes on duty?"

"No problem."

"Thanks. Bye."

On that note I returned my attention to the papers in front of me, and in particular the problems of getting a stem cell unit trust fund off the ground.

* * *

On my way to the ward later that morning I ran into Johnny Frobisher in the corridor. He had been discharged from the ward and was looking quite pleased with himself.

"So, you finally beat poor old Jean into submission. Where are you off to now? What's it to be first? Feed the pigeons, or a visit to the tobacconist? It must be terrible, having such a difficult decision to make!" I said, as sarcastically as possible.

He decided to ignore the latter remark. "Don't know what you mean, Andrew. We get on very well really. She was a bit annoyed with me at first, for not having mentioned the old hobby but she eventually calmed down. All things considered I think she's pretty reasonable. Well, as reasonable as is possible for a female doctor." He definitely was feeling more perky. I think now I prefer him more when he's wheezing.

"Steady on, Dr Frobisher! That's chauvinist talk. *Equal opportunities* and all that. This is the twenty-first century you know, not the middle Ages." I was appearing for the defence this time. Not my natural role I know but perhaps I was mellowing with age, like a good bottle of wine. And, like a good bottle of wine, it was not destined to last long.

"Well, you know what I mean. The sort of woman who survives and reaches the top in our system has to be tough and relentless, not to mention resilient. I didn't mean any disrespect."

"I'm sure you didn't, old darling."

"I do wish you'd stop calling me that. Here, I gather old Boris has put in a complaint about you to the Chief Executive. Someone in the Trust office leaked the news to Jean," he said, with concern in his voice.

"That's par for the bloody course. Not so much the complaint.

You know how I simply *cherish* them. But, being the last to hear about it. Sneaky bastard, old *Boring*. I don't know why he doesn't confront me directly. Anyway what's his beef this time?"

"Apparently, he's accused you of malpractice," Johnny replied.

"What! Malpractice!" I couldn't help laughing. I would willingly confess to most of the deadly sins but malpractice certainly was not one of them. "What have I done this time, been caught sleeping with the enemy!"

"If you mean by that, *patients*, no. He's accused you of accepting bribes from various drug companies to use their drugs." Johnny was obviously very worried. Far more worried than I ever thought I could be about such a preposterous accusation.

"What drug companies? What drugs?" I shouted, indignantly.

"Keep your voice down. People will hear you."

"What does it matter? They've probably heard everything else about it already, anyway." I was trembling with anger. I had a good mind to have the whole thing out with old *Boring* in front of his embarrassed junior staff but then thought better of it. "What companies?" I veritably whispered.

"I don't know. Jean didn't get that information."

"That's because it's not true," I said. "Malpractice! What a bloody cheek. I mean, that ignoramus spends most of his cushy, protected life sitting on his fat arse in one committee after another while some poor bastard has to do his work for him. I bet he doesn't see more than a handful of patients all week. Now *that's* what I call malpractice. Sanctimonious old swine! What sort of bribery is he talking about anyway?"

"He said you've been receiving various direct payments from the companies in return for using their drugs, which of course *do* happen to be very expensive," Johnny said, glancing at an attractive nurse as she passed down the corridor, and he fiddled nervously with his bow tie and started to blush.

"I might have guessed money was at the root of all this. He should have been a bloody bank manager!" Funny how the haematologist's favourite adjective is *bloody*.

"Every drug I use is the best one available for the particular problem I'm dealing with, regardless of the cost. If this Health Service cannot afford the drug, it's hardly my problem. This government got itself elected largely on the strength of the promises it made regarding the *National Health Service*, *Education* and so on.

If it has no intention of living up to its promises, then it should move over and let the other lot have a go, not that it would probably make any difference.

"They didn't seem to have any problem affording the Millennium Dome, fat lot of good that was to my patients. And we're talking about a sum of around a thousand million pounds, so they obviously don't have any real problem with money these days, do they!" A fiendish grin crept across my face, as I began to feel pleased with my little outburst.

"But what about the money Boris was referring to, Andrew?" Johnny continued to look worried.

"The money that old sneak's talking about happens to represent legitimate expenses incurred by me whenever I attend a medical meeting, such as the annual American Society of Haematology meeting every December. Since I'm invariably presenting some research involving one of these infamous drugs he's been going on about, the relevant company happens to sponsor my attendance at the meeting.

"That way, everyone's happy. The company, because hopefully my research is going to show what a truly useful and wonderful drug they have. The hospital, because the miserable bastards won't have to shell out any *study leave* allowance to me and instead can spend the money on carpets, furniture, and expensive plants for the Trust Board offices. And, last but not least, me, because I get away from this sweatbox for a few days.

"All perfectly legitimate, as I said. I make sure I keep all the relevant receipts and have even declared it all to the Inland Revenue, bless their little cotton socks. What I didn't realise was that I also had to declare it all to dear old Boris as well!"

"Then I don't see he has a leg to stand on," said Johnny, relieved at last.

"If he has, then I'll sure as hell kick it from under him."

"Well, that's a relief. You are a strange beast at times Andrew, but your heart's in the right place."

"Thank you for those few kind words Dr Frobisher. You're not a bad old stick yourself. I'll bring my sick kidneys to you anytime!"

"Don't mention it. Hey," he said, staring at his watch, "I must be getting along. See you back at the infirmary next week." And with that he was off down the corridor.

"Cheerio……Oh wise one!"

* * *

The rest of the day was relatively uneventful. By late afternoon I was on my end-of-the-week ward round with Hugh Schofield and the houseman on Manvers ward. I was pleased to find Mr Bremner looking decidedly better since starting his antibiotics. His blood pressure had come back up and he was feeling more comfortable.

"Better start the growth factor injections today Hugh. That might get his white cell count back a bit sooner," I said, pointing to his drug chart.

"Yes, Dr Ryan."

"It'll also help spend a little of that precious money old Boris and Douglas Whines are meticulously trying to stash away for the administration," I whispered to myself, obviously not quiet enough.

"I beg you pardon, Dr Ryan?" Hugh inquired.

"Oh! Er, nothing, Hugh. Well, is that all of them?"

"Yes, that's the last patient," he replied.

"O.K. Thanks, Hugh. You on call this weekend?"

"Yes, from tomorrow morning."

"Well, give me a ring if there's any problem. I really don't mind being phoned. Makes me look very important in restaurants. Like a used car dealer!"

"You won't forget to switch the mobile on this time will you Dr Ryan!" It was Sister Cannon piping up with her usual invaluable advice.

We'd known each other for nine years, ever since she had been appointed as our new ward sister. A diminutive-looking woman, she had become a terrific asset to the unit and knew all her consultants like the back of her hand.

She kept a firm grip on the ward and protected her nurses like a mother hen. On arrival on the ward for the first time, all new male junior doctors were given the standard ten-minute lecture, the gist of which was that fraternisation with her nurses would result in instant castration or worse.

No one yet had fathomed out what *worse* referred to and not one of the junior staff had dared venture to find out. Although she was firm, she was also extremely fair and consistent, and you certainly knew where you were with her. We had always got on famously, sharing a similar slightly bizarre sense of humour.

"Certainly not, Mary. As if I would ever be guilty of such a thing!" Only last week I had gone to play tennis one evening with our usual four and had forgotten to switch the damn thing on. When they needed me, it was Mary who finally sussed where I was. It's a long time since I've had such a peaceful game. Perhaps that's why we won. Hugh was grinning at the houseman, a little embarrassed, whilst I received this subtle warning.

"Of course not, Dr Ryan. As if you'd be guilty of that," she smiled to herself, as she returned to the ward desk with the note trolley.

I bade farewell to my team and set off back to the department.

CHAPTER SEVEN

There is at bottom only one genuinely scientific treatment for all diseases, and that is to stimulate the phagocytes
– George Bernard Shaw

"I put Victoria Hall in your room when she arrived. That was about ten minutes ago. I hope it's alright, Dr Ryan," Anne said, looking up from her desk as I entered the department.

"Fine," I replied. "Any messages for me?"

"No messages. But the Chief Executive's secretary wanted me to make an appointment for you to see him early next week. I made it for 10.30 on Monday morning if that's alright. The coffee should have worked by then!"

"That's O.K. by me you old cynic. Anyway, if it's about what I think it is, I'll probably need something a lot stronger then coffee for this particular meeting. Somehow I think it is going to require all my powers of tact and diplomacy. Luckily, they happen to be my middle names! It's almost as if I invented the expression!"

"Been rubbing the establishment up the wrong way again, have we? You do realise that if you get the shove I'll have to go and look for another job as well. I mean, it's taken me years to get used to you and I really don't think I could go through all that again with someone else."

"Come on, Anne, you love me really, don't you?" I enquired, complete with my special hangdog expression.

"No. But I'm used to you!" And with that she returned her gaze to the work in front of her. Suitably dismissed, I headed for my room.

"Victoria, how lovely to see you." She was looking breathtaking as usual, in a dark blue silk suit and white blouse with her long blonde hair cascading off her shoulders. She wore the minimum of make up, just sufficient to accentuate her natural beauty and was sitting in the easy chair across from my desk.

"And you, Andrew." She had a lovely, sensuous smile that took me back nearly twenty-five years, to when I was a houseman and had fallen madly in love with a staff nurse on my ward. Of course, she hardly ever noticed me, having eyes only for one of the surgical registrars, who I gather she eventually married. I couldn't help thinking that she'd probably be fat with varicose veins and a gaggle of screaming grandchildren by now and obviously far too old for me.

"Did the jjourney down ttake long?" I stammered, half blushing. She was doing it to me again. My knees felt like jelly and I couldn't find my words. I was a dumbstruck teenager again.

"No. A little over the hour. Bit of a problem getting out of London but then the traffic flowed smoothly. How was the ward round? Got many in?"

"Not too bad. You look terrific. Can I get you anything, coffee, tea?"

"No thanks. I'm fine. Have you finished for the day, or do you want me to leave you for a while?"

"Oh! No. I've nothing particular to do. If I start anything new now I'll be trapped for hours. Anne's finishing off the letters, so we might as well go."

"Where shall we go? Do you have any particular restaurant in mind?" she asked, brushing her hair from over her forehead; an act that, routine as it was, nevertheless caused me to catch my breath rather suddenly.

"Who's paying, if it's not a rude question?"

"Cytotech. I told you on the phone"

"Ah, yes. I forgot. In that case I know the very place. It's a little French restaurant not too far from here. Quite expensive but well worth it. Terrific atmosphere. I'm sure Cytotech would greatly approve!"

"Sounds perfect," she said, doing that manoeuvre with her hair again, and producing yet one more bout of apoplexy deep within me. "Will it be open at this time?"

"Probably not. I'll get Anne to book us a table, and perhaps we could slip out to a pub for a drink first."

"Fine by me. I'll drive if you like. Is it alright to leave your car here till later?" She smiled again, and I was instantly transported to another planet.

"Now you're talking, Victoria. You know, I knew I was going to like you when we first met, all those years ago. And there's certainly no problem leaving my car here. It probably could do with the rest anyway!" I managed a reciprocal smile.

"Some men are easily satisfied," she teased. "And it can't be all that many years ago. You make me sound ancient."

"That's the last thing I want to do," I said, finding my confidence slowly returning. "O.K. You drive and I'll navigate. I know a great watering hole a little way out in the country and it's not far from La Petite Chaumière."

"You've got a deal," she said, as she got to her feet, grabbing her briefcase off the floor in the process.

We headed out of the office, pausing only to ask Anne to book us a table for later. We drove in her new company BMW, much more comfortable than my old banger, and decidedly cleaner.

The conversation flowed easily and within minutes I'd put all the turbulence of the previous few days out of my mind. She explained what a busy week it had been and how much she had managed to accomplish.

In no time at all we were in the car park of the *Dog and Parrot*. As soon as she'd parked the car I was out of the passenger seat and round the car so as to open the door for her.

"Why thank you, Dr Ryan" she whispered whilst rolling her eyes with an expression of amazement. "It would seem the age of chivalry is not dead after all. By the way, is this yours?" she asked, handing me my mobile phone. "I noticed it on the floor as you got out."

"Yes," I mumbled, half blushing as I took it from her and switched it on, before placing it safely in my top pocket.

"I'd imagine it's a bit difficult being on call without that switched on," she grinned.

"Yes, so I've been told!"

We entered the bar and made for a quiet corner, where she settled into a chair by the window, withdrawing some papers from her briefcase as she did so. While she placed them on the table and started to scan through them, I wandered over to the bar and got a white wine for her and a large gin and tonic for myself.

"The only way to finish the week," I grinned, raising my glass and adding, "Cheers. You know, Victoria, I would just like to say that it really is lovely to see you again and also a big *thank you* for all your help and support with this trial I've been pushing to get accepted. I must say it seems so long since you were last down this way."

"Cheers, Andrew. And thank you for your kind words. It's lovely to see you again too" she said, slowly sipping her drink.

"You look whacked," she added. "Has it been a bad week?"

"You could say that," I replied, between gulps of my gin. "Some of the patients were barely tolerable, which is more than I can say for the administration. To cap it all, earlier on I received a summons to see the headmaster on Monday morning. Got a feeling he's not too happy with me at the moment. I'll probably get six of the best!"

"What have you done this time? Anne told me you're never happy unless you're causing mayhem for the managers."

"*'Mayhem for the Managers'*, Sounds like a song, or even a play!"

"Trust you! Yes, I suppose it does."

"Anyway, my good woman, the dictionary definition of *manager* is *a person who directs or manages an organisation, industry, shop, etc.* These guys couldn't organise an orgy in a free Paris brothel!"

She laughed, brushing her hair from off her forehead as she did so; a manoeuvre that nearly resulted in me swallowing the lemon slice in my drink.

"It also has another meaning, you know," she fired back. "*A person who controls the business affairs of an actor, entertainer, etc.*, and, no doubt, that's their role in your case. I can see you now, doing your full Laurence Olivier bit in front of the committee."

"Touché! Let's not waste time talking about that lot. After all I have managed to survive a whole week of them relatively unscathed."

"And vice versa, no doubt! Fair enough. Then it's down to business," she said, picking up the papers she had sorted on the table in front of her.

We talked for nearly an hour about the drug trial I had proposed. Her company was definitely interested and had made various suggestions with regard to the drug protocol and the patient information sheet.

The latter is such an important piece of paper, as it is the main way we have of getting the patient to understand the basic concepts of what treatment we have chosen to use in their particular case. It is vital that it also includes all the necessary information on the possible side effects to expect from the drugs we will be administering.

For obvious reasons the wording of this piece of information has to be precise and must not leave any possible loopholes which may give the patient or their relative a chance to make a major complaint regarding the patient's management.

The company had insisted that I act as principal investigator and were prepared to offer us the drug free on certain conditions which are standard for this kind of trial. It was now up to me to draw up the treatment protocol and get it through the medical ethics committee.

Our ethics committee is a strange affair, its members representing a broad cross section of the community. It includes doctors, nurses, a pharmacist, my pal Douglas Whines, and a few lay members, most prominent of whom is a local vicar. Over the past few years he and I have had a number of run-ins, usually regarding what I considered to be relatively trivial issues to do with my research. All good sport though, and I'd say the score currently stands at fifteen all!

The conversation then moved on to more pleasant topics. In particular, the weekend and what we would each be doing with our free time.

"I've no doubt your other half will have some exciting pursuit lined up. An unexpected trip to Paris, or shopping in London followed by a show and dinner," I ventured.

"There is no other half," she said, staring at the young couple giggling in the far corner.

"No other half. Somehow I find that incredibly hard to believe," I said, with a lift in my voice.

"I don't see what's so surprising about that," she said, raising her glass and staring blankly at it for a while, before taking a sip. "Sometimes it does you good to be on your own for a while. Gives you the chance to take stock of your life and decide what you really want to do with it."

"But looking at you it seems hard to believe you're not swamped with admirers pestering you day and night for your company."

"I didn't say there wasn't the occasional one who has tried recently. But somehow, they don't quite seem to fit the picture that I have of myself at the moment," she volunteered.

"Well there doesn't seem to be anything wrong with the picture from where I'm sitting," I managed to say, without blushing. *Smooth talking bastard*, I thought to myself.

"Thank you." Now it was her turn to do the blushing.

"But tell me. There must have been someone back there in the not so distant past," I enquired, not wishing to appear too inquisitive.

She took another long look at her glass and then back at me. "Yes there was someone once." She seemed to hesitate for a while, as if she wasn't sure that she wanted to discuss it. Then she took a deep breath and proceeded to tell me the whole story.

She took her time and didn't seem at all embarrassed as she related the events that had led to their relationship, their wonderful time together and the tragic way it had ended. For the first time that day she appeared to lose her composure, but only for a short while and she soon brightened up by the time she had finished, her beautiful smile returning once again.

Paul had been an airline pilot working for British Airways. He was a first officer and flew mainly the European routes. Not surprisingly they had met in the air, when she was flying to Rome to represent Cytotec at a major European medical conference. This had been not long after she joined the company.

He had slipped away from the cockpit to stretch his legs and had brushed past her, knocking her drink into her lap. He was most embarrassed and couldn't stop apologising. And while he was struggling for the words, he picked up the glass but then managed to drop it onto the arm rest, where it proceeded to deposit the rest of its contents onto her dress.

She couldn't help laughing at the sight of this very attractive pilot, a most responsible person who was capable of flying hundreds of people safely all over the world but incapable of sorting out a minor accident without making it worse.

When she ran into him again at the airport, soon after arrival, she took one look at his pathetic, doleful expression and immediately burst into laughter once more. Naturally, they got into conversation. He begged her to let him take her out for dinner by way of an apology for the trouble he had caused. She willingly accepted, and was soon captivated by his charm.

The relationship blossomed and it was not long before they were sharing a flat together in West London. Her whole life changed. They were passionately in love with each other and couldn't bear to be separated, even for those few days when he was away flying. She had wanted to get married there an then but he was more cautious at first. He didn't like the idea of being away so much and felt they hadn't known each other long enough. She couldn't help thinking how unusual it was for it to be the man who thought in these terms.

In the end, even he couldn't bear it any longer and they fixed the date of the wedding for spring the following year. As winter approached they became very preoccupied with the arrangements for the ceremony.

She was blissfully happy and in her own world. Nothing could mar such wonderful feelings locked deep within her; feelings she had never experienced before.

Or so it seemed, until one Saturday evening early in December, when there was a knock on the front door. At first she thought it was Paul returning early from the football match having forgotten his keys. Then she realised it couldn't be that, since he had needed his keys for his motorbike, which he had taken on this occasion, as it was an away match and out of town.

The police sergeant at the door was very kind and compassionate. He broke the news as gently as he could, although the manner of his delivery failed to stem its impact on Victoria. Paul had been in a collision with an on-coming car on a particularly dangerous bend. It had all happened so quickly and he had been killed outright. The policeman added that the witnesses to the accident all stated it had happened so quickly, that they didn't believe Paul would have known anything and certainly would not have suffered.

Victoria's whole life fell apart. Her friends all rallied round with offers of support, but she largely declined their help, choosing to remain alone with her happy memories. Over the following months she threw herself into her work, in an effort to blank out her inner feeling of sadness and despair.

Slowly she recovered, but she still would spend long periods alone with her thoughts, gradually coming to terms with the events of that winter. Later, there had been other friendships, but nothing that had lasted any length of time. When she eventually finished relating the story she smiled, as if it had been a great relief to have had the chance to discuss it after all this time.

"I am so sorry Victoria. I had no idea," I blurted out, wishing I'd never mentioned the subject of anyone else.

"Oh! That's alright. It's a long time ago now and, as they say, '*Life goes on.*' Besides, I think it has done me good to talk about it after keeping it bottled up for so long. Here, I do sound morbid don't I. Lets talk about something a bit more positive," she suggested.

"Like you taking me to dinner," I suggested. "That reminds me," I said, glancing at my watch, "We're a bit late, so we'd better hurry."

"Right," she said, reaching for her papers and stashing them back into her case. "Then perhaps over dinner I can hear a bit about what makes Dr Ryan tick."

"Not much to hear, really. Bit of a rusty clock, I'm afraid." I replied, blushing once more.

And with that we left the Dog and Parrot and made our way through the winding country lanes to the restaurant.

* * *

"So, what skeletons lurk in your cupboard then, Dr Ryan?" We had finished the rack of lamb and were enjoying a magnificent glass of *Les Forts de Latour, Pauillac 1985* whilst waiting for the crème brûlée.

"A veritable graveyard, if truth be known," I sighed. "But it's all pretty boring really, compared with your globetrotting life."

"Is there anyone else at the moment?" She had heard about the divorce from Diane and, on more than one occasion, she had commented on the photo on my desk.

"Apart from Beethoven and Bach, no. I'm resting, as the actor says when he's out of work. Completely unliveable with, that's me."

"I'm sure that's not true," she interrupted. "Anne said you put up this front deliberately to keep people away. She certainly seems to know you very well."

"I'm afraid she does, too damn well. You know, I've spent fourteen years trying to insult that woman and haven't got through once yet. I've virtually given up on that one."

"You are funny, Andrew. You know she's invaluable to you. And you don't really mean it anyway. It's all a bluff. A front, to keep people at bay. And it's all very strange because, deep down, you really do enjoy company. In fact, you can be the life and soul of the party when it suits you, which isn't often these days according to Anne."

"Sounds like you've been researching my whole life story!" I interrupted.

"Not really. It's only that you don't seem to add up sometimes. On the outside you put up this hard, slightly cynical, even brash barrier. And all the time, on the inside, there lurks a very soft, kind, sensitive, and caring individual. You don't fool me and you certainly don't fool Anne." I was sure the wine was getting to her.

"Hey! Steady on, you're ruining my street cred." I felt insulted. "No one can live up to that image and you well know it. Besides, that wouldn't get me anywhere at the infirmary. They'd run roughshod over me in a week. Old Boris would have me on weekend sluice duty."

"Tell me about your wife?" She changed the subject, and not a moment too soon.

"There's not much to tell. I met Diane when I was specialising as a registrar in London. She had only recently qualified and was doing her pre-registration house jobs. We hit it off from day one and started going out, typical hospital romance really.

"We were married within eighteen months and by that time she was intent on becoming a GP. But the children came along and soon put paid to that idea. Shame, we needed the money!" I added, quite unnecessarily.

"Andrew!" Victoria wasn't going to let me get away with that.

"Sorry. Well, the children were great fun of course, but all the time I think that, deep down, she bore some resentment over losing out on her career. But that's women for you, they want it all."

"There you go again. And men don't, I suppose!"

"Anyway, as the children got older and more off her hands, she started a refresher course. Eventually, after I'd been at Eastwich a few years she got herself a place in a practice on the other side of town. By this time we had drifted apart and were in our own worlds.

"The first few years had been particularly difficult for me at Eastwich. The department was very low key when I arrived, offering a diagnostic service, but very little else. There was no clinical haematology; all the serious cases were referred to London. It took me years to build the clinical side up, but obviously it didn't do much for the marriage, especially when Diane was so busy with he own work."

"How did you eventually come to separate?"

"It was about five years ago. The atmosphere had become so strained and it was obvious that we had to make the break. We talked it over for a week or two and even discussed it with the children, well the two older ones. We tried to make it as amicable as possible, but you know how these things are. It never quite works out how you want it. Especially when the bloody lawyers get in on the act. Do you know what the definition of *alimony* is?"

"No."

"It's *the screwing you get for the screwing you got*!"

"That's pretty crude and definitely unnecessary," she said, giving me an expression that left no doubt she meant it. It was not something I had witnessed before and I knew it was definitely for real.

"So is divorce," I added." I wouldn't recommend it."

"Not a problem for me. I'm not married."

"Whoops! I'm sorry. There I go again with my size nine mouth." I pleaded for clemency.

"Have there been any significant others since?" she appeared genuinely interested.

"It all sounds so formal when you say, *'significant.'* No, not really. Bit like you. The occasional fling, but nothing to hang a marriage certificate on."

"You sound so cynical Andrew. I'm sure it's not like that. It's probably more likely that you don't want anything to happen. Sort of a defence. That well known Ryan barrier. Keeps all well known invaders out; particularly the female of the species."

The dessert finally arrived and, as far as I was concerned, not a moment too soon.

Saved by the crème brûlée!

"Would you like another glass of this gorgeous wine?"

CHAPTER EIGHT

Love's like the measles – all the worse when it comes late in life
– Douglas Jerrold

After dinner, we agreed that I had better not drive as it had been a long evening with the drinks flowing somewhat freely and mostly in my direction. Victoria suggested dropping me off at my place when I told her I could easily pick my car up at the hospital in the morning.

"Would you like a night-cap," I asked, as she swung into the driveway.

"Perhaps a coffee would be sensible. I've probably had more than I should. It certainly was a lovely evening. I can't remember when I last laughed so much. And the meal was excellent."

"Me too, I enjoyed it very much. It's been so long since I've been out to dinner. I love talking with you. Conversation seems to flow so easily. I can't help thinking that, if you were on some of these committees I have to attend with monotonous regularity, I'd probably end up a veritable pussy cat." Boy, the drink was certainly loosening my tongue.

"Thank you. I see the age of flattery is not dead," she grinned as she locked the car.

Once inside, I took her coat and showed her into the lounge. She sat beside the inglenook fireplace as I lit the fire and fetched some logs from the kitchen. Even though it was early spring the temperature drop during the evening was still sufficient to require heating.

"Are you sure you wouldn't like a brandy?" I asked, as I built up the fire.

"I'd love one but I really mustn't. I'd probably lose my licence and with it my job with Cytotec." She looked at me with those wonderful soft, warm eyes.

"Well, you could always stop here for the night. The house has plenty of rooms. Unless of course you really need to get home."

"That's very kind of you, Andrew. I've nothing special on tomorrow, but perhaps I ought to go," she said, sounding slightly tempted.

"Oh! Come on. You've nothing to lose and perhaps, if I play my cards right, I may get a decent breakfast in the morning for once."

"I see. I should have guessed. With men there's usually an ulterior motive," she smiled appearing even more tempted. "Well, put that way how can a woman refuse. In that case I'd love a brandy."

"Now that's what I like, a woman who can change her mind! One brandy coming up for my lady." I had been rejuvenated. "Napoleon alright?"

"Well, not according to Nelson, but it sounds fine to me!"

"Oh! A comedienne in our midst. Perhaps you have had too much to drive. Women never can hold their booze," I jibed.

"Just because *you* drink for England, you think the fairer sex can't handle it. Typical of the male chauvinist. One day I'll take you on at a contest, but right now I could do with that brandy." She looked at me with menacing eyes that made me laugh out loud.

"Right you are my lady. One brandy coming up, shaken but not stirred."

"I can't believe that, knowing you! I mean, it's not in your nature to miss any opportunity to stir it, now, is it?" she retorted.

"I can't win. Hopeless to even try. Back in a jiff," I said, as I disappeared in the direction of the kitchen. I think it is better known as *'retiring to regroup.'* Whatever it is, I poured two generous brandies and set the coffee machine in motion, before returning to the lounge to find Victoria sitting on the carpet staring into the flames.

"Penny for your thoughts," I asked, handing her the glass.

"I was miles away," she said, glancing back at the fire. "I always get mesmerised by the flames. Tell me, Andrew, don't you ever get lonely sitting here all by yourself at night?"

"But I'm not on my own," I replied

"But you said there were no others."

"I lied."

"Ah! A liar, as well as an alcoholic. There is no hope. And pray tell me, who are these mysterious guests? Or would you rather not say?" she enquired.

"Beethoven, Bach , Chopin, you know. I slap them on the old CD player and I'm instantly in the company of friends. Transported into oblivion. There can be no equal."

"You are a hopeless case," she whispered, gently sniffing her brandy. "And what of real, live people. Don't they get a look in?"

"Who are they?" I replied, rolling my eyes. "I think I've heard of them, but they don't qualify, since they'll only try and make me mend my ways. Or else they'll be complaining of some symptom or other. No ma'am, not on your life. I'll stick to the BBC, you know… Beethoven, Bach, and Chopin. They always behave themselves and don't try to change anything in me."

"Yes, and we can't have that can we. Dr Ryan is not allowed to be dragged back into the land of the living. Strictly forbidden." She was sounding serious.

"That's not absolutly true you know, Victoria," I said, striking a slightly more serious note. "I know I tend to put on this flippant act and in some ways it is a sort of defence. But in truth I get so annoyed with many of the things I see happening these days. Not only in her Britannic Majesty's Nationalised Health Service, but in the world in general.

"People and governments really do not seem to act logically most of the time. And usually it's got something to do with greed or power. I mean, sometimes I think it would drive me to drink……that is, if I wasn't already there!"

"That was quite a nice speech, till you got silly at the end. You are not as big a drinker as you make out. You get hangovers too easily. Well, according to Anne anyway. And that's certain to guarantee you don't drink that regularly," she lectured.

"Tell me Victoria, did you major in psychology by any chance?" I questioned.

"No, but in your case one doesn't need a degree to work you out," she said, draining her glass. "I don't suppose I could have another could I? I think I've got some catching up to do, not that I'm implying anything." That grin swept over her face once again and I completely melted.

"No problem ma'am." I took her glass and turned for the door.

"How about some music," I said, as I switched on the player and selected Elgar's Enigma Variations before disappearing back to the kitchen. I returned a minute later, not to the strains of Nimrod, but to the dulcet tones of Whitney Houston singing *Something in Common*.

"Where did you find that?" I asked, with genuine surprise in my voice, as I handed her the drink.

"It was over there on the book case. Why, don't you remember it?"

"Not really. I think someone must have left it here some time ago."

"Aha! A dalliance from the past. So life still exists deep down in the old haematologist after all. Well, at least she had good taste I must say." She smiled, as she clinked her glass a little clumsily on mine.

"Maybe. But don't let it get out. You know, street cred and all that," I whispered in her ear as I added, "quite a nice tune really."

"To hell with the tune! What about the words? They say everything. What is it about men that totally prevents them from taking in the important messages these songs are trying to convey?" She looked decidedly angry, in a tipsy sort of way.

"What words?" I said, dodging her right cross and catching her as she tripped on the edge of the carpet.

"You're hopeless, Dr Ryan," She giggled helplessly in my arms.

At this moment instinct took over, as I slowly bent forward and kissed her gently on the lips. To my complete surprise there was no indication of any resistance. After what seemed minutes I straightened up, about to offer a semi-drunken apology. But before I could say anything she lifted her hands, clasping the back of my head and drew me down to her lips once again. When we had finished I felt suddenly embarrassed and suggested we sit on the sofa by the fire.

"Victoria," I mumbled, "I don't know what came over me. You must forgive me."

"Why, what did you do wrong. I didn't exactly decline your advances. It has been a long time since anyone kissed me and I must say it's still a lovely feeling."

"If it's been a long time for you, it sseems like decades for me," I stammered, at a loss for words.

"Well, you didn't give that impression. And I bet you wouldn't get that from Beethoven! Or if you did it would probably be *Pathetique,*" she quipped, taking another sip from her glass before reaching over and kissing me once again. "You know, you taste quite nice for a musty old haematologist!"

"Victoria, you're a very beautiful woman and I really care a lot for you, but don't you think this is all a bit silly."

"What, kissing an old haematologist. No I don't. I've never done it before and obviously didn't know what I've been missing." And with that she leant forward once again and kissed me. A long, hard and very passionate kiss. Suddenly, I was that houseman again, madly in love but somehow unsure of what to do next. I needn't have worried as she seemed to be calling all the shots.

"Shall we take the coffee upstairs?" she asked, with a seductive glint in her eye.

"Look Victoria, I have to tell you. You know, it's been a long time…."

"For me too," she butted in. "But don't worry. I won't tell anyone, if you don't." She grinned at me for a second and I was totally gone. Then she slowly leant over and gently started to undo my shirt.

That night we made love in front of the fire. She was warm and passionate, and so tremendously giving of her love. She had so much to give and it was as if she had longed to do so for some considerable time. Now it all flowed out. I felt completely transformed and at peace as she gently caressed me and whispered sweet, soothing words in my ear.

Feelings of love, I had never before experienced, were kindled deep within me. As I entered her I experienced feelings of passion and arousal I would never have believed possible. As if with an innate and immaculate sense of timing gained from a lifetime of experience together we came as one, melting in a sea of frenzied passion in each other's arms. Exhausted, we lay there speechless, but obliviously happy and at odds with the world. Somehow words were not required.

After some time we stirred and went upstairs to bed where we made glorious love again, taking great care to please each other as sensuously as possible. At long last we fell into a deep sleep locked in each other's arms. It all seemed so wonderfully natural.

I was the first to wake, probably due to the presence of a mild earthquake in the region of my frontal cortex. Glancing to my left I could see Victoria at peace, with her head resting lightly on my shoulder. She looked so beautiful with her long blonde hair scattered over the pillow.

I kissed her gently on the forehead and she blinked one eye at me. A satisfied grin crept over her face as she moved slowly across and kissed me lightly on the lips. At the same time I could feel her hand moving slowly and carefully over my thigh. In an instant the earthquake was replaced by a nuclear chain reaction, as we began to make rampant love once more.

* * *

As we sat eating breakfast and sipping coffee, Victoria caught sight of my worried expression.

"Something troubling you, Andrew?"

"Only a minor earthquake going on in my head," I replied, with my much rehearsed, sorry-for-myself expression covering my face.

"Ah! A hangover. What a surprise!"

"I'll have you know, my good woman, that a hangover is God's way of telling you that you're still alive," I volunteered, with an obvious air of experience and authority. "Albeit, only just!" I added.

"I am not your *good woman*, you chauvinist pig!" she laughed, sliding round the table to give me an affectionate peck on the cheek.

"Victoria."

"Yes, *old man*!"

"Last night was a wonderful experience for me. After so long, I never thought something like this would ever happen to me again."

"You mean you've experienced this before," she said, feigning insult.

"Not quite like this, no."

"That's alright then!" She was smiling again.

"Seriously Victoria, I didn't want you to think that I do this sort of thing every day." I pleaded.

"I should hope not. You'd probably be dead within a month if you did..........*old boy*!" she teased, by now obviously enjoying the advantage.

"I wish you'd be serious for a moment, you infuriating drug rep, you," I retaliated.

"Ah! Shoe on the other foot is it. *You* can be flippant, whenever it suits you to switch off, but I can't, is that it?" She had me in a vice, and was slowly turning the screw.

"O.K. I give in. You win. But will you listen to me for a minute, please," I pleaded.

"What's on your mind?"

"I'm trying to tell you, in my own inimitable and clumsy way, that I love you Victoria. More importantly, I am *in love* with you. In fact, if truth be known, I think I've been in love with you for some time. Every time you visit Eastwich I crumble at the knees at the very sight of you. I know I've probably embarrassed you, but I just had to tell you. And I would fully understand if this tirade frightens you off forever, but I'd never forgive myself if I let this moment pass without telling you." Somehow I felt a great sense of relief in getting all that off my chest.

"You big softy, Andrew. Do you think you are the only one with feelings? I also have felt strongly attracted to you for sometime. I don't know what it was, but there was something about you that turned me on from the start. Perhaps it was your deep-seated sense of caring, carefully hidden behind that defensive Ryan wall and that incredible air of vulnerability that accompanies you wherever you go. And then of course there's your cute ass!"

"My *what*?"

"Your cute ass," she repeated, playing seductively with the lapel of my dressing gown, as she gave my backside a pinch.

"Want to go upstairs again.......you sex maniac?"

CHAPTER NINE

I'm not unwell. I'm fucking dying
– Jeffrey Bernard

It was 8.30 when I arrived at the hospital on Monday morning. As I walked toward the entrance I caught sight of Johnny locking his car. He was carrying a bundle of notes under his arm and looking at his watch as he coughed out loud.

"Been at those bloody pigeons again?" I shouted across the car park.

"Andrew," he looked startled. "No need to shout. If you must know I've been showing the girls how to look after my little feathered friends this weekend. They picked it up quite well actually. So, from now on I can sit back and delegate," he said, with real pride in his voice.

"You're sounding more and more like a bloody surgeon! Anyway, I'm proud of you. You'll make an administrator yet," I smiled at him. "Guess who's got to see the headmaster this morning?" I teased him.

"Andrew, I'm really worried about you and I must say my piece. Some of our colleagues are saying that you've not been acting in a civilised manner recently and are seriously questioning your sanity. I'm sure one or two of them are already conspiring behind your back."

"I've no doubt they are. In fact, I'd be positively hurt if they weren't. You want to know what Ghandi said when he visited these shores in the '30 s and was asked by some twee reporter, *'what do you think of civilisation in Britain?'"*

"I don't suppose there's any way I can avoid this and I know you're just itching to tell me," he smiled.

"He replied, *'I think it would be a good idea!'"*

"I never doubted you'd have an answer, you always have."

"On certain occasions circumstances can arise that really do require a suitable answer there and then." I tried to respond, with conviction. "But you know, although it was a very amusing retort, I can't help feeling that there's some degree of truth in its message.

"We appear to be surrounded by hypocrites. Whether they genuinely believe in what they say or are merely opting for the easy way out, I'm not sure. I don't even believe I care, but I do question why some of these charlatans ever took up medicine in the first place, if all they were after was the easy life."

"All the same, I've warned you before and I mean it. I am very concerned, Andrew. You can be most infuriating sometimes but, all in all, you're one of the good guys and we can't afford to lose the good guys. There, I've said my piece. Now I must get to work. I've got some catching up to do."

"Thanks for the advice, I appreciate it, really. I'll make every effort to be more constructive with my crusade in future," I said, accompanying him into the building.

* * *

Since I was the first to arrive in the department, I went straight to collect the mail, pausing only to switch on the coffee machine. While sifting through the envelopes scattered over my desk I dialled Victoria's mobile phone number and got the answering service. I did not particularly want to record what I had hoped to say and so, hung up.

The mail contained the usual boring mix; a couple of GP referral letters, some information from a drug company on a new AIDS drug, the agenda for the forthcoming hospital consultants committee, and a copy of a complaint about the anticoagulant clinic. This had reached me via the Director of Nursing and Quality, who was asking for my comments. It seemed strange to me that they should have one person to be the Director of Nursing *and* Quality, almost as if the two don't normally go together!

Anne appeared and asked if there was anything I needed doing before she went off in search of some files I had requested on

Friday. I couldn't think of anything and she disappeared, after reminding me of my appointment with the chief executive at ten.

The phone rang and it was Victoria. She had arrived earlier than usual at work and called to see how I was doing.

"Now, you are going to be a good boy in that meeting aren't you," she mothered.

"Not you as well. I've already had headmaster Frobisher on at me. Yes dwarling, I promise to be the prince of tact!"

"As I remember it, the word is darling," she giggled.

"Absolutely right as usual my little cherub. I have a few things to do before that meeting so I'd better go. I'll phone you later. That is, if you can remember to switch it on. Don't know how you could ever forget! Be in touch.......Dwarling!"

* * *

The Trust office is situated on the other side of the hospital and I arrived a few minutes early, carrying a bulky folder under my arm. The chief executive was standing at the door to his office, discussing something with his secretary.

David Marshall was in his late forties. He was a little over six feet tall with square, strong shoulders, and the first signs of grey appearing in his dark hair. I had always got on well with David. An extremely fair man, he was genuinely concerned regarding the heavy responsibilities thrust upon him as a result of his lofty position.

He was always available and on occasions had been most helpful with his advice. Not that he couldn't be firm if the situation demanded it and I wondered if this would turn out to be such an occasion.

"Hello, Andrew. Good of you to make it. Come in please," he gestured towards the open door.

"Hi, David. Thank you." I slipped past him into the office and eased myself into the upright chair beside his desk. David followed, closing the door behind him. As he sat at the desk he looked at me with a solemn expression that gave me the impression I was in for the high jump.

"I appreciate you sparing me the time. I know you're busy these days. Sometimes I wonder how you manage to fit in all your various work commitments," he half smiled.

"That's alright, David. Anyway, I think I know what it's all about," I said, opening up my folder and looking for some papers.

"You do?" He looked puzzled.

"Yes. I presume it's about that complaint I gather Dr Baldwin has levelled against me."

"Oh! That. No, that's not why I've called you here. Dr Baldwin managed to get hold of the wrong end of the stick I'm afraid," he replied, instilling in me a sense of instant relief.

"No. I'm fully aware of the circumstances associated with your academic trips and can see absolutely no cause for suspicion. I'm afraid Dr Baldwin is apt to get carried away sometimes when dealing with his administrative affairs. He tends to be a little overzealous when he feels he has a cause to follow and sometimes forgets to check the facts. No, there's no problem there."

"Then why *did* you ask me to see you?" I enquired.

"Something serious has cropped up and I would greatly value your advice. That is, if you don't mind sparing me a few minutes of your precious time." Once again he was looking more than a little concerned.

"By all means. How can I help?"

"It's a little difficult to know how to start," he said, nervously fiddling with a pen lying on the side of his desk. "I've not been feeling too well lately, the main problem being that of excessive tiredness. As you probably know, I've been under a lot of pressure these past few weeks, dealing with a number of important issues. Many of these have required a rapid solution and as a result I've been putting in some very long hours both here at the desk as well as up at regional health authority.

"Well, it eventually got to the state that I was finding it extremely difficult to keep up with the volume of work. Naturally, at first, I put it all down to the pressure I was under. However, since it had been going on for some weeks, with no sign of improving, I eventually decided to see my GP last week. He examined me and did all the usual blood tests.

"As you know, I live outside the district, so the blood tests would have gone to another hospital. Then, on Friday he phoned me with the results. Apparently, I'm fairly anaemic and was told this would require further investigations to be carried out at the hospital. To be perfectly frank with you, they suspect it may be some form of leukaemia."

"I'm very sorry to hear that. How can I help you with all this?" I asked, completely stunned by the news.

"I was wondering if you would mind taking over the further

investigations. You see, if this is confirmed and I'm going to require treatment with chemotherapy and so on, I would rather that I be confined here for the treatment.

"It may sound strange to you but, if I am going to need hospitalisation for what would probably amount to some weeks, I feel that if it could possibly be here I would at least be able to keep an eye on what's happening on my patch. I do have a number of problems running at the moment and only I know exactly what's happening in many of these situations." He was certainly putting a brave face on it all and I could not help but admire him for his courage and dedication.

"Of course, I'd be only too happy to take over your case, David, but let's not jump the gun. It may all turn out to be something quite simple. If you like, I'll call your GP this morning and square it all with him. Then I'll get back to you and arrange to repeat the bloods so that I can take a look at the results."

"That's fine by me. Thanks, Andrew." He looked relieved.

"No problem. Can I ask you one thing though?"

"What's that?"

"Does anyone else here know that you are ill?" I asked.

"No, not yet. I thought I'd wait to see what you said."

"Well, I'd keep it under your hat, at least, for the time being. We can discuss what's best when we know exactly what we're dealing with," I said, getting up. "I'll get back to you as soon as I've spoken to your doctor. Can you let me know his name and telephone number?"

"Thanks again, Andrew," he said, handing over a card with the particulars on. "I really am most grateful for your help with this matter."

"Don't mention it," I replied, as I opened the door and set off back to haematology.

* * *

"Was it the cane then?" Anne enquired.

"Yes, but not too serious. I may live to fight another day. Any messages?"

"No. It seems no one loves you," she sniffed, blowing gently into her hankie.

"Thank God for that. I wouldn't know how to handle that sort of thing! Got yourself a cold I see."

"No it's my hay-fever. Nothing seems to work."

"Then I'd better keep my door closed," I chuckled to myself, as I moved on to my room.

It took only a few minutes to get through to David's doctor. He was perfectly happy for me to take over the further investigations and I promised to keep him informed of the results.

Then I phoned David and arranged for him to pop up to me for the tests. Within half an hour they had been completed and the blood was in the laboratory being analysed.

While it was being processed I shot down to the ward to have a word with Sister Cannon. We had been having problems with hospital night-security recently, and our ward was one of those that had been severely criticised. As a result, I had agreed to try to help and wanted to have a few words with sister before making my suggestions public.

By the time I got back the results were on my desk, together with a blood film. The figures did not look good and the appearance of the blood film was indeed strongly suggestive of a diagnosis of acute leukaemia.

I got back on the phone and discussed the results with David. He agreed to come up at two o'clock for me to do a bone marrow test to confirm the diagnosis. I felt pretty lousy all of a sudden and was in no mood to see people. I wandered off to the library to catch up on some references I needed for a paper I was in the middle of writing.

It doesn't matter how long you've been at this game, every now and again it gets to you and this was just such an occasion. I even began to feel a little mean at the way I had been going on about the administration lately. I knew it was unlikely to last, but right now I needed to be on my own, surrounded by peace and quiet.

CHAPTER TEN

It's not that I'm afraid to die. I just don't want to be there when it happens
– Woody Allen

Events moved swiftly over the next two days. David's diagnosis was confirmed with the bone marrow examination, and some special blood tests. After a brief period during which he set in motion the procedures necessary for his deputy to take over the effective management of the hospital, he was admitted to an isolation room in Manvers ward.

There followed considerable discussion with him and his wife, Anna. I attempted to explain as best I could exactly what was involved in the treatment of his condition, and the sort of complications to expect. They both had a number of pertinent questions to ask relating to his management, but eventually appeared satisfied with the arrangements.

We all realised that it would not be possible to keep the facts of this *special* case from the rest of the hospital. However, all the ward and junior medical staff were lectured on the need not to discuss the case with anyone off the ward. If anyone was to push the issue I gave instructions that they were to be referred directly to me at whatever time of the day or night.

Furthermore, I made it known that if I found anyone to be guilty of a breach of confidentiality in this issue I personally would see to it that they were severely reprimanded at the highest level. I was at odds to point out that this is what I normally expect of my staff with every case, but that I fully expected in this particular situation there would be more pressure on them than usual to discuss the case. With that I left them to organise the treatment and to get the chemotherapy started.

*   *   *

Back in my department I was busy reviewing the latest batch of bone marrow slides at the microscope when the phone rang.

"Yes," I barked down the mouthpiece.

"Sounding a bit abrupt today aren't we!" It was Victoria. She had phoned to check on me, and to see if I felt like going up to London at the weekend to catch a show. "There's that play on that Oscar Wilde wrote with you in mind, *An Ideal Husband*! It's only on for one more week. What do you say?"

"I'd rather see the one he wrote with you in mind."

"What's that?"

"*A Woman of No Importance*!" I quipped.

"Bloody cheek!" she bellowed down the phone.

"You know I didn't mean it," I interrupted. "But you started it. Seriously, I'd love to go but unfortunately I've got too much happening on the ward at the moment. Also, until my new colleague arrives, I've got no medical cover. But why don't you pop down here and we could go out for a meal, on me this time?"

"I'd love to, but my mother is coming over on Sunday first thing, and I really can't put her off. She's been going on about this visit for weeks. And besides, she has offered to help me with some dress alterations I've got stuck with."

"Ah! *Lady Windermere's Fan*," I whispered to myself.

"What's that? I couldn't quite hear."

"I said, *Oh! Damn.* Never mind. Perhaps we can arrange something for the weekend after," I suggested.

"I'd like that. Take care, Andrew. And don't go getting yourself into any more fights. Stay calm," she mothered.

"Indubitably, oh wise one! I'll phone you later in the week," I said, replacing the receiver and returning to my work.

*   *   *

The haematology out-patient clinic that afternoon went relatively smoothly and, surprisingly for me, on time. Towards the end of the clinic I received a new referral from one of Eastwich's more competent GPs.

Mrs Lynn Harris was an attractive thirty four year old lady whose general health had been very good recently. Her only complaint was that she had noticed a lump on the right side of her neck, which had been present for about two months and appeared to be getting slowly bigger. There was no pain or tenderness and, on examination, no other abnormality to find.

I had explained to her that this might all be due to some simple problem, such as a recent viral infection. However, I had also pointed out that this could be something more serious, such as Hodgkin's disease and that the only way to be sure was to ask the surgeons to carry out a lymph node biopsy.

She had remained quite calm throughout and, when I explained that even if it was the latter there was every chance of a cure with the modern treatments available, she willingly agreed to the procedure. I also explained that in view of the position of the lump the surgeon would more than likely decide on a general anaesthetic for the operation. As she was leaving I told her that I would arrange her admission in the next few days since she would require an overnight stay.

Back in the laboratory everything was quiet. Anne was finishing off for the day and was unusually pleasant, considering my slightly gruff mood. On my desk I found a message from Johnny asking me to call him in the morning as there was something he wanted to discuss.

Carol Donnelly called into my office to tell me that she was more than ever convinced that there was something going on between her two juniors, Julie Webber and Alan Makepeace. Apparently there was obviously bad feeling between Alan and Julie's husband and tempers nearly flared at lunchtime in the common room. I promised to have a word with them the next day and then turned my attention to dictating my clinic letters.

It was a little after six thirty when I finally finished and left the department heading for the ward.

* * *

I sat in David Marshall's pokey little isolation room thinking how vulnerable he suddenly looked, sitting propped up in bed with his Hickman venous line protruding from his chest wall, attached to a bottle of fluid on a drip stand. He had seemed cheerful enough when I entered and was busy browsing through some enormous administrative document making notes as he went. It was almost as if he were in bed at home without a care in the world. I couldn't help thinking that within a few days such a thing would be far from his mind.

"How's it going?" I enquired.

"Well, I know it's early days obviously, but I'm feeling O.K. and I'm determined to give it my best shot. In other words I feel quite positive and glad, in a way, that at last we've started the treatment." Indeed, he was looking very positive and I instinctively knew that he was going to be one of those patients who would do everything that was expected of them with the minimum of fuss.

"Do you mind if I ask you a question?" I said, glancing at the chart on the end of the bed.

"Fire away. I'm not going anywhere," he grinned.

"How do you do your job? I mean, it's well known that our overall funding is utterly ridiculous for the work and productivity that is expected of us. Every year we are set impossible targets to achieve, given our budget, and yet we somehow manage the impossible, despite Boris Baldwin's efforts to keep the money away from the patients.

"In many ways I really do not envy your job, though I'm not always sure what exactly motivates some of your colleagues."

"I think when considering this issue one has to take a more global view of the problem," he replied, appearing almost relieved to get onto a topic he felt he had some control over. "The issue is how best to utilise the national health budget for all concerned given that it *is* a fixed sum."

"But the government has been elected by the people largely on the strength of its promises regarding the health and education services. It would appear to me that they are fully aware, during the election campaigning, that they have no intention of fulfilling those promises once they are in office," I protested.

"I don't think it is quite as cynical as that, Andrew. They must be realistic when it comes to the rationing and fair distribution of what is, in effect, a fixed budget for the health service. The resources are not limitless and, as I'm sure you are well aware, the cost of the service continues to rise astronomically with the rapid advances in medical technology that we are experiencing. No government can be expected to afford all the new advances. It would simply bankrupt any administration within months." David was sounding horribly logical.

"Then they shouldn't make promises they know they can't keep," I interrupted, but not with great conviction.

"That, I'm afraid is the nature of the beast," he said, getting into his stride. "Politicians have a different definition of *honesty* compared with the average member of the electorate. I really don't believe they think they are lying to the people. In their case they genuinely feel that they are fulfilling their responsibilities in the best possible way, given the scope of the problem"

"What you are telling me is that we are interpreting our language in different ways, and therefore that makes it alright." I was on the attack.

"Yes. In many ways that is exactly it. In reality few people can comprehend the full funding requirements of a comprehensive, modern, state-of-the-art health service. No nation can realistically expect to afford, directly from its tax system, such a service. Many don't even try. The USA, for instance, has the barest of systems compared with ours. It is certainly not the place to be both poor *and* ill.

"No, our system may well have its faults and I'm the first to admit that, but nevertheless I firmly believe it is still the best and fairest health system going. No wonder it is still the envy of the rest of the world," he concluded, pointing his pen in my direction.

"I can accept many of the points you make, David. However, at the end of the day that service, of which we are both justly proud, is as good as it is largely as a result of the continuing sheer hard work and dedication displayed by its employees. And I'm not referring solely to the doctors and nurses. It includes all the technical and support services, all the way down to the humble cleaning lady. Yes, and even many of its administration who, I agree, in many ways have a very difficult role to fulfil.

"It's only that sometimes I am convinced that the wretched government takes all that for granted. You know the scenario. Because we are all dedicated to the job we will make every effort to ensure it is done efficiently. The patient must never be allowed to suffer as a result of the political manoeuvring that goes on. And, all the time, the government is fully aware that we will do everything in our power to protect the patients from the potentially disastrous effects of the ever-increasing *cut-backs* thrown at us. And because that is the case, we continue to achieve the objectives in the face of ever increasing hardship, while they continue to find every excuse to cut the dwindling budget even more.

"At times it seems like a downward spiral and all the time it gets harder to keep up the standards. I wouldn't mind if the bastards would only use the service themselves when they were sick, instead of running off to the private sector for their cures! I mean, it's not exactly a good advertisement for their precious baby, is it?

"Perhaps one way of improving the situation would be to insist at the general election that all new MPs sign a declaration that throughout the time they are in parliament their families will only receive their medicine on the National Health Service and their education through the state system and without privilege. That way, at least they would get to witness and suffer the failings of the impoverished services for which they are directly responsible. Now, that would give them something to think about and test their *dedication!*" I had said my piece and felt decidedly better for it.

"Tell me, did you by any chance fake my diagnosis, in order to trap me in here where I couldn't escape your anger," David laughed.

"I'm sorry, David. I must admit that at times I have been known to stoop to some pretty low tactics when all else has failed but, as yet, not that low! And I certainly do go on sometimes and allow myself to get carried away. Forgive me, it's unfair under the circumstances," I blurted out.

"That's alright. Does you good to blow off steam sometimes."

"Excuse me, Dr Ryan." It was the staff nurse speaking through the open door.

"What is it staff?"

"I'm sorry to interrupt you but Mr Marshall's next treatment is due to go up," she said.

"O.K, I was about to leave anyway." I turned to David. "I hope you didn't mind my little tirade. I sometimes need it to keep my motivation fuelled," I said, in defence.

"Think nothing of it. I've often heard second hand of your ability to focus minds on a committee, but this is the first time I've been privileged to have a ringside seat, as it were. Albeit one without an available exit!" David was enjoying making me feel a little embarrassed.

"Thanks for listening anyway. Perhaps it's all best summed up in that quote, the circumstances of which escape me, that goes *I think it will be a clash between the political will and the administrative won't*! See you tomorrow David."

"I will look forward to the next lesson," he smiled, as he reached for his administrative papers, and safety.

* * *

The wine that evening tasted especially good. It had been a long and hard day, but I felt some important goals had been achieved. And it had been lovely to hear Victoria's voice again. I missed her very much and was longing to see her again. My need for her had grown with every day we were apart.

Something I would never have believed possible a few weeks before. Somehow the age difference, a feature I would normally have considered an insurmountable barrier, seemed irrelevant. Although there were many differences in our interests, in many ways they only served to give us more to talk about. And, without doubt, we shared a similar sense of humour; a feature I have always considered essential for any relationship to survive.

I resisted the temptation to pick up the phone and dial her number, but instead poured myself a generous glass of wine and settled back to the sound of Whitney Houston singing *I Believe in You and Me.*

CHAPTER ELEVEN

GRONTE: It seems to me you are locating them wrongly: the heart is on the left and the liver is on the right.
SGANARELLE: Yes, in the old days that was so, but we have changed all that, and we now practice medicine by a completely new method
- Molière

I called Johnny early the next morning and arranged to meet him later in the Blue Boar. Then I asked Alan Makepiece and Julie Webber in for a chat. They appeared, wearing a worried expression and sat nervously fidgeting in front of me, looking as if they were about to be sentenced at a murder trial.

Following a brief preamble concerning their respective jobs and responsibilities, I ventured on to the subject of the gossip regarding them that, according to a reliable source, was currently doing the rounds of the laboratories. However, I quickly pointed out that, in a busy hospital environment, gossip is always rife, albeit usually unfounded and is often the result of some petty jealousy or rivalry. I deliberately avoided any discussion concerning the specific details of the rumours and did not attempt to accuse or cast blame upon them. I merely stated that they had a responsibility to themselves to ensure that these rumours were laid to rest, even though they were no doubt groundless.

To their credit, neither tried to deny the flirtation, or even to side-step the issue. They both agreed that perhaps there was some reason for the gossip and that they would ensure that there was no further cause for concern.

Under the circumstances I felt very sorry for them, particularly since I was convinced that nothing serious had ever taken place. But, more importantly, because I really did not believe it was anything to do with me what two adult individuals chose to do with their lives.

It seemed to go against every principle I held dear. It was a classic example of the double standard; the one you have to show the public because that is what they deem to be right and proper and the other because it is what your heart says is right.

They left my room looking decidedly relieved that it was all over. Personally, I felt a complete heel.

* * *

The Blue Boar was even more packed than usual as I pushed my way through the crowd, clutching my beer tightly whilst searching for Johnny. I found him in his usual corner and to my utter surprise he was perusing the latest issue of the *British Medical Journal* instead of one of his ornithological magazines. The obligatory cigar sat in the ashtray in front of him, issuing a long plume of smoke spiralling its way to the ceiling. He was sipping his gin and tonic and seemed completely oblivious of my approach, let alone the presence of anyone else in the bar.

"Stooping a bit aren't you, reading the BMJ. What's up, someone purloined your birdie magazines?" I enquired.

He jumped as I spoke. "You shouldn't creep up on people like that Andrew. You startled me."

"Sorry. You looked so engrossed in whatever it is you are reading, I didn't want to shout across the bar. Whatever could have grabbed your attention in *that*?" I asked, pointing at the journal." The only use I ever found for it was the advertisement section for jobs and the obituaries. Now, at my age, it's down to the latter to see which of my colleagues has finally shuffled the mortal coil and gone off to meet that great pharmacist in the sky or, more likely now, heavenly hospital accountant, I suppose."

"There's a very interesting article in here that caught my eye. It's about sudden unexplained death in young women."

"How morbid," I grimaced.

"Well, after that young diabetic lady who died the other day, it seemed rather relevant. I don't suppose we'll ever know why she died. But that's no reason for being complacent. This article is really very interesting." He was obviously still very disturbed over this particular case.

"I can't help remembering what Stan Laurel said in one of his films when asked by Oliver Hardy what his aunt died of."

"Do we really have to? Oh, go on then, what was his reply?"

"I thought you'd never ask! He said, *'She died of a Monday!'*" I volunteered, in a feeble attempt to lift his spirits.

"Very funny. Won't you ever be serious?"

"Not if I can help it," I replied, with all honesty. "What did you want to talk to me about?" I continued. "You left a message on my desk yesterday. Very mysterious I must say!"

"Oh! Yes. I saw Mavis Heggerty in my clinic yesterday. She's doing fine. No further problems and her kidney function is back to normal. She told me that she was very grateful to you for all the interest you took in her problem. Seems you made a good impression with her..."

"Better not let her talk to Boris about me," I interrupted.

"Quite," he agreed. "Anyway, she went on to say that she wanted to help in some way and asked if there were any schemes or projects going that required financial support, as she would like to make a donation. I immediately thought about your plans for a stem cell unit and said I would have a word with you."

"How kind of her," I said, somewhat taken aback. "Trouble is I haven't been able to get the fund off the ground yet."

"It doesn't really matter. She said she'd talk about it with you when she sees you in your clinic in a few weeks."

"Thanks Johnny. I'd better get on with it soon." I was thrilled at the news and it was exactly what was needed to stimulate me into action.

The conversation turned to other matters, including his health, which had picked up tremendously since he had roped his daughters in on his hobby. I thought it a good time to mention my meeting with Victoria and how things had progressed, including my feelings for her.

He was delighted that at long last I had taken the plunge and committed myself to a relationship once again. He sounded like my father, almost relieved that he wouldn't have to watch over me again. He also ventured to suggest that I might like to bring her over for a meal one evening, now that I was back in the land of the living and almost civilised. I wasn't sure I liked his tone. It was never my intention to be civilised, only partially restored.

I really didn't want to lose too many of my unsavoury characteristics in one foul swoop. Too much too soon could render me non-functional or worse, impotent, in my *cause célèbre* at Eastwich General.

I agreed to contact him early next week regarding dinner. It felt a bit like bringing your first real girlfriend home for the ritual parental inspection and approval. For a change I was the first to leave, since I had someone waiting in my office for a meeting. As I retreated towards the door, I heard him cough that cough only smoking can produce, blaspheme quietly to himself, then settle back to his journal.

* * *

That afternoon I made arrangements for Lynn Harris to be admitted on Tuesday for the lymph node biopsy. I had discussed the case with Matthew Bryant, the general surgeon who dealt with most of the surgery required by my patients. He was happy to fit her into his Tuesday operating list and agreed that she would probably need a general anaesthetic and an overnight stay.

Anne approached me with a request for a few days holiday as she wanted to visit her niece in the West Country. The thought of her taking a holiday always filled me with dread. She organised the department so efficiently that her temporary absences usually meant a few days chaos for me. Apart from the usual secretarial role, she played a major part in protecting me from the various interruptions throughout the day that threatened my very work and sanity.

Reluctantly I agreed and made a note of the dates in my diary. Before she left for the weekend she reminded me that my new colleague, James Kennedy, would be starting on Monday and that I still had to sort out his office.

With all the excitement of the previous few days I had completely forgotten about James starting at Eastwich. My previous colleague, Neil Forrester, had decided a few months ago to take early retirement. He had suffered a mild heart attack before Christmas, having previously been in the best of health. Not unnaturally, this had greatly worried him and he never really got over the shock of such a sudden attack out of the blue.

His decision to retire had been helped by the fact that he had only recently inherited a tidy sum of money from an aunt. Needless to say, it came as a severe blow to me and I hadn't been that optimistic about our ability to replace him with anyone as good and helpful as he had been to the department in general and me in particular.

Neil had been a veritable pillar of strength to the department, having originally been single-handed prior to my arrival. It was he who had recognised the need for a second haematologist, and, more importantly, for a clinically orientated haematologist to effectively turn on the clinical side of the speciality. Prior to my appointment, most of the haematology patients had been treated by the general physicians.

The more complicated problems, such as the haematological malignancies including the leukaemias, had been referred directly to the neighbouring teaching hospital. The physicians, to their credit, were the first to admit that they were unable to keep up with this rapidly advancing subject, and were only too pleased to add their support to the case for the establishment of a second haematologist.

Apart from his role within the department, Neil had also been a great support to me during my early years at Eastwich. Like many new consultants I had rushed in, bright eyed and bushy tailed, full of new ideas about how to transform the department. And, like so many new consultants, I had run slap bang into a seemingly impenetrable wall of lethargy and financial restraints imposed by the administration.

New consultants are not meant to spell more money was the stock answer to my pleas for essential funding. It was the older and wiser Neil who had painstakingly shown me the way forward. How to charm the powers that be. How to inveigle my way onto important committees where my voice could be heard. And, perhaps most important of all, when to shut up and stop annoying the very people capable of supporting our cause. With regard to the latter, he was never capable of completely silencing me, but he did manage to curb my early impetuous behaviour, to the extent that my energies were focused with much greater effect.

I was already missing Neil. Most of all, I missed our quiet chats about the department, the patients and how we saw the future of haematology. He was a calming influence on me to the extent that, within a few short months of his leaving, Anne had already noticed the lack of *control* I was displaying on occasions when pressured. I had made a mental effort to curb these outbursts in the absence of my mentor, but it wasn't always proving too successful.

James was going to be different. Young and ambitious, he already had a few good ideas with regard to improving the department. He was coming to us from Guy's Hospital, where he had been a senior registrar for the past few years. His references were excellent and spoke of him in glowing terms. I had had the chance to meet all the short-listed candidates for the post in the weeks leading up to the interview. It had been a very strong field and I was sure that any one of the candidates would have been capable of doing a fine job.

However, at the interview it was James who had impressed me the most. He displayed a fine understanding of the subject in general and of the challenges to be addressed at Eastwich in particular. His answers to the many searching questions put to him had been succinct and well thought out. He had displayed the very confidence I was seeking in my new colleague, without any evidence of cockiness or conceit. In a word, he possessed the degree of humility I consider essential in a good doctor.

In addition and in my book almost as important, he had shown that he had a keen sense of humour. Very early on in my career I had realised that if one is to survive in this job this is without doubt one of the most important qualities to possess. In the end the decision had been easy and he was duly appointed following a unanimous vote.

The weekend after the interview he had popped down, with his wife and two young daughters, to look at the property in the area. I was pleased to have the opportunity of meeting his family and had got on very well with his wife Joanne. I looked forward to welcoming him on Monday, but couldn't help feeling, perhaps understandably, a little nervous at the prospect of this new partnership.

*   *   *

After completing my tasks in the laboratory, I looked in on David Marshall on my way home. He was sitting up in bed surrounded by files and dictating a letter to his ever-faithful secretary, seated across from him in the corner chair.

He was in good spirits and had no problems. I got the distinct impression that he quite liked the privacy afforded by his current predicament. Certainly, it would be very difficult to get hold of him without coming up against Sister Cannon and I had no doubt who would win any such encounter.

I bade him farewell and set off home after first phoning my children from the ward desk. I invited them over for the weekend and told them to bring their tennis rackets.

CHAPTER TWELVE

The kind of doctor I want is one who, when he's not examining me, is home studying medicine
– George S. Kaufman

I arrived at my desk a few minutes after seven on Monday morning, anxious to make an early start. I had to sort out James' room before he arrived and wanted to see how things were on the ward before starting the out-patient clinic. By eight, the room was in order and I was sitting at the desk, sipping my coffee, and recalling the events of the weekend.

The children had arrived a little after one on Saturday afternoon. Mark had come down the previous evening but, true to form, had not struggled from his bed till noon. I was convinced he had been bitten by the tsetse fly when on his elective period in Africa and was now suffering from chronic sleeping sickness.

Jane was even more caustic, suggesting that the only job he would possibly qualify for would be testing mattresses for the Dunlopillo Mattress Company. Emma was quick to add, *'in sleeping mode of course. Definitely not anything to do with activity! That',* she had said, with great sarcasm, *'would require a different kind of athleticism.'*

One was never really sure that any of this ever registered with Mark, as he was, by nature, incredibly laid back and difficult to ruffle. This didn't prevent his younger sisters from trying whenever the situation presented itself. Despite all this they remained devoted and would defend or protect each other if ever threatened.

In the afternoon we had wandered over to the tennis club for an *'F' Cubed,* as Mark insisted on calling it in his scientific terms.....*a Family Friendly Fixed Foursome.* Though where exactly the *Friendly* fitted in I was never quite sure. They had all achieved a good standard at the game, having represented their county at the junior level and were naturally very competitive in any event; even that most dreaded of club games....*the friendly.*

I had realised very early on that if you ever wanted to lose a friend, all that was required was to take him on in a *friendly* at the club and all your troubles would be over. Why this should have been the case I could never work out, but even the most timid of old ladies is instantly transformed into a veritable fire breathing dragon, upon inclusion in a *friendly* game. For this reason I avoided them like the plague, preferring, instead, a regular *fixed four* with three close friends every Thursday evening. It had proved quite a useful escape valve from the pressures of the week, the most important part of the proceedings being the social drink in the bar after the game.

After our game we had shopped in the local supermarket, where we collected the food and wine for the evening meal and then stopped off to hire a video film as part of my promise to the girls who had agreed not to wander off to the local disco after dinner.

The evening had been very enjoyable. It was not often that I had the chance to see all three of them together and I relished every moment of it. Even when they attacked me for being *old-fashioned* and *moody,* which is their standard way of trying to provoke me into an argument. On this occasion, I wasn't rising to the bait and they soon gave up the attack.

We talked of their future and what they wanted of life. There was the usual light-hearted argument about which one of them would be saddled with me, or *Aged P,* as the insisted on referring to me, in my grumpy old age. They finally agreed that no one could possibly be expected to put up with that, and that the only solution would be for them to club together and pay for a nursing home.

I thanked them for their concern and questioned why anyone would have children in the first place. This brought on the usual tirade from my youngest, who was always most indignant about me referring to them as *children. 'Children'*, she had said with great indignity, *'have to be in bed by eight!'*

"That's only because they have to be home by eleven!" Mark

interrupted, grinning at his sister.

I was not amused by his contribution, but suggested that her eight o'clock one was a pretty good idea. Needless to say, it did not go down too well. I also pointed out that whatever age they were, they were still my children, and that I couldn't be expected to introduce them every time as *'Have you met my two daughters, Emma and Jane and my son Mark? '* We had agreed to disagree on that one.

The conversation eventually got round to the subject of their mother and I enquired if she was alright. It was when I moved on to inquire about her possible male friends that they smelled a rat and accused me of being mercenary. It was true that were she to cohabit or remarry I would be relieved of a generous portion of the monthly alimony payments, but I hastened to add that had been far from my thoughts when enquiring after her happiness. It fell on stony ground and I was glad to get off the subject relatively unscathed.

They eventually left after lunch on Sunday, and I got on with the mundane business of cleaning the house and writing those letters and paying the bills that were weeks overdue.

The gentle tap on the door jetted me back from my dreams..

"Come in," I shouted.

"Sorry to disturb you Dr Ryan." It was James appearing round the door, looking a little nervous at his interruption. "I seem to have arrived a little early and there doesn't appear to be anyone around. I hope I'm not disturbing you."

"Not at all James," I said, getting up and offering him my hand. "But, please call me Andrew. No formality in this department. Your predecessor, Neil Forester, insisted we leave it out and I always agreed. Welcome to Eastwich. I hope you're all going to be very happy here."

"Thank you Andrew. I'm sure we will."

"Now I'll show you your room first. Then you had better get yourself over to personnel for all that paperwork they insist on. After that, they'll take you on a tour of the hospital introducing you to the various departments and will get you your passes and all the bits and pieces you're going to need.

"That should take you most of the morning. By that time I should have finished my clinic and we can pop over to the canteen, if I can remember where it is, and I'll introduce you to some of your colleagues." With that I ushered him out of the room and into his office.

By the time he had frequented himself with the layout of the department Anne had arrived. She had decided to postpone her trip to the West Country by a couple of days in order to help James settle in. She had obviously decided that I was incapable of such an act. I introduced the two and she agreed to take him over to personnel, disappearing ahead of him through the door.

I made my way over to the ward to check on the patients and have a word with Hugh before my clinic.

* * *

Returning from the clinic later that morning, I found James sorting out his room. He had rearranged the furniture as he wanted it and was busy loading some books onto the shelves. On the table stood a flowering plant that looked familiar, the name of which I couldn't remember. A pile of folders rested on the desk beside an expensive looking stethoscope. Everything looked so neat. I couldn't help wondering how long that would last.

We made our way over to the canteen, where we found Matthew Bryant, John Lindsey, and Johnny Frobisher deep in conversation as they tucked into their food. I introduced James, as I took the seat beside John.

"It's nice to meet you." Matthew offered his hand over the bowl of mushroom soup sitting in front of him. "Johnny here tells me you've been appointed to keep an eye on Andrew. Sort of mediator, to prevent him reaching meltdown and going critical. Sounds like a full-time job to me," he added, with a sideways grin at John.

"I didn't quite say that Matthew. I merely pointed out that it would do Andrew good to have the calming influence of a colleague once again," interrupted Johnny, a little nervously.

"Rumours of my volatility and irascibility are *greatly* understated," I joined in, smiling at James, who must have started wondering what it was all about.

"For the uninitiated, James," John volunteered, "Andrew here has a well earned reputation for stirring it. In the nicest possible way of course. But he has a habit of attacking on sight anything remotely associated with the administration. And *doctors* associated with the administrative process, woe betide them, are his number one pet aversion. Red rag to a bull, I'm afraid. There really is no way of stopping him. You do of course, James, have my deepest sympathy." He offered his hand in mock condolence.

"I suppose it's too late to get out of it now, is it?" James smiled, entering into the spirit of the conversation.

"Afraid so," said Matthew shovelling the soup into his mouth. "You've already signed the contract. Binding agreement and all that. Like to help. Know what I mean. But it's more than my job's worth!"

"Well, in that case, I suppose I will have to accept the challenge," James jested, producing a solemn expression that fooled no one.

"You know, I think the new boy's going to make it," added John, feigning surprise. "Definite potential there, I'd say. Real courage and fortitude under fire." Changing tack he added, "When you're free why don't you drop down to the oncology department. I'd be pleased to show you over the sharp end of the hospital as it were."

"I'd love to. Thanks."

John bade farewell and set off for his department. Johnny started chatting to James, as Matthew made to get up.

"Your lady's first on tomorrow afternoon. Is that O.K. Andrew?" he asked, reaching for the notes he'd left under his chair.

"Fine. Thanks Matthew. There shouldn't be any problem. She's very fit and no other medical problems as far as I'm aware. It all looks very much localised with an extremely good chance of cure."

"Good. Must rush. Welcome to the sweat box James. And remember, when you've tried everything you know on your patients without success, you only have to give me a ring and I'll cut it out. In the bucket, that's the place for it. In the bucket!" With that he was gone, manoeuvring his way through the growing crowd with speed only a manic surgeon can generate.

"Why is it that surgeons never have time for lengthy conversations," I questioned. "Everything is dealt with in such an abrupt fashion, with none of the fineries or subtleties of conversation. Slap, bang, wallop. *'That's it, in the bucket.'* Whoosh! Off they rush in a dust storm. All drama. As if they were on the stage of the Old Vic. I wonder if surgeons' wives have a higher incidence of duodenal ulcer."

"Probably," laughed Johnny. "But he's a real character, our Matthew. Complete workaholic. And he fulfils his NHS contract with plenty to spare. Nothing's too much trouble. I wish I could say the same for more of his surgical colleagues."

"Ah! Now what makes me think you're talking about the illustrious Mr Whetherby! Rumour has it he was seen on an NHS ward last week. Obviously lost his way, or visiting a sick relative!" I said with venom in my heart.

"A dying, rich one, no doubt," Johnny added.

"I've obviously got a lot to learn." James was plainly enjoying the entertainment, without appearing too shocked.

"Masses I'm afraid, James. Could take you a lifetime. That's why we thought you'd better start now."

"One thing I would warn you about in all seriousness," Johnny touched James's arm. "Andrew has managed to cause a lot of trouble over the past few years, stirring up the administration and a number of his medical colleagues. Not that I'm saying he's wrong. But a number of people have really got it in for him now and are hanging in there waiting for him to make a mistake so that they can pounce. You'd do well to bear this in mind. Because in many of their eyes you are going to be looked upon in the same light, being associated with him in the department."

"I appreciate you concern and advice Johnny," James replied. "In fairness, I had heard of Andrew's reputation before I applied for the job. Haematology is a relatively small speciality and it doesn't take long for such facts to filter down the old grape vine. In many ways it only served, if anything, to attract me even more to the job."

"Why, thank you dear boy!" I intoned with glee." I knew the day we met I was going to get on with you."

"Well, it's good to meet you at last James," Johnny continued, pushing his chair back." I've heard a lot about you from Andrew. Some of it good!" he joked. "Any kidney problems and I'm your man."

James laughed. "Thanks. Not one of my strong points. I'm sure I'll be seeing you fairly soon."

"See you, my ornithological friend," I said, as he made for the door. "By the way. That's the first time since I don't know when that I haven't heard you wheeze. I should charge you double for my advice!"

"On the contrary my friend. It should be free on the NHS!"

" See you,..........smart ass!"

* * *

I left James to himself most of the afternoon, in order to sort out his schedule and meet the staff. I also suggested that he might like to leave early as he had to get back to London. He hadn't been able to sell his house yet and would therefore have to commute for the time being.

I had gone a whole weekend without speaking to Victoria and it had seemed like weeks, I missed her so much. By early evening I managed to get hold of her at the office. She had had a busy weekend and there was a lot to talk about. Once again, the sound of her voice lifted my spirits and completely revitalised me. I yearned to see her again and to hold her in my arms and make love.

Most of all, though, I wanted to wake in the morning with her beside me, feeling warm and complete once again. I promised to ring again on Tuesday and she agreed to come down for the weekend.

CHAPTER THIRTEEN

The longer I practice medicine the more convinced I am there are only two types of cases: those that involve taking the trousers off and those that don't
– Alan Bennett

As I drove to work the next morning the car radio dispensed the eight o'clock news, with its usual air of doom and gloom. There had been yet another terrorist plane hijacking, the third in four months and a hurricane had struck Florida leaving eighty people dead and causing widespread damage. French farmers were blocking their roads in protest over English lamb exports.

What's new, I thought; Nelson and Wellington remained two of my greatest heroes! A hospital in the midlands was being sued over the unexpected death of a patient last year and the Bank of England had announced it would have to put the bank rate up yet again, the third hike in six months. The only piece of remotely positive news was the announcement from a group of unknown quacks in America that they had discovered a new wonder drug that appeared to offer a cure for leukaemia. Some hopes, I pondered.

Every year, some loony came out with such a statement, falsely raising the hopes of thousands of patients and their relatives around the world. And, in nearly every case, further research would fail to corroborate any such effect for the drug. But, of course, not before some unscrupulous businessman has taken millions off numerous unfortunate sufferers who, quite naturally, would clutch at anything that might possibly offer them a cure for their condition.

It was all so predictable. Very occasionally, the news is founded on an element of truth, such as promising early results suggesting a possible role in controlling the disease, rather than an out and out cure. But, of course, such news isn't nearly sensational enough to sell to the public and therefore has to be hyped up for human consumption, and profit!

Profit! The word certainly has a peculiar ring to it. I couldn't help thinking back thirty years or so to when a certain drug became all the rage for its antiemetic and sedative role in pregnant women. Tragically it was later associated with horrific physical deformity in some of the children born to the mothers who had taken the drug in early pregnancy. At the time of its use in pregnancy it was a relatively cheap drug compared with many of its rivals..

Recently, however, the drug had shown itself to have a very real and important role to play in the treatment of certain malignant diseases, including some haematological conditions. In fact, the results of a lot of the preliminary studies involving patients with advanced, relapsed and otherwise resistant disease had been so promising that it has already been included in a number of medical trials for the treatment of certain types of malignancy currently being conducted around the world.

Although a relatively cheap drug when used in pregnancy all those years ago, amazingly it has suddenly become quite expensive and, as such, is causing a big headache for the administration when it comes to the funding of our cancer units and their drug budgets.

Regarding the item I had just heard on the news I had no doubt there would be numerous calls from my patients and their families over the next week or so, enquiring after this new *'cure'*, and asking why they hadn't been offered the drug.

I had long ago decided that, if I was ever to inherit a massive fortune, I would buy my very own TV news station putting out news bulletins every hour on the hour. The only stipulation I would make would be that every alternate item of news had to be one of good news and each bulletin would have to start and finish with good news.

So, for instance, following the blowing up of parliament the programme would commence with the news of the quintuplets born to a happy mother in Scotland, to be followed by the Guy

Fawkes episode. And the news could conclude with a picture of the happy mother surrounded by her screaming piglets.

All very simple, really! And I bet the health of the nation would take a dramatic turn for the better. My only hope would be that it didn't put me out of a job!

I sauntered into the department humming quietly to myself and secretly relieved that my new colleague had at last joined me. Anne had arrived a little earlier, having decided that it was the only way to ensure that she would be able to get away on holiday on time.

"Did you hear the news Dr Ryan? Another terrorist hijacking. Where will it all end, I wonder?" She was obviously getting her concerned mood ready for holiday.

"Yes," I replied. "I gather it's a plane load of hospital administrators, off to some convention or other, no doubt at great cost to the tax-payer. Apparently, the terrorists are demanding a million pounds, or they threaten to release them."

"Very amusing, Dr Ryan." She was retrieving a set of notes from the filing cabinet as she added, with a definite hint of sarcasm in her voice, "Dr Kennedy is in already; been in for over half an hour, in fact! He asked me to let you know. You must be thrilled to have such a keen, young colleague at last. A real breath of fresh air too, if you ask me. In my opinion, it's exactly what you needed, Dr Ryan. He's decided to pop down to the ward to meet Sister Cannon, as he missed her yesterday."

"Fine, Anne, and once again, thank you for your undying support," I said, nausea welling up deep within me, as I wondered if this was going to set a new precedent. I didn't think I could possibly make it to work at eight every morning. At least, not without some major rearrangements in my social life. Particularly those concerning Beethoven and Chateauneuf-du-Pape.

* * *

"I'm not getting on that couch, and that's final," shouted the tall middle-aged man in bay three in the A&E department. He was remonstrating with the young casualty officer, who was trying to persuade him onto the couch, so that he could examine the knee that was apparently causing all the trouble.

"What's the problem," I asked, putting my head round the curtain.

"It's Mr Sampson, Dr Ryan." The poor casualty officer looked quite flustered. "He's complaining of pain in his knee and is demanding an injection of morphine. But he flatly refuses to let me examine the knee. Says it's the same as before and that every time he has to have an injection, and that I'm wasting valuable time."

Colin Sampson was one of my severe haemophiliacs, who had been on my books ever since he moved to Eastwich a few years ago. I felt considerable sympathy for him, as he had suffered numerous problems over the years. Consequently, he had required an enormous amount of treatment for spontaneous bleeding episodes, which had occurred fairly frequently, this being the case with the severe form of this condition. Not surprisingly, he had contracted a number of the complications associated with this condition and, in particular, it's treatment with large volumes of blood products.

Although these blood products are fairly safe nowadays, this sadly was not the case many years ago, when it had not been realised they could contain a host of viruses passed on by the donors.. These included the AIDS virus and others that could severely affect the patient, such as the ones causing hepatitis

It was not surprising that he was now HIV positive, which he had contracted at some stage from contaminated blood products. He had been aware of his positive status for nearly three years, but had not yet manifested any of the features or signs of the full-blown condition.

It was simply impossible to imagine what degree of mental anguish and torment he must have experienced over the past few years, armed with the knowledge of his situation, just waiting for the inevitable Added to all this he had become dependent on the strong pain killing drugs that are often required to control the severe pain associated with the bleeding episodes he suffered, particularly those into his weight-bearing joints.

As a result, he would often pitch up to the A&E department complaining of severe pain and demanding pain-killers from the unsuspecting junior doctor.

"Now come on, Colin," I said, placing my hand on his shoulder. "You know the rules. This doctor has got to examine you, or he can't possibly be sure what to give you. Besides, if it's a bleed into the knee you know you're going to need some Factor VIII replacement," I continued.

Factor VIII was the specific blood clotting factor haemophiliacs lacked and therefore needed whenever they had a bleed. It was now genetically engineered in the laboratory and as such was a safe product, completely free from any form of contamination with viruses. The down side was that, as a result, the product was extremely expensive to produce, resulting in yet one more financial headache for the administration, not that it gave me any sleepless nights!

"Dr Ryan, I don't think it's a bleed this time. It doesn't feel like that at all. It's more like a severe pain due to the arthritis. You know how it gets me sometimes." He appeared a little surprised to see me and a look of guilt was showing in his expression. Although he could be very devious and manipulative when his craving for the drugs became intolerable, he was also well known for playing down his symptoms at times, whenever he thought his condition might require admission to the hospital.

"Colin," I began, "You must understand that this young doctor really wants to help you. But he does have certain cardinal rules to follow. In the first instance, if he doesn't examine you he will be seen as neglecting his primary duty towards his patient. That in itself could lead to all sorts of medico-legal problems, which we can all well do without. Now, be a good chap and hop on the couch and let's see if we can find out what this is all about."

He really didn't have any choice and he knew it. With a grimace he shrugged his shoulders and struggled onto the couch. Within a few minutes it was obvious to me that he had sustained a fairly severe spontaneous bleed into the knee joint and that it would require his admission to hospital for aspiration of the blood from the joint, Factor VIII replacement, bed-rest and the addition of properly supervised pain-killers. Later, when the pain was under control, he would require physiotherapy to keep the joint as mobile as possible.

Although initially reluctant to be admitted, he eventually relented and I made the necessary arrangements for his transfer to Manvers ward.

* * *

Arriving on the ward later in the morning I made a point of seeing Lynn Harris to reassure her about the procedure she was due to undergo that afternoon. I was able to confirm that she should be able to leave early next morning. Before leaving the ward I put my head round David Marshall's door to say hello and to tell him that I'd be back later in the afternoon to see him.

I met up with James at lunchtime and took him over to the

Blue Boar by way of his initiation. It also provided a chance to have a quiet chat without the intrusion of hospital colleagues and all their medical talk.

Once we were settled in the corner I began by asking after his family. Joanne, his wife, had trained as a nurse but had given up work following the birth of their daughter three years ago. A second daughter had followed soon after and now she was quite naturally, in his words, 'anchored to the house, playing the young mother and housewife.' She had no ambition to return to nursing and was blissfully content with her family life.

They both enjoyed the outdoor life, and were hoping to find a house in the country away from the 'smoke,' as he put it. Sport also featured on their agenda and although James' favourite pastime was cricket, it appeared that they both enjoyed tennis. I promised to arrange an unfriendly four, as soon as I had managed to round-up one of my wayward daughters. James had laughed when I explained to him my theory regarding friendly fours. He explained that a similar situation often arose in the cricket world and that his opinion was similar to mine in that he didn't believe there was such a thing as a friendly match.

They were also lovers of music and Joanne apparently was a good pianist, having taken lessons from a very young age. James played the guitar and was more into rock and what I refer to as '*modern forms of music.*' I mentioned that my interests in this sphere were limited to listening, as my playing talent had been officially zero-rated by my astute music teacher at school.

We soon got onto the subject of the haematology department and I was able to explain my plans for the future. James made some very constructive suggestions regarding the development of the service, with particular reference to the clinical side. We concluded by agreeing his time-table and eventually made it back to the department a few minutes after two o'clock.

* * *

On my desk, propped against a set of notes, I found an envelope marked *Strictly Confidential.* It had been addressed by hand using a black biro, but I was unable to recognise the style of the writing. Intrigued, I reached for the letter opener and gently sliced it open.

As I removed the contents Anne appeared with some letters

to sign. I asked her if she had been in the department when it had been delivered, but she denied having seen the letter or anyone delivering it. She did point out that she had been away from the department for half an hour getting a bite to eat in the canteen and concluded that it must have been delivered while she was away from her desk.

The letter consisted of two sheets covered with neat, close handwriting in a simple style that was easy to read. I read through the letter very slowly and then went back and read it again, before replacing it in the envelope and locking it carefully in the bottom drawer of the desk.

At first I was completely taken aback and not too certain what to do next. Then, after giving the problem some thought, I decided upon a line of action, which included keeping the contents of the letter completely to myself for the time being. At least, until I could corroborate a few facts.

Having put it from my mind I got on with my afternoon's work, including the outstanding bone marrow reports that Anne had been bullying me over earlier. When I'd cleared the decks I shot down to Manvers ward where I was informed that Lynn had returned from theatre but was still very drowsy.

I found Hugh who informed me that he had successfully aspirated Mr Sampson's swollen knee and that he was now resting and quite comfortable with the pain well controlled.. The other patients were all quiet, so I thanked Hugh and headed off to see David Marshall.

"Everything O.K.?" I asked, entering the room wearing the plastic apron and gloves required in the isolation section.

"So far, no problems," he replied.

"Good," I said, glancing at the folders strewn over the bed. "Won't you ever let go of work?"

"I could ask the same of you," he smiled. "I'm informed there's a bit of the workaholic in you leaping to get out."

"Yes, but that's real work," I continued, grinning in his direction in an obvious attempt to provoke him into argument.

But David was too experienced a professional and too hardy a campaigner to be drawn into argument that easily. "You're absolutely right, of course," he said, completely taking the wind out of my sails. "I couldn't possibly concentrate on your sort of work trapped in here. Luckily, it's only administrative chores. The sort of thing you could do with your eyes closed. Or I suppose you could always run out and get a ten-year-old to do it! Isn't that what you were suggesting to the Resource Management committee the other day?"

Ouch! I felt that. "What a sneak that Boris is! Alright, I give in," I laughed. "Anyway I think Oscar Wilde had it pretty well summed up."

"How?"

"Well, when he said, '*Work is the curse of the drinking classes.*'"

"Now you're talking. I could do with a gin and tonic right now, if the truth be known. But, I'll have to exercise restraint," he said, with resignation in his voice.

"Ah! My middle name. Andrew *Restraint* Ryan," I volunteered.

"Hardly, from what I've heard," he chuckled.

"I can imagine what you've heard," I said, "And who you've heard it from. But, as I'm sure you are aware, there are always two sides to every story."

"Quite so. And you must realise that people in my position will always be the recipient of gossip and rumour concerning the hospital. Some of it will, no doubt, have an element of truth to it but most is obviously completely unfounded. On occasions it results from petty in-hospital jealousy. Another time it arises, driven by malicious intent. And then, of course, there's the complete crank. I get to see it all." David looked across at me and gestured for me to sit in the chair beside him.

As I took the seat I asked, "And what category would you say Boris Baldwin fits."

"Oh! Probably jealousy. Possibly tinged with a misplaced sense of loyalty to the establishment. I'm no analyst, but I wonder if, in his case, it might all have stemmed from his youth. I gather he was an only child and he once mentioned to me that he soon realised that whatever he did he was never able to please his father, who it seems soon tired of him and packed him off to boarding school at quite an early age. Also, as I'm sure you're aware, you have a tremendous reputation within your profession. I wouldn't be putting my faith in you right now if you hadn't. But such a reputation rarely appears without a great struggle and much sacrifice. It is also quite natural that one will make a few enemies along the way; it goes with the job and the role you've set yourself.

"Dr Baldwin on the other hand is probably equally capable as a physician, but for some reason early on he has decided that that was not primarily for him. He has chosen to continue his development more along administrative lines for reasons that are best known to him. As so often happens, the converted become more zealous, even righteous, than those responsible for the conversion. The difference makes you two appear as chalk and cheese. Clashes are probably inevitable, especially with your ability to stimulate differences of opinion, shall I say!" Ever the diplomat, David was showing exactly why he had been selected as our Chief Executive.

"I see all that, David. But somehow, he always manages to get under my skin. I fully understand I should know better, but the very sight of him sets me off."

"Well, it's called professionalism. You both have to learn to exercise restraint, difficult though it may seem. After all, you are both supposed to be on the same side. Differences of opinion are bound to arise. But in most instances there's a constructive solution."

"Well, I will try to forget the habits of a lifetime and make a Herculean effort to control my emotions where he's concerned," I said, with some considerable reluctance.

"That's as well then," he continued, "As I've just had to make him the acting Chief Executive for the time being." He was staring me straight in the eyes as he delivered this little exocet, knowing full well exactly what my reaction to this red hot snippet of news would be.

"You wwhat?" I stammered.

"I really had no choice. I'm afraid the only other possible candidate is really not up to it. He came to see me yesterday to discuss the situation. In the end I was forced to accept his resignation. And, as the Medical Director, Dr Baldwin was the natural choice as his replacement in the current circumstances. In view of the situation I am sure I can count on you to give him all the support he is going to need." The last sentence was delivered more as a statement than a question.

"Indubitably," I moaned, incapable of hiding the sudden onset of misery I experienced deep within me. As I rose to leave, David coughed that nervous cough one often hears from government ministers before they are about to lie to the nation on television. In his case, I knew he wasn't about to lie, but he did appear decidedly uncomfortable.

"You know, Andrew, this business with me couldn't have come at a worse time for the hospital. I was in the middle of a number of very tricky negotiations with both the Health Authority and the Region. Things are finely balanced at the moment and I feel extremely frustrated that I'm not there to guide these issues through. I know I can count on you for your support." He was beginning to look very concerned and for the first time since his admission he was actually beginning to look ill.

I shook his hand as I made to leave. "You know you can, David," I said. "Why! Who knows, perhaps I'll be able to get a job at the United Nations when all this is over."

"Let's not completely lose sight of reality," he grinned, reaching for a fat folder at the end of the bed.

CHAPTER FOURTEEN

Cured yesterday of my disease, I died last night of my physician
– Matthew Prior

"What do you mean, 'she's dead.'" I was sitting bolt upright in bed. The digital clock on the bedside table read 3.06am and I had been fast asleep for over three hours. I had been rocketed back to consciousness by the shrill ring of the phone, which was positioned less than a foot from my right ear.

"It's Mrs Harris, Dr Ryan. I'm afraid she's dead." It was the night sister, Sister Green, sounding very distressed. "I was doing my routine rounds when I noticed her lying there staring at the ceiling. At first I thought she had trouble sleeping and as I approached the foot of the bed I asked if she would like a sleeping tablet. But she remained motionless with a fixed expression and then I knew there was a problem." She sounded close to hysterics.

"Anyone with her now?" I enquired.

"Yes. Dr Gibson, the duty medical registrar. I called him straight away. And I also called her husband who is on his way."

"O.K. Fiona. I'll be right over," I said, replacing the receiver and swinging my feet out of bed.

I was in the ward within a quarter of an hour. The scene at the desk was one of utter confusion, with Sister Green, her juniors and Dr Gibson all chattering away excitedly but not actually listening to each other. I quickly calmed them down and asked if Mr Harris had arrived. Fiona said she had placed him in the visitors' room, together with a Staff Nurse to help console him. After examining Mrs Harris I ushered Fiona and Dr Gibson into the staff room.

"Someone had better tell me what happened here," I demanded, looking for a pad to make notes.

"It's as I told you on the phone Dr Ryan," Fiona began. "I found her at about 3 o'clock. There had been no problems before that. She hadn't buzzed the desk for anything."

"Who was the last to see her alive?" I asked.

"It was Dr Gibson. I called him some time around midnight, as her intra-venous drip was leaking and needed re-siting," Fiona was looking extremely distraught. Despite the fact that she was one of the hospital's more experienced nurses, this episode had obviously deeply affected her.

"Tell me what happened, Paul."

"As Sister said. I was asked to see her because she was complaining of pain in the left arm. On examination it was obvious that the drip was tissuing. So I removed it and re-sited a new venflon in the other arm. At first, I wondered whether she really needed it to be replaced, as she had done so well post-op. I nearly didn't bother, but then I thought, as she was not one of our patients I didn't know what the policy would be in her case. Since there were no instructions in her notes and it was very late to contact anyone from her team I thought the easiest thing was to replace it, which I was able to do in a few minutes. She was in fine spirits while I was doing it and seemed very well. Then I left to see a patient on Creswell ward."

"Did Mrs Harris complain of anything else when you saw her? You know, headaches, chest pain, fevers, anything at all?" I was searching for any possible clue as to a cause for her demise.

"No. As I said, she appeared very well. In fact she even joked about wasting my time, since she was going home in a few hours anyway."

"She was right. And since she was fully conscious by now, she obviously didn't really need the drip replacing. But, I cannot blame you, Dr Gibson. As you said, there were no specific instructions to the contrary. Were the vital signs all normal?" I continued.

"Yes. Temperature, pulse, blood pressure. The lot."

"I just don't understand it," I said, staring at the note-pad in disbelief. "A perfectly fit young woman, whose only problem was a small lump in her neck, comes into hospital for a simple biopsy procedure and dies suddenly that same night. And not a single clue as to a possible cause. I mean, what can I possibly say to her husband?"

The others could only stare at me, unable to offer even the remotest of solace. There were no answers to a situation of this making. Most doctors, at some time or other, will experience occasions when they cannot explain what has happened to a patient, or they will know the problem but simply won't have an answer to offer. That goes with the job. But in no way can anyone prepare for this type of situation. The young, fit patient experiencing sudden unexplained death whilst undergoing a simple medical procedure. We all know such problems occur in medicine, but somehow you never believe it will ever happen to you or your own patients.

I slowly picked myself up from the table, thanked Fiona and Paul for their efforts and made my way to the relatives' room to meet Mr Harris.

* * *

"Andrew. There you are." It was Johnny, approaching with a pint in his hand. "I went to the lab, but no one knew where you were. Might have guessed you'd pick the Blue Boar to hide your sorrows. Come on, buck up."

"Johnny, I'm not exactly in the mood for company." I was in fact feeling profoundly depressed and worse, extremely sorry for myself.

"I heard all about it from my registrar. Dreadful business."

"You *could* say that," I said, sarcastically.

"Come on, Andrew. These things happen. It's not your fault."

"I'm not sure it's anyone's fault," I whispered. "But she was my patient and I was responsible for bringing her into hospital for the biopsy. And for persuading Matthew to go for a general anaesthetic so she would have to stay overnight," I added, feeling even more guilty.

"You don't even know what happened. Only the other week you were saying the same thing to me about that lady with the diabetes who died suddenly." Johnny was doing his best to console me, but I was in no mood to be consoled. I'm afraid I was wallowing way down in the depths of self-pity, guilt, and even doubt over my clinical judgement.

"Yes, well, no one was able to explain why she died either,"

I hissed into my beer. "The P.M. gave no clue. As you said at the time, it's all so very final and unfair. It's completely without reason."

"How did her husband take it?"

"How do you think? There was not a single thing I could say to him by way of explanation. How do you console or comfort a man in such circumstances? Woken from his sleep in the middle of the night to be told that his wife, the mother of his two young daughters, has died so suddenly and unexpectedly. A beautiful woman he greatly loved, and with whom he had shared a large part of his life. A woman who, until the day before, had never suffered anything more serious than a bout of flu. A fine mother and loving wife. No words exist that can possibly cope with such a situation.

"He was, as with so many relatives confronted in this way, magnificent. He listened quietly and very carefully to everything I had to say, without a single interruption. And all the time he maintained his composure, and displayed great self-control. At last, when I had finished, he managed to ask a number of questions as to the possible cause of her sudden deterioration.

"There were, of course, no answers, apart from mentioning that under the circumstances the coroner would undoubtedly be ordering a post-mortem examination that we hoped would reveal the cause. This was the only occasion when he showed any sign of breaking down. But he soon regained his composure, thanked me for my time, and left to collect his wife's effects. Why? What could possibly have happened to that poor woman so suddenly to deprive this family of such a fine wife and mother? And, why, oh why, did I have to persuade Matthew to go for a general anaesthetic?"

"Come on, Andrew. It's no good blaming yourself. I'm sure the post-mortem will show what happened and I'll bet you we'll find there was nothing you could have done whether she had been in hospital or at home. Probably a massive pulmonary embolus."

Despite his good intentions, Johnny was not improving my state of mind. I had an overwhelming desire to be on my own, in order to adjust to the events of the past few hours.

"Forgive me, Johnny, but I must go. Have to pop into town and get a few things before the afternoon session. Thanks for your support. I really do appreciate it." And with that I was up, and pushing my way through the crowd by the bar before he could manage a reply.

* * *

"Can anyone give me five causes of macrocytic anaemia?" I asked, trying my hardest not to convey my feelings of despondency to the students facing me in the main lecture theatre. They were quite a bright bunch and were half way through their three-month attachment with us at Eastwich. Coming from Guy's Hospital there was often an initial problem with *adjustment* when seconded for attachments in *District Hospitals*. The misconception among many medical students is that only *Teaching Hospitals* should teach medicine, leaving their district associates to do the *dog's body* job of *routine* medicine.

"When you say, *'macrocytic anaemia,'* Dr Ryan, do you mean when the MCV is above 96 fl., or are you merely referring to the morphological appearance of the red cells when viewed down the microscope?" the tall, spotty male in the front row enquired. There's always one in every class, but to me they were becoming more obvious. Perhaps it was all related to my current sense of persecution, or perhaps he was just the average *know-all*. Whatever he was, I was in no mood for semantics.

"Well Jenkins," I started, glaring at him. "I can tell you are an academic. So, tell me, in what specialty do you eventually hope to spend the rest of your life inflicting your own particular brand of healing and whit upon the unsuspecting public? That is of course when the examiners eventually take leave of their senses and decide to convey a medical degree upon you?"

"I intend to become a dermatologist," he volunteered, cockily, smiling straight at me, whilst his colleagues started to giggle.

"Ah! The perfect speciality for those interested in private practice."

"Why's that, sir?" he said, grinning inanely in my direction, to further giggles from the crowd.

"Because you are unlikely to cure any of your patients, who will swell your out-patient clinics to bursting. And, what is more, they rarely ever die of their skin diseases. The net result is that the poor old patients will eventually fill your private clinic to bursting, having got fed up waiting for ever and a day to be seen on the NHS. The perfect set-up for private practice. Hilaire Belloc summed you lot up in his famous poem that went:

Physicians of the Utmost fame
Were called at once; but when they came

They answered, as they took their fees,
'There is no Cure for this Disease.'

The group broke into guffaws of laughter, as poor Jenkins started to blush with embarrassment. I began to feel a twinge of guilt over my actions. Hot headed as usual, I had unfairly rushed in to attack a relatively inexperienced and defenceless beginner. I started to feel pretty mean about my insensitive actions. After all, it wasn't his fault I felt so down and desperately sorry for myself.

"It could be worse Jenkins," I added, in an attempt to salvage the situation, and with it some of his dignity. "You could have chosen surgery!"

At this, the audience started to fall about and Jenkins picked up, visibly relieved at the outburst, as I winked at him and continued, "Tell you what. If you like, when we've finished, I'll show you some blood films that illustrate what I've been talking about."

"That would be great," he said, obviously only too relieved that the pressure was finally off him.

"Now. What about the rest of you, you idle bunch. Can't anyone give me five causes of macrocytic anaemia? It's not asking too much now, is it?"

* * *

Later in the day I was mulling over some notes in my room, feeling lower than ever, when James tapped on the door and wandered in. In his left hand he carried a half bottle of Glen Merangie. In the other were two glasses.

"I know how you must be feeling," he said. "Thought a spot of malt whiskey might help. It always seemed to do the trick for me."

"James. I didn't know you were still here. I thought everyone had gone long ago."

"I thought I'd attempt a spot of settling in. Also, I was wondering if you might like some company." He handed me a glass, removed the cap from the bottle, and poured a generous shot. After pouring his own, he raised his glass and continued, "Here's to the devil you know."

I took a healthy gulp of the welcome drink, settled back in my chair, and focused on my new colleague. "Thanks James. Just what the haematologist ordered. I really do appreciate that."

"Don't mention it."

"Silly isn't it. There's always one case that gets to you. After all these years you'd think I'd be able to handle it a little better." I looked at him, suddenly feeling very vulnerable.

"If it didn't get to you at times you couldn't be the caring physician you are," he said, staring past me at the photo on my desk. "Your children?" he asked, looking back at me.

"Yes. My daughters, Jane and Emma, and my son Mark," I replied, reaching for the photograph, and holding it out in front of me for a few moments before continuing, "Even though I don't get to see them that much these days I feel very close to them. They were over at the weekend, giving me the usual lectures on how to be a father. You know the scenario. Three years ago they couldn't understand how they could have been saddled with such a backward thinking, tyrannical, dominating, ignorant parent such as me. Then, the other day, they told me they were at a loss to understand how much I'd managed to learn in three years! Who wants to grow up? But right now I miss them tremendously."

"I look forward to meeting them. They sound as if they have you taped," he said, freshening up my drink.

"It's good of you to pop in James. I appreciate it right now. That drink has done a power of good. I knew I was going to like you!"

"Steady on. Let's not go too far. You don't really know me yet. You haven't had the pleasure of seeing me when I don't get my own way." He made a grisly face, as he raised his glass in my direction.

"I have that pleasure to come, James. But, right now you're tops in my book. Thanks again." I raised my glass, returning the salute, and downed the contents in one gulp.

* * *

The ward was quiet when I looked in on my way out of the hospital. Hugh Schofield informed me that Colin Sampson, the haemophiliac, had discharged himself against our advice. Apparently, he had said that he couldn't sleep as there were so many distractions and disturbances during the night, with doctors coming and going, screens being pulled and people talking. Hugh made sure he placed the patient's signed, official discharge note in his medical record and that a suitable summary was forwarded to his GP.

Back at home, after finishing the mediocre pizza I had collected on the way, I settled into the armchair by the fire, with the statutory glass of wine by my side and phoned Victoria. I felt guilty because I hadn't had a chance to phone her the day before, as promised. It was answered, after five rings, by a sleepy sounding voice.

"Victoria. You alright?"

"Yes, fine. Why?"

"You sound so distant," I said, wondering if I had disturbed her.

"I'm O.K., really. It's just that I've had a bad day. Only got in half an hour ago." She did sound unusually tired and I began to regret having phoned her.

"If this is a bad time to phone? I could always call back tomorrow," I volunteered.

"Don't be silly. It's lovely to hear your voice again. I thought you were going to phone yesterday." She sounded a little brighter now.

"Yes, I had meant to, but somehow circumstances conspired to get the better of me last night. By the time I had finished everything it was a bit too late."

"How's your day been?"

"Absolutely bloody awful."

I proceeded to relate the events of the past few hours in detail. When, at last, I had finished I took a deep breath and followed this with a sip of wine.

"Sounds really terrible," she said. "Poor lady. And that poor family. How ever could you bring yourself to speak to her husband? I wouldn't know what to say."

"There isn't anything you really can say. I felt dreadful. And he was so good the way he handled it." I was back in the doldrums.

"You poor darling. I wish I was there to comfort and cuddle you right now. You sound so down and in need of company." The sound of her soothing voice, itself was a comfort, and I told her so.

"Well, it will soon be Friday and you are still coming down I hope." I tried to sound as if suicide was an option if she had changed her mind.

"Nothing would stop me. I've been looking forward to this weekend so much." The spring in her voice told me she really meant it and a warm feeling kindled deep inside me.

"Good," I said." Otherwise I would have had to put in a formal complaint to your company."

"Oh! Please spare me," she giggled. "Anything but that. What are you doing tonight?"

"I had thought of going down to the pub to drown my sorrows. It seemed the most appropriate thing to do under the circumstances."

"You'd better not," she warned. "Or I'll forget the weekend. I don't like the thought of you in this mood, drinking on your own. Remember what Dean Martin once said."

"What's that?" I enquired, slowly emptying my glass.

"He said, *If you drink don't drive*.............. *Don't* even *putt!*"

I burst into laughter. "Hey! I'm supposed to deliver those lines," I said, my academic pride badly wounded. "That's the first time I've laughed today. I really needed that. It only goes to show, I can't do without you."

"Exaggeration from the eminent Dr Ryan, yet again. Well, I don't care. I think I'll hang on to that attempt at flattery till I see you on Friday."

"You do that. Now you'd better go and have yourself a well-deserved long, hot soak in your bath. You're sounding tired," I bullied her.

"Oh! Alright *dwarling!* What ever you say. By the way, in case I forgot to mention it, I do love you." Click! The line went dead.

My spirits had been lifted to new heights and I was back in the land of the living once again. With mixed feelings of sadness and joy, I poured myself another glass of wine, and drank a slow, silent toast to Lynn Harris.

CHAPTER FIFTEEN

People are not content with a simple hernia or a fracture of the finger. They turn everything into the rarest of diseases. It gives them immense satisfaction to think that their illnesses are different from everyone else's
– Anton Chekhov

I had slept well, the conversation with Victoria having greatly soothed my troubled brain. As a result I was up early the next morning and at my desk by eight. Gulping down my black coffee, I was busy sorting through a rough draught of my proposed leukaemia trial.

Somehow, things had not been too bad around the office with Anne away in the West Country. Her colleague, Louise, who had been with us a little over two years, was coping remarkably well, considering the pressure she was under. To my relief James was not in his room when I arrived. Much as I enjoyed being at work early, I realistically accepted that such a phenomenon was not practical on a permanent basis. And, *keeping up with the Jones'* was not my idea of a reasonable sport.

I had just poured myself a second cup when the phone burst into life, causing me to jump for the umpteenth time that week and, in the process, spill coffee all over the papers in front of me.

"Andrew. How are you?" It was my older sister, Jill, virtually whispering into the phone.

Jill had only recently reached that black milestone in a woman's calendar, her fiftieth birthday. For many, this would have been an occasion of great joy and celebration. For Jill, however, it served only as a reminder that her sick and ailing body was hurtling inexorably and even faster toward ultimate decay and destruction. For, ever since I could remember, my poor sibling had been almost totally preoccupied with the symptoms and signs of all the various illnesses it had been her misfortune to acquire. As an example, a simple three-day cold would easily be strung out the full fortnight, possibly to include a mild bout of pneumonia requiring copious amounts of antibiotics.

When she eventually ran out of her own symptoms she would proceed to commandeer those of her friends and associates suffering from genuine ailments. Nothing was sacred to her when it came to suffering. As far as she was concerned it had become an art form, and she was forever having an exhibition.

All this did not mean that I did not love my sister. Far from it. But through some Machiavellian twist of fate her younger brother had decided to become a doctor. Some had believed this to have been the ultimate sacrifice of a caring brother for his beloved and doomed sister. Some futile attempt to protect and prolong the miserable life of a disease-ridden older relative. The ultimate act of dedication and sacrifice. Whatever the reasons, the stage had been set. It had become like Christmas every day for someone who craved presents.

Jill was well aware of the cruel joke running within the family that she had had the misfortune to suffer from every disease going, except hypochondria. Even this had no effect on her relentless pursuit of cures and treatments for a range of ills, from bunions to boils, from pre-menstrual tension to inoperable brain tumours. We had even ventured to suggest that she become a research chemist. That way, we had said, she would have been able to make a fortune by, as Victor Borge had once put it, *'inventing the cure for which there was no disease.'*

But all this, of course, was firmly brushed aside. For, very early on, it had become apparent to me that to be a successful, fully fledged, accredited, practising hypochondriac it is imperative that one develop that most fundamental of associate requirements...... the ability not to listen to anything you don't want to hear. The art of *'discriminate aural reception,'* we had coined it. When she had enquired what that had meant we had all shouted,....*'deaf!'*

"Hello Jill," I said, trying to conceal the deep sigh I felt within me. "What's the problem?"

"What do you mean, *'problem'*? There's no problem," she intoned, sounding distinctly affronted. "Why is it that you always seem to think that I only ever phone you when I have a problem? Really! It's only that I've not heard from you for some time and I was wondering how you were getting on. Adam and I were talking about you only last night. He misses you and was wondering when we are going to see you again."

Adam, her long suffering husband, was a very kind man who had been reduced to a quivering wreck over the years. This had largely been the result of the continuing loyalty he had shown his wife throughout this period, with all her various medical problems. The reason they had not had any children, according to Jill, was due to a mysterious illness involving recurrent episodes of chronic salpingitis over the years. A little uncharitably, I had believed it was more likely due to the fact that childbirth required a certain amount of pain and real suffering, and that might have got in the way of, or even taken precedence over, all her other *'problems.'* And nothing was going to be allowed to do that.

Poor Adam's one and only other love in life was his vintage car, a gleaming Lagonda with over two hundred thousand miles on the clock. Once, over a pint at his local pub, I had joked that half of that mileage had probably been accumulated over the years driving Jill backwards and forwards to the numerous GP surgeries and hospitals she had graced with her various maladies.

He had found in me a friend with whom to swap anecdotes; a fellow sufferer to act as father confessor, councillor and general all-round psychoanalyst. It was not that he did not love Jill. But, all the years of support he had provided his spouse had taken its toll and he badly needed an ally. For my part, I greatly enjoyed his company and looked forward to our conversations. We shared a similar sense of humour, a fundamental prerequisite for anyone saddled with a relative of Jill's predisposition.

"I'm sorry I haven't been in touch," I said. "Trouble is that I've been so busy at the hospital lately. There's been so much to sort out and my new colleague has now joined me, and has taken a lot of my time showing him the ropes."

"That's no excuse for forgetting your relatives," she chided. "It doesn't take much to pick the phone up once in a while." She was now acting the big sister.

"Yes, well, I've also had numerous problems on the wards that have required a lot of my time. And, as if that wasn't enough, I had to admit one of our senior administrative staff who has only recently been diagnosed with leukaemia. The poor chap has been struggling on at his post for some weeks now feeling very tired with severe anaemia." As I uttered the words, I knew intuitively that I should have avoided the subject of symptoms. But it was too late. The damage had been done. The die was cast.

"In fact, it is true, I haven't been feeling too good recently, Andrew," she waded in. "I've been feeling excessively tired and run down."

I sometimes wish you would be, I thought to myself, a little unkindly. *Preferably by the Lagonda. How poetic.*

"It's probably nothing much," I suggested, as positively as I could bring myself to sound. "There are a lot of viruses about at the moment. They're having a veritable holiday."

"Oh! It's worse than that, I'm certain." She was in, and nothing was going to stop her. The locomotive was on the track, and raring to go. "I wouldn't be surprised if it wasn't something like BSE coming on."

She had a habit of assuming that even the most severe form of incurable disease was in the habit of *'coming on'* whenever it suited her, and then vanishing again as quickly, only to reappear sporadically over the ensuing years, like a menstrual period for a woman approaching the menopause.

"Jill, for God's sake. Even if you have been unable to give up eating British beef, the chances of you contracting BSE are about as likely as me having a baby," I remonstrated.

"It's all very well for you to say that. But where's the proof? And, anyway, it's me who has the symptoms. Only I know what I'm suffering. Sometimes I think you don't care."

"Jill, Jill, Jill. Of course I care. But you must be reasonable. Every time someone has an illness, you have to top it. You are, in fact, a very fit person for your age, which, for the record, does not happen to be that great.

"You really must try to take a firm grip on yourself and stop thinking that every slight cough, or twinge is the result of some dreadful incurable disease. After all, there is a limit to how many times a person can die. And, in the end, even you can only die of one particular cause and that should, of itself, be some sort of comfort to you." The doctor had spoken. But he might as well have saved his breath.

"You are obviously not in the least concerned about my feelings," she interrupted, indignantly. "I really don't know why I bother talking to you about my problems. As a specialist I would have thought you would show more concern."

"You don't need a haematologist, you need an expert in euthanasia," I whispered to myself.

"I didn't catch that. What did you say?"

"I said, '*You don't need a specialist. What you need is a spell in the gymnasium.*' You know, aerobics and all that. To get you in trim."

"Oh! Don't be ridiculous. I have given up trying to get any sense out of doctors. Anyway, I must go. I need to make an appointment with my practitioner before this gets any worse."

"O.K. Hope you're feeling better soon. Give my regards to Adam. Tell him I'll be in touch soon about meeting up for a drink."

* * *

Touring the ward at lunch-time I came across Hugh at the nurses' station writing up a patient's drug chart. He pointed out that David, whose blood count was now virtually non-existent, because of the chemotherapy, was feeling unwell and was developing a high fever.

Following a brief examination, I ordered the usual investigations and got him started on broad spectrum intravenous antibiotics. I then phoned his wife to inform her of the situation.

On my way out of the ward I ran into Mr Bremner, the other leukaemic patient, who had made a good recovery from his bout of septicaemia, and whose bone marrow had regenerated and was now in complete remission. He thanked me profusely for all my help and then departed, after collecting his follow-up out-patient appointment from the Staff Nurse.

Back in the department, Louise nervously approached me as I sauntered through the door.

"Dr Ryan. I'm sorry to disturb you, but Dr Baldwin's secretary phoned a minute ago. Dr Baldwin was wondering if you could spare him a few minutes this afternoon. She didn't say what it was about."

Poor Louise, who was of a slightly nervous disposition, almost backed into the wall as she delivered the message.

"Thank you, Louise," I said, trying my hardest not to convey my instant sense of anger at hearing Boris' name. The mere sound of it brought out the rottweiler in me. "I'll give his secretary a ring and fix a time."

* * *

"Boris, how are you doing?" I positively breezed into David's office as if I owned it. "I gather you wanted to see me. What can I do for you?" I said, in my most malevolent tone.

"Ah! Dr Ryan. Thank you for coming," he said, in his typically condescending way. "As I gather you know, in the circumstances, I am acting Chief Executive."

"It had filtered down to me. But I preferred to believe it was merely a bad dream." As I said the words I realised that I had already forgotten what I had promised David such a short time ago. It was obviously going to be very difficult to live up to that promise.

"How is poor David doing?" he asked, with the minimum of feeling.

"As well as can be expected," I replied. "But, of course, I cannot discuss my patient's illness with anyone but his relatives," I added, by way of a snub.

"Quite so. Dreadful business. Couldn't have come at a worse time."

"You can say that again, and with you as the only alternative!" I whispered, under my breath. "What can I do for you, Boris?" I was becoming impatient already.

"I've asked you down to discuss a very serious matter that has only recently been brought to my notice."

"And what might that be? My houseman been caught *flagrante delicto* with his trousers down again? I've already spoken to him about it twice. Or, could it possibly be all my drug sponsored trips abroad?" I'm afraid I could not resist having a go.

"Dr Ryan!" After all the years he'd known me, this pompous old twerp still couldn't bring himself to use my first name. "That's most uncalled-for. I merely reported what, to all intents and purposes, looked like a possible case of bribery. There was no personal animosity involved. I was only doing what I plainly saw as my duty in the circumstances."

"Any decent human being, Boris, would have confronted the culprit directly, and given him a chance to explain the situation, before rushing off to the headmaster like your average school sneak. Anyway, I'm extremely busy. So what's your beef now?"

"It has been brought to my notice that your department is accruing a considerable overspend on the allotted drug budget." He started to shift a little uneasily in his chair, as he balanced his prinz-nez spectacles precariously on the end of his bulbous nose and shuffled the papers on the desk in front of him.

"What overspend?" I replied, feigning complete surprise.

"Dr Ryan, you must be aware that your current drug bill has accumulated to about double your allotted budget. Why, your use of broad spectrum antibiotics alone has driven it through the roof."

"Oh! Is that all it's about. For a moment I thought it was going to be something important." I was beginning to find the whole business very tiresome. "Boris, my old darling, all the drugs I use, and the occasions on which I use them, are in keeping with the agreed protocols. Protocols, I might add, that have already been fully accepted by your *Wineing* pharmacy colleague, as per hospital policy."

"How irresponsible can you be," he said, a little hysterically. "Even you should realise the importance of good housekeeping."

"For God's sake Boris, I'm not making a soufflé, or building a ruddy rock garden. A large part of my life is spent trying to save the lives of a number of extremely ill patients. How can you possibly place a price on that?" I really had had enough of this sycophantic twit. "The real problem is that one simply cannot predict with any certainty how many patients are going to present with leukaemia in a given period. And, since it is a relatively rare disease, just two more cases in a month would be enough to severely rock your so-called *'budget'*. As a responsible physician I really cannot allow myself to become restrained by this illogical, kindergarten-type thinking."

Boris was obviously doing his utmost to control his emotions. "You know and I know, that at the end of the day there is only so much money in the health budget. And we all ultimately have the responsibility to make sure that it is fairly and properly meted out for the overall care of all the patients."

"Exactly how much money appears in the National Health budget is not a matter for my concern," I interrupted. "What is my concern is the overall welfare of my patients. And we would all do well to bear in mind that every one of them has been made a promise by this godforsaken government on its way into office. For those of us with short memories, that promise was to make available to the general public the best medicine going.

"As a consequence, I see it as my fundamental duty to ensure that they are not allowed to forget that promise and, not only what it means long-term but also what it will require realistically when it comes to implementing and maintaining it on a national level. In other words Boris, me old darling, I aim to see to it that they keep their bloody promise, even if *they* don't!"

And with that I was up on my feet and halfway out of the office before the red faced Boris could find a reply.

* * *

I had felt particularly invigorated following my meeting with the deputy *obergropenfuhrer.* I sailed through the out-patient clinic in the afternoon, finishing well in time to complete a short ward round with Hugh. There were no real problems, and David was feeling a lot better since starting him on those '*shockingly expensive* antibiotics.'

Later, back in my room, Matthew Bryant looked in to discuss the dreadful business of Lynn Harris' death. He obviously felt as badly about the whole affair as I had and was finding it hard to accept. In the end we both agreed that there was probably some other underlying condition we were unaware of and that we couldn't possibly have anticipated. No doubt all would be revealed following the post-mortem.

James was finishing off the lab reports for the day as we discussed my meeting with Boris. He smiled as I recounted the conversation, having virtually heard it all before when he had been working at Guys, where his boss had also run foul of the administration over the '*overspend*'. It was obviously a universal problem within the world of haematology. When he had finished we retired to the Blue Boar for a quick drink and debrief of the day's events, before heading off in different directions home.

As I drove through the heavy rain, windscreen wiper thrashing at full speed, I couldn't help feeling very happy with James' appointment. He was without doubt going to prove a fine colleague and a very important piece in the overall jig-saw.

CHAPTER SIXTEEN

I'm dying. I need a doctor. Take me to the nearest golf course
– W. C. Fields (attributed)

"Fore!" my partner, Nick Forsyth, yelled at the top of his voice, as he badly sliced his tee shot on the third hole. Unfortunately, it was a little late, as the curving ball had already crossed the intervening rough and was coming to earth between a group of four elderly ladies, slowly making their way up the seventh fairway. As he shouted, the old dears were already scattering in all directions, arms held aloft, having abandoned the golf trolleys to their fate.

"Have you any idea how many people are killed on our golf courses every year?" I enquired, as our other two colleagues made a bad attempt at hiding their laughter.

"Oh! God. I'd better get over there and apologise," he stammered, grabbing his bag and scurrying off in the direction of his ball.

Nick was one of our histopathologists at Eastwich General. These are the guys who do the post-mortems and look down their microscopes at all the biopsies and various organs that get removed from our patients from time to time. He was an excellent pathologist and had only been with us three years.

In addition to a recently appointed forth specialist, there were two, more senior, colleagues in the department. However, I had gathered from various sources that there was not a lot of love lost between Nick and his most senior partner. I knew a bit about the problems but had deliberately not pried into the situation. The moment Nick had arrived on the scene I had taken a liking to him and we had struck it off from the start.

As far as his senior colleague was concerned, I considered him to be extremely competent and good at his work and I had always enjoyed a good working relationship with him. However, that is where it had ended. Socially we were miles apart and there had always been that inexplicable *something* between us.

I knew that, although he had always spoken to me in the nicest of ways and had never shown any obvious sign of dissent, behind my back he had done what he could to undermine me with the administration and some of my colleagues. None of this had been of much importance to me but when Nick had appeared I realised I'd found a good friend in the histopathology department.

He finally caught up with us as we approached the third green. Gasping for breath, he looked at me rather sheepishly and said, "Boy, were they angry with me."

"Well, you did very nearly kill them," I volunteered. "And to think, if you had succeeded, you'd probably be doing their post-mortem on Monday." The others started chuckling again. "Anyway, let's forget it. Isn't it great to be out in the open air, enjoying the beautiful countryside on this lovely Saturday morning? It sure beats that sweat box of a hospital."

"Under any other conditions I would agree with you. But, who was it who once said, 'Golf is a good walk spoiled'?" he asked.

"Mark Twain." I replied, smugly.

"Well, he was right. At least, in my case."

"Come on, Nick," I said. "What's up? Your senior colleagues been annoying you again?"

"You could say that," he said, selecting the pitching wedge for his next shot. "I caught them yesterday interviewing a new junior technician for our lab. And they hadn't even had the decency to discuss the appointment with me beforehand. I didn't know they had advertised the post and I'm one of the consultants in the department. How would you feel?" He really was feeling aggrieved and I had to agree with him.

"What did they say when you confronted them?"

"Oh! You know. They pretended it wasn't important and that they didn't think I would have wanted to be bothered with such a trivial matter. It's very difficult to tie them down, but all the time they simply brush me aside.

"I'm never considered when it comes to the policy-making

decisions in the department. And yet, in a few years time, after they've retired, I'm going to be the senior member of the department. And I'll be left with staff I may not have chosen if I had been involved in the selection process in the first place. It's really beginning to get me down."

It was obvious to me that he was coming to the end of his tether with his colleagues and was badly in need of some support. I was prepared to do what I could, and decided to discuss it with him later.

He took his shot, but caught the grass in front of the ball, sending it scurrying off course and leaving himself a tricky twenty foot, downhill putt from the right side of the green. The silence from his companions was deafening.

"Good one to win," I said, in my most encouraging tone.

Fuming, he removed the putter from his bag and approached his ball. As he sized up the putt and prepared to strike the ball, a horse neighed in the nearby field. He stepped back, straightened up, and snapped in disgust, "It's like trying to play in the middle of a godammed circus." Exasperation was written all over his face.

"You know Nick," I said. "You remind me of that P. G. Wodehouse character. You know, the one who, '*The least thing upset him on the links. He missed short putts because of the uproar of the butterflies in the adjourning meadows.*'"

There was a moment's silence following which, he burst into laughter, having seen the humour of the situation, and we all joined in.

Needless to say, he missed the putt!

* * *

The sun was shining brightly as we crossed from the eighteenth green towards the clubhouse. We had already bid farewell to our companions and Nick was in a much happier frame of mind. Having managed to tee off around seven it was still quite early, with the clock registering a quarter to eleven. As Victoria was not due to arrive till after noon we had time for a quick pint in the bar, and Nick hadn't taken too much persuading.

On our way to the golf course earlier Nick and I had discussed Lynn Harris and the post-mortem that had failed to identify any obvious cause for her sudden death. He had pointed out that, every now and then a cause was not evident from such an examination. He had explained that the heart can stop for any number of reasons, not all of which will leave a positive clue as to the underlying cause.

As an example he mentioned certain cardiac arrhythmias, sudden changes in the natural rhythm of the heart that can occur for a number of reasons and can, in certain cases, effectively stop the normal flow of the blood, cutting off the vital supply of oxygen to the brain. He also mentioned conditions such as epilepsy that can occur at any age and is a known cause of sudden death on rare occasions.

In certain conditions or circumstances the chemical composition of the blood can be altered, thereby affecting the normal function of the heart muscle, and leading to irreversible cardiac arrest. Although these instances are rare, they do occur and undoubtedly account for a number of such *'unexplained'* deaths in the country every year.

He went on to tell me that it was even the subject of a one-day symposium already booked for later in the year at the Royal College of Pathologists. All this had made me feel a little easier over the episode, although I still felt a tinge of guilt.

Snuggled in the corner of the bar, our pints on the table in front of us, I decided to open the batting.

"Nick, the other day I received an anonymous letter that had been left on my desk, whilst I was out of the department," I began, looking him squarely in the eye. "It was concerning one of your colleagues, and made a number of serious accusations, including what would amount to plain fraud."

He looked at me with an inquisitive expression. But he made no effort to speak, as he reached forward and picked up his glass.

I took a large gulp of my beer and continued. "It wasn't you who left it was it?" I kept my eyes on him as I asked the question.

"No it wasn't," he said, returning my stare in such a way that I instantly believed him. "What did it say?"

"It mentioned that one of your colleagues is party to a fraud. And that this fraud is to do with the private work associated with the pathology service you offer the local BUPA Samaritan Hospital. In some detail, it stated that this colleague was in the habit of reporting certain biopsies for his surgical colleagues up the road and then signing someone else's name to the report."

Nick looked carefully at me for a moment, and then took a

long sip from his drink.

"Did you have any idea of this?" I asked.

"Yes, I did. But I didn't realise anyone else knew." He carefully placed his glass back on the table and looked across at me. "I've been aware of this for some time, but I didn't dare tell anyone. Mostly, because I didn't think anyone would ever believe me."

"But, why would he do it, and whose name is he signing?"

"As you know we are all employed by the Eastwich Hospital NHS Trust on *Full Time* contracts. These allow us to do a little private work on NHS time without being penalised financially."

What he was alluding to was that up to a certain amount we were officially allowed to do some private work in the NHS hospital without it affecting our Full Time NHS salary. If, however, the value of that private work amounts to more than ten percent of the NHS full-time salary, then you are honour-bound to declare this to your employer who will then put you onto a *Maximum Part-Time* contract. This means that you will lose about ten percent of your NHS salary. All this, of course, also means that your eventual NHS pension will be affected, since the amount is directly related to your final salary.

"But why go to such lengths?" I questioned.

"Because Patrick's private practice is brimming. If he is seen to accept any more he'll be driven into a Part-Time contract."

"Are you telling me that he's working an elaborate fiddle for the sake of a miserable few thousand pounds?"

"That's about the measure of it. I can't see what else it could be."

"But whose name is he using? And how does he *possibly* get to benefit from the cheating?" I was intrigued.

"He's signing the name of our esteemed Consultant Cytologist."

"What, *Tony Knowles,*" I gasped, in complete astonishment.

"The very same. I have actually witnessed Patrick, on a number of occasions, openly signing Tony's name on a number of histology reports. And I know it's been a closely kept secret, but these two have been living together, ever since Tony decided to *'come out of the closet,'* as it were, the year before last, and left his wife. I suppose the divorce must have cost him a pretty packet, and he really can't bear to lose any more. And since he's already on a part-time contract he's entitled to unlimited private work." With that he finished off his beer and looked across at me. "Would you like another half before we go?"

"I think I'm going to need it," I said, staring him blankly in the face, then added, "Under the circumstances I think you'd better make it a pint!"

Once he'd returned with the drinks and was settled back in his seat, I leant across and asked, "Tell me, is your other, recently appointed, colleague also involved?"

"I don't think so. But I'm sure he knows what's going on. Though, I don't for one moment think that it was him who left the letter. I can only presume that it was one of the technicians, or possibly even a secretary. It's no secret they can't stand Patrick, what with all his mean ways and dismissive treatment of the staff."

"You know, Nick, it would be lovely if only we could deliver the proof to the administration. But that would not be easy. You know how one's colleagues soon close ranks when they smell a rat. Especially the one's into money. I can't help thinking there's quite a number of them out there who are well aware of what's going on, but they're perfectly happy to carry on regardless and simply ignore the fact. I really find it difficult to understand them sometimes. Tell me, Nick, do you play chess?"

"Yes, why?"

"Do you know how many different chess games are possible?" I asked.

"Can't say I've ever bothered to try and work it out," he replied, with a grin.

"I once read somewhere that there are more possible variations of a chess game than there are atoms in the *whole* universe."

"So?" he said, looking quizzically at me.

"So," I continued, "Every time you think you're beaten with no way back, with all the infinite possible moves available to you it's more than likely that there must be a winner there that you haven't seen. In other words, my advice to you in your particular situation is not to give up. There most likely *is* a move that will turn the tables. Sometimes you must summon up the discipline to sit and wait till it presents itself to you, before you can strike at the enemy."

"Isn't there some clever Biblical saying about enemies?" Nick primed me.

"You mean the one that goes something like,' *Always forgive thine enemy.*' I cannot help thinking some of the original saying got lost along the centuries, and that the piece finished off something like, '*but never forget their name!*'"

CHAPTER SEVENTEEN

He was a very fine doctor. Very little he couldn't put right when he set his mind to it. Rita's knee got the better of him, though
- Alan Ayckbourn

I was busy cleaning my golf clubs when I heard Victoria's car pull up beside the front door. Trying not to display my obvious sense of teenage joy at the sound of her arrival, I slowly replaced the putter in the bag and started to tidy the kitchen. I waited for the bell to ring before setting off to open the door. My heart was pounding as I slipped the latch and pulled the door open.

"Hi." I said, taking her leather holdall and giving her a big hug. "How was the journey?"

"Almost bearable. The roads were blocked with carloads of children heading for the sea. It's taken me nearly two hours to complete a one hour journey." She was obviously very harassed, and badly needed to unwind after the drive.

"Why do the wrong people travel, travel, travel,
When the right people stay back home?
What compulsion compels them?
And who the hell tells them
To drag their cans to Zanzibar
Instead of staying quietly in Omaha?"

"Are you alright?" she enquired, looking at me a little puzzled, as she slid out of her coat and placed it over the back of a chair.

"Oh! Sorry. Noel Coward. Summed it up rather well, don't you think."

"I thought for a moment that the administration had finally got to you," she said, leaning forward and giving me the most sensual of kisses.

"Bugger Bognor," I whispered, staring straight into her deep blue eyes.

"I beg your pardon," she giggled, grabbing my arms and placing them firmly around her beautifully shaped hips.

"Oh! Sorry." I repeated. "George V's dying words, apparently," I stammered. "I think the Royal family used to holiday there a lot, but he hated it. It would seem he had to wait till he was dying before he could admit it to anyone. At least, that's one theory."

"You're a veritable mine of useless information," she said, a little uncharitably I felt. Then she redeemed herself with, "But I still love you, just the same."

"That settles it then," I said, grabbing her hand, dropping the holdall and dragging her towards the stairs.

"And where do you think you are taking me?" she asked, like a good barrister in court, who only asks questions of the witness to which he or she already knows the answer.

"To my boudoir," I said, hissing through my teeth, rolling my eyes, and generally trying to look menacing.

"Oh! That's alright then. For a horrible moment I thought it was to the kitchen, to wash-up," she said, in her best Little Miss Riding Hood voice.

We positively rushed headlong up the stairs, removing garments as we fled, arriving at the bedroom breathless and semi-naked. The combination of nearly two weeks separation, two pints of beer, and Victoria's erotic perfume had proved too much, even for the most perfectly controlled of haematologists.

As we crossed the threshold of the room I tripped on Victoria's skirt, which she had hastily discarded and we both slipped to the floor, rolling as I hit the carpet. I ended up on top of her, my face a few inches from her giggling countenance.

Our lips met, and we were consumed with passion. Slowly I began to play with her supple body, as we lay there enjoying the touch of each other. It had seemed so long since we were last together, enjoying each other's company. The time apart had only served to confirm, more than ever, our passionate desire for one and other, and our very real need to be together. I was aroused as I had never been aroused before.

The lovemaking was slow and highly sensuous, as we savoured every single moment. We were blissfully unaware of time passing, as we lay there locked in each other's arms, moving in complete harmony. The very touch of her vibrant, supple body triggered new emotions deep within me, propelling me to unbelievable heights of ecstasy.

For what seemed like hours, we lay there in each other's arms, only half conscious, but somehow aware of each other's presence and feeling that great inner warmth that two people experience only rarely in life. Her body felt part of mine, the whole fused in some inseparable way. I had no inclination to move. I had been transported and had no intention of returning to reality. This was heaven as I had envisioned it, and I had no desire to leave. I was.....*converted.*

* * *

We spent the afternoon in town doing some shopping and browsing through books in the large department store off the high street. There were no pressures on us and we were able to glide from shop to shop, stopping to inspect whatever took our interest, totally oblivious of the time.

I bought Victoria a floppy, wide-brimmed straw hat with a colourful ribbon trailing off the back, but it kept blowing off her head in the stiff sea breeze that had blown up during the latter part of the afternoon. We eventually took refuge in a picturesque little coffee shop I knew that was off the beaten track. Here we sipped our cappuccino, and slowly munched our way through the most fattening of cream cakes, giggling to ourselves as the cream smudged our faces.

We were a million miles into space and not a rescue ship in sight. The ultimate ship-wrecked couple, with everything they desired, including that feeling of cosy isolation and peace. Complete bliss.

We completed a wonderful afternoon with a stroll through the park that was situated on the outskirts of town. As we walked along, enjoying the scenery and marvelling at the way nature had of waking up every spring, we discussed the possibility of getting away for a few days.

I had suggested Paris, but, at first, Victoria was not too keen on the idea. However, she eventually agreed when I explained all the places we would visit, including the little out-of-the-way bars and restaurants I knew and how lovely it would be to stroll, hand in hand, along the banks of the River Seine in early summer.

We were back at home by six, giving us plenty of time to get ready for the evening. I had booked dinner at a little candlelit restaurant in town and we weren't due there till eight. In the interests of economy and in anticipation of that perennial of English problems, the national water shortage and hose-pipe ban, we shared a bath. Needless to say, I got the tap end!

Why two grown adults cannot learn to behave and show decorum and respect under such circumstances of hardship and deprivation I'll never know, but we were no exception! As a relatively innocent middle-aged haematologist I would not have believed what two people could possibly have got up to in a communal bath. I decided to make notes for future reference, in case by some cruel twist of fate senility, with its associated short-term memory loss, decided to pick me out earlier than anticipated.

* * *

The restaurant was nearly full when we arrived dead on eight o'clock. It was starting to rain as we pulled into the car park and we had had to sprint the forty yards to the entrance. As we entered, Victoria whispered into my ear that we hadn't needed to share the bath after all. I half blushed at the memory, as the slightly effeminate waiter greeted us and led us to the bar. After handing us the menu and wine list, he took our order for drinks and minced his way over to the barman.

"It doesn't matter what you do in the bedroom as long as you don't do it in the street and frighten the horses," I whispered as he departed.

"O.K., Sir Laurence, so what was that all about?" Victoria asked.

"It was a comment by Mrs Patrick Campbell on the subject of homosexuality," I answered.

"Andrew! Because he walks a little delicately, and speaks softly, it does not necessarily imply anything to do with his sexuality. And even if it did, it has nothing to do with us." It was my turn to be lectured.

"I didn't mean to be critical. Far from it. It's only that seeing him move that way reminded me of that rather humorous quote.

But I stand corrected. Under the circumstances my lady, I throw myself upon your mercy. Give us a kiss," I implored, with my repentant eyes fixing her stare.

She grinned that sexy grin only she could manufacture, leaned carefully over the little table and planted the most delicate of kisses gently on my cheek.

"Surely you can do better than that," I grunted.

"Not now. Not here. Later," she promised.

"I want one now," I insisted loudly, in my most spoilt, schoolboy tone.

"Behave," she hissed quietly, staring over my shoulder at the other diners sipping their drinks in the corner. With a smile that transfixed me to the spot, she leant over once again and delivered the real McCoy, tongue searching and all.

"Now you're pumpin' gas," I said, as a broad smile spread slowly across my face. I reached under the table and gave her thigh a gentle stroke.

"That'll be all for now, Dr Ryan! You'll get the rest later." She straightened her skirt and started looking over the menu as the waiter reappeared with the drinks.

Once we had ordered and the waiter had retreated through the door beside the bar, we settled back in our seats and took in the scene. As we sipped our drinks I updated Victoria on the events of the week. I finished with the discussion I had had with Nick that morning and with the anonymous letter I had received.

"It's obvious to me," she said, "that someone feels strongly enough about the situation, and the people involved, to have informed the one person they feel may eventually be inclined to get up off his backside and do something about it."

"Meaning me?"

"Yes. Because your reputation for taking on so-called *'good'* causes precedes you. You are renowned for the trouble you're prepared to make for others if you consider the cause to be a just one, and the people concerned to be guilty of involvement. Someone has singled you out because he or she knows that you won't allow yourself to be bought off. And, what's more, you won't let go until you have succeeded in bringing the situation to the notice of the administration and seen that something positive has been done about it."

"The whole thing seems a bit of a tall order to me," I said. "I have no doubt that these two are guilty of fraud and cheating the system and for relatively small amounts. But proving it would not be easy. Experience tells me that the moment anyone gets anywhere near the truth, one's colleagues have a habit of closing ranks and obscuring the view. A perfect example of the *'old pals act'* at work."

"I'm sure many of them are not like that really. When it comes down to it, they're probably like most people and don't want to get involved, preferring to keep out of it in the hopes that it will all simply go away." She reached forward to retrieve her coaster that had fallen to the floor.

"Perhaps I am being a little harsh on some of my colleagues. But I find it difficult to believe they can merely sit there and pretend nothing has happened," I said, frowning at her across the table

"You know, you're probably greatly overestimating their knowledge of these events. But I know you when you have that look on you face," she said. "You have no intention of letting this go. Whatever happens, you must be careful. This type of person can be pretty ruthless. I've seen it all before. Where money's involved, they tend to lose all sense of proportion. Ouch!" She exclaimed, clutching her stomach.

"Victoria," I gasped, jumping from my seat and moving round to her side. "Are you alright?" I placed my hand on her shoulder, as I knelt down beside her.

"Yes, fine," she answered, straightening up and smiling at me. "It's only a slight twinge. Didn't last more than a few seconds. Probably all those cream cakes!"

"Are you sure. If there's any problem we could easily forget the meal."

"Don't be silly," she said. "I wouldn't hear of it. I've been looking forward to this evening for ages and I'm not going to miss it for anything." She turned sideways, grasping my hand and giving it a big squeeze. "Now, what were we talking about?"

"Cheats!"

"What, no quotes? You haven't possibly run out have you?" she teased.

"*'Thou shalt not steal; an empty feat, When it's so lucrative to cheat.'* Arthur Hugh Clough." I offered, triumphantly.

"Never heard of him. Bet you made it up. You'd do anything to impress."

I shrugged my shoulders in defeat, as our waiter sidled up and, mincingly, showed us over to our table.

* * *

The meal was a delight and we took our time, cherishing every moment together. The wine and the atmosphere blended to make it one of the most enjoyable evenings I could remember.

It was raining heavily when we left and we got soaked getting to the car. I drove slowly as we chatted about our common interest in the theatre and eventually arrived back home at eleven.

I poured a couple of brandies and lit the fire in the lounge, while Victoria slipped upstairs to get out of her wet clothes and into something a little more comfortable.

I sat sipping my brandy, staring into the flames and contemplating the busy week ahead of me. Completely lost in my thoughts, I was unaware that Victoria had been gone so long, until I heard a loud crashing sound coming from upstairs.

I dropped my glass instantly, throwing myself through the door and up the stairs two at a time, shouting out Victoria's name as I ran. I found her sprawled out on the bathroom floor, groaning and clutching her stomach. She was ashen faced and perspiring profusely.

"Victoria," I shouted. "Victoria," as I knelt beside her, cradling her head in my arms.

CHAPTER EIGHTEEN

Who shall decide, when doctors disagree,And soundest casuists doubt, like you and me?
– Alexander Pope

The middle aged man facing me across the desk in out-patients slowly leant forward on his chair, and proceeded to ask the most difficult question for a doctor to answer.

"'Ow long 'ave I got then Doc? Bott'm line."

He had been a patient of mine for over seven years, during which time he had received numerous courses of chemotherapy for his Hodgkin's disease. Following his last relapse, nearly two years ago, he had undergone an intensive bout of treatment, followed by stem cell transplantation; a procedure that had gone a long way to replacing the need for formal bone marrow transplantation. The procedure had gone well and, up to his last visit twelve weeks ago, he had remained in perfect health and in remission. At last, we were all beginning to believe that we may actually have achieved a cure.

Then, his symptoms had begun to recur, initially in the form of profuse sweating at night. Following this, he began to lose his appetite and his weight started to slip. Eventually, he noticed the appearance of a few small, painless lumps on the right side of his neck and under his left arm.

He had always been one of those patients who bore his illness and the treatment extremely well, displaying great bravery and fortitude and rarely ever complaining. He was totally compliant with whatever his medical team had suggested and he never once questioned our decisions. He was, in fact, the model patient. This made it all the harder to sit before him on this occasion and admit that we had not succeeded in curing him.

"Peter," I began, "you know as well as I do that it really isn't possible to give a specific time interval in these situations." I was trying my hardest not to sound over- pessimistic. But, like so many patients in his situation, over the many years of hospitalisation and treatment he had managed to acquire a vast knowledge of his condition with its various treatments and its prognosis.

"Come on doc. It's no use tryin' to dress it up for me. I know all about the disease. I probably know more 'bout it by now than old 'odgkin 'imself." He gave his nervous little laugh that I had become so used to over the years. "It's plain to me the writin's on the wall. It's only that like, wivout me specs, I can't read the bleedin' small print." He gave another laugh, bolder this time, as he gained a little more confidence. It was his attempt to spare me any embarrassment.

"Peter, you're great," I said. "I'd like to believe I would be able to be as brave as you when my time comes. What's your secret?"

"Well Doc. When yer've been dyin' as often as me, it gets to become part of yer life, if yer see what I mean, like. I've fought abaut it so much over the years that I'm bored wiv it now. So, when it eventually 'appens it'll be a bleedin' blessing, in some ways."

"Well Peter, it's not going to happen yet. Your particular disease has always been fairly low grade in its activity and there are plenty of things we can do to keep it at bay for a while. Besides, speaking selfishly, I want you around a lot longer. You make me laugh and feel good.

"Your uncomplicated sense of logic is very important to me. It makes my day and helps me in my life-long fight with bureaucracy. So there, I'm sorry to disappoint you my friend but I do not consider you are ready for the knacker's yard yet.

"That your disease will eventually take you there can be no doubt. And when it is your wish to give up the fight you have only to tell me. But, as long as we can keep you feeling well and able to look after yourself, I'm your man."

"Whatever yer say doc. I trusts yer, yer knows that. So, what's next?"

"Well, in the first place we need to get some more scans to see exactly how much disease you may still have around and whereabouts it's situated. Then we can decide what is the best approach. If it's not too widespread we may be able to get away with some relatively simple treatment such as localised radiotherapy," I said optimistically, handing him the request form for the CT scans.

"O.K., I know the drill. When do yer wanna see me again," he asked, reaching for the form.

"Two weeks. They should have done the scans by then."

Slowly getting to his feet, he thrust his hand in my direction. "Fanks again doc. I really appreciate all yer 'elp," he said giving me the firmest of handshakes.

"You're welcome," I replied, massaging my fingers back to life. "See you in a fortnight."

* * *

When he'd left I settled slowly back in my chair, my hands clasped firmly behind my head and stared blankly at the ceiling. It had been a very long two days and I hadn't managed all that much sleep.

The ambulance had arrived within twenty minutes of my call on Saturday night. Poor Victoria was delirious as the ambulance men carefully loaded the stretcher into the vehicle. Although I demanded to accompany her to the hospital, I don't believe I was of much use as a doctor on this occasion.

Some doctors find it very hard to be objective when it's their own family or close friends who are ill and I'm definitely one of that group. All I could think of was how much she was suffering and how useless I felt in this situation.

I was immensely relieved when we eventually arrived at the hospital and I found that the duty surgeon was Matthew. He arrived within twenty minutes of my call, by which time his registrar had done all the preliminary work-up and got the investigations under way.

Matthew examined her and came over to inform me that she had what we term an *'acute abdomen'*, but that he couldn't be sure what the underlying cause was from the test results. Under the circumstances, there was nothing for it but to operate as soon as possible. However, since she had only recently eaten a meal there might have to be a slight delay.

It had seemed hours before she was eventually taken to theatre, and the long wait began. I spent a nerve-racking hour and a half pacing up and down the deserted corridors, thinking the worst. Only the most complicated of possible causes for Victoria's collapse came to mind.

My inability to act rationally was triggered by the thought that I could not stop reminding myself we had only just found each other and how important she had become to my whole existence in such a short time. I could not allow myself to entertain any thoughts of losing her so soon after the discovery of our mutual love. I was totally inconsolable and wandered about the hospital like some lost pilgrim in search of a sacred place.

The slightest of sounds had me looking up in expectation of some good news. I tried very hard to be positive about the problem but I felt mentally drained and totally irrational in my approach to the situation that now confronted me. I had been so preoccupied with my thoughts, and had become totally disorientated as to where I was, that I hadn't heard Matthew calling to me down the corridor.

"Andrew! Andrew! There you are. I couldn't find you. Are you alright?"

"Matthew. How is she?" I asked, as my eyes began to water.

"She'll be fine," he said, placing his hand on my shoulder. "I thought it was going to be an appendicitis. But I was wrong. It was a ruptured ovarian cyst. No problem really, except she decided to start bleeding again as we went to close. Had to go back and tie off the offending artery. She'll be back asking for the champagne by tomorrow night," he joked.

I stared at him in disbelief, as a solitary tear trickled slowly down my cheek.

"You alright old chap?" he asked, leading me over to a seat and sitting me down.

"Yes, fine," I replied. "God, I was wandering around in a trance fearing the worst. For the past two hours I've been the world's most useless doctor."

"Well, what do you expect for a physician," he quipped, smiling enticingly at an attractive, leggy blonde night nurse as she passed on her way to the canteen.

"Touché!" I said, removing my handkerchief and wiping the tear from my cheek. "Can I see her now?"

"She's pretty groggy still. You look all in. Why don't you get on home and get some sleep. Then you can see her first thing in the morning."

"I suppose you're right Matthew. Be sure and give her my love. And, thanks for all your help," I said, struggling to my feet.

"By the way, I suppose surgeons do have their uses.....sometimes! Perhaps I've been a little harsh on your breed over the years. You're not all that bad......when one gets to know you!"

"Beware physicians bearing compliments! You'd better get going. I'll see you in the morning..........my poor love-sick friend!"

"Are you alright, Dr Ryan?" the out-patient staff nurse asked, as she entered the room.

"Oh! Yes thanks. I was miles away I'm afraid. Reliving the past," I replied. "Was he the last patient?"

"Yes, Dr Ryan."

"Good. I suppose I better get back to the lab," I said, getting up from the desk and grabbing my white coat as I headed for the door.

* * *

Johnny was busy dictating his out-patient letters when I eventually tracked him down in the renal dialysis unit around lunchtime. He had an enormous set of notes lying open on the desk in front of him when I sauntered in.

"Andrew. I heard all about it. Busy weekend I gather. How's Victoria?" he asked, laying his dictaphone on the desk and gesturing for me to take a seat.

"She was feeling a lot easier when I looked in on her earlier. She was complaining of a very sore abdomen, not surprisingly."

"Glad to hear it. I don't know, the things you do to get your women to stay!" he joked. "Why can't you use the usual methods like the rest of us? You know, flowers, sweet talk, and all those wonderful lies they absolutely love to hear."

"Ever since I kept you away from that pigeon loft of yours you've become much more perky and even a trifle cynical into the bargain. I'm not so sure I like the new you," I said, with a note of caution in my voice.

"Well, you'd better get used to it. Because it's here to stay, like it or lump it," he said, with a new-found confidence.

"Poor old Jean. Who's she going to lay into now? Now that her favourite punch bag has been cured."

"I don't care," he said nonchalantly. "I saw her in the car park on Friday evening when I was on the way home. She actually asked me, in her superior way she uses pointing the tip of her nose at me, how I was coping without cigars. That was all I needed to stimulate my need. So I lit one up in front of her, as I was getting into my car. She gave a grunt of disgust, shrugged her shoulders and, turning on her heels, headed off in the direction of her car without another word."

"You're very unkind, Johnny," I said. "After all she's done for you too!"

"She'll get over it. Once she's found another victim to suffer her sanctimonious lecturing on the evils of smoking," he replied, removing his glasses and placing them in his top pocket. "Word has filtered back about your meeting with old Boris last week. Have fun did we?" he smirked.

"It's always fun watching that over inflated, self righteous, bag of wind go red in the face," I answered. "What else have you heard?"

"Well, it's only rumour. You know, whispers in corridors. But, apparently, he's keen to start imposing some system of restrictions on those directorates guilty of exceeding their budgets."

By now I was getting interested and was anxious to hear more. "Like what for instance?"

"Well, rumour has it that he's considering reducing the number of acute unit hospital beds in an attempt to recoup the money lost in the overspend." Johnny was enjoying watching me get worked up. I could tell by the sinister glint in his eye.

"You mean he's prepared to close down a ward, or part of a ward, in order to save money to balance his miserable accounts?" It was my turn to go red in the face.

"Apparently," he answered, rummaging for his cigars and lighting up, as he sat back in his seat and grinned in my direction, watching for my reaction.

"But that's preposterous," I shouted. "The beds are full to the brim as it is. If he succeeds in closing beds there's bound to be problems. He'll have deaths on his hands, and then what? He'll never make it stick."

Johnny stared me straight in the eye as he puffed on his cigar. "Well, it would seem he has the support of a number of his colleagues on the Trust Board," he said, lighting the blue touch paper.

I was on my feet in a second. "We'll see about that," I said, making for the door. "How dare the man presume to call himself a doctor?"

"Calm down, Andrew. It's no use getting all worked up. If you don't watch out you'll be the next one to get yourself admitted."

"Hardly, if they're closing beds! Where would they put me?" And with that I stormed out of his office.

* * *

David had asked to see me and it was not until early evening, after the ward round, that I found the time to get along to his room. I found him sitting in his bedside chair browsing through some documents. He certainly looked well enough and I noted from his charts on the way in that his temperature had been stable over the weekend.

"Ah! There you are Andrew. Good of you to spare me the time," he said, laying the documents on the bed and looking up as I entered.

"No problem, David. How are you feeling?" I asked, perching myself on the edge of the bed.

"Fine now, thanks. Wasn't so good towards the end of last week, as you well know. I never could have imagined what it would feel like to suffer such an infection. You almost feel like jacking it all in when you're feeling so wretched."

"Well, you look good now. All the parameters are stable and the temperature's down. Thanks to all those wonderfully expensive antibiotic drugs." I couldn't resist the dig. Nothing like a top administrator suffering the problems we deal with every day and then experiencing first hand the desired results of our therapies, however expensive they prove.

"That's why I asked to see you," he interrupted. "I have heard about your meeting with Dr Baldwin last week. And about his proposals for stabilising the budget."

Now I began to feel bad. "I didn't want you to get involved with this sort of thing. Not right now, with you in this position. This is not the time for you to be bothered with problems of this nature," I said. "We should be able to handle them ourselves and leave you in peace. You have enough on your plate right now." I was genuinely concerned about his welfare. However strongly I had felt about my meeting with Boris, it had never occurred to me to raise it with David in discussion at this time.

David grinned at me that superior, rank-pulling grin of a Chief Executive. "Ah! But I have my loyal spies strategically placed throughout the hospital and I make it my business to know exactly what's going on while I'm stuck in here. While I'm up to it I still mean to be involved as best I can."

"You carry on in this way David and you could succeed, where others have failed dismally, in getting me to change the habit of a lifetime regarding my treatment of the administration," I grinned back.

"Even I wouldn't believe myself capable of anything as drastic as that," he interjected, laughing at the ceiling. "But, getting back to that meeting. I have had a word with Dr Baldwin on the subject and put a stop to his proposals for bed closures. I pointed out that, although it is undoubtedly one possible strategy, we must put it to the back of the file as a last resort. One to be considered only if we really cannot find some other way of funding these expensive treatments. I have asked him to reappraise the whole situation including all the other possible options and then to report back to me."

"That sounds good news," I said, trying, not too successfully, to stifle my obvious joy at having got one over on Boris.

"So, as you can see, it's in your interests to keep me going. At least, for the next few weeks. I can't think of a better incentive, particularly in your case." His grin reappeared.

"Neither can I," I said, getting up to leave. "And there was I, prepared to let you rot with nothing but cheap drugs for company!" On reaching thc door I turned and added, "Joking apart, I really appreciate your support, David."

"I'm merely doing what I think is right in this issue, Andrew," he said, with genuine conviction. He added, "Much as I respect you, this decision was not taken to endear myself to you, nor specifically to assist you in your differences with Dr Baldwin."

Suitably informed, I added, "Nevertheless, I'm grateful when that decision coincides with my beliefs." Changing the subject, I continued, "Is there anything I can get you?"

"No thank you, Andrew. I've got all I need. The treatment and nursing is excellent. But then, I never doubted it."

"You are now five days post chemotherapy," I continued, giving him a run down on the state of play with his treatment. "I wouldn't expect to see much in the way of a decent blood count for at least another seven to fourteen days, so it's the boring old waiting game I'm afraid."

"We administrators are used to that," he replied.

"Well, we're doing what we can to speed things up," I added. "That's why we'll be starting those horrendously expensive growth factor injections in a couple of days," I said cowering away, with my specially perfected innocent expression.

"You'd better get out while you're winning," he said, reaching for the empty glass on his bedside locker and making to chuck it in my direction. "Before I throw something at you. And, don't forget to close the door on your way out, Dr Ryan," I had been dismissed and decided to leave him to his documents.

* * *

On my way back to the department chance, or could it have been providence, put Boris Baldwin in my path as I approached the stairs. Childish though it undoubtedly was, I couldn't suppress the broad, victorious grin that began to creep over my face as we met.

"Boris, my old darling. How have you been?"

"You're looking very smug Dr Ryan. But it won't be for long," he said, scowling at me with a fierce look of anger in his eyes.

"Come on Boris. Closing the beds was a bad idea and you know it. It should be the very last thing a busy acute hospital should ever contemplate. Why, it's actually playing into the very politicians pockets," I said, trying genuinely to appease the situation.

"There's more to it than that and you well know it," he said. "You've never liked me for some reason. Just about everything that I propose on the committees you do your best to criticise and undermine. You're never satisfied until you've got your own way, which invariably means shouting me down and belittling me at every possible opportunity in front of my colleagues. Well, we'll see."

"Oh! Come on, Boris. Stop being so paranoid" I said, in an attempt to rectify the situation.

"Go to hell!" he shouted, turning down the corridor and storming off.

"Well, in that case," I continued, my own anger rising within me, "In the immortal words of Groucho Marx, 'I never forget a face, but in your case I'm prepared to make an exception!'"

CHAPTER NINETEEN

This cough I've got is hacking,
The pain in my head is wracking,
I hardly need to mention my flu.
The Board of Health has seen me
They want to quarantine me,
I might as well be miserable with you.
- Howard Dietz

The morning could not have looked lovelier, as I drove to work on Tuesday. The sun was shining brightly, the trees were positively bursting into life and there was that wonderfully fresh spring smell in the air.

At the other end of the scale I could not have felt worse. My head was throbbing from a combination of an overdose of Cotes Du Rhone and the occasional cigar the night before. Coupled with this, I had a cold coming on and I was feeling decidedly sorry for myself as I pulled into the car park at seven thirty.

I had made a Herculean effort to be in early in order to see Victoria before starting work. My head recoiled with pain as I slammed the car door and slowly made my way to the hospital. I had taken a couple of paracetamol the moment I had lifted my head from the pillow, fat lot of good they had been!

I dragged my weary body all the way to the lifts, where I found one waiting with its door open. As I pressed for the fourth floor, that animated voice fitted for the blind, that informs them that they have just stopped at the floor that no one had requested, blared out, "Doors closing. Going up." I winced as I clung onto the side rail for support. After what seemed an age the car came to a sudden halt without any attempt at controlled deceleration, sending my head through the roof with pain. As the doors opened and I made to exit, I passed a couple of giggling night nurses on their way off duty. The sight of me stopped them dead in their tracks, concern written all over their faces.

"Are you alright?" they enquired.

"About as well as can be expected under the circumstances but thank you for your concern anyway," I replied, as politely as possible, making every effort not to move my head any more than was absolutely necessary.

They brushed past me continuing their giggling as I headed for Victoria's ward. Passing the ward kitchen, the clashing of the breakfast trolleys being manoeuvred brought further pain to my troubled skull, and I momentarily closed my eyes in an effort to steady myself.

I proceeded slowly past the sister's desk, where she was conducting the early morning hand over with her juniors seated around her like piglets waiting to be suckled. I greeted her with a cursory nod of my troubled head and a softly spoken, "Hello", to which she dutifully returned the nod before getting back to the business at hand.

I tapped gently on Victoria's door before pushing it open and entering. She was sitting propped up in bed, with the newspaper open in front of her. She looked up, somewhat surprised, as I entered. Having caught sight of my pained expression, together with my greyish complexion, she immediately sussed the situation. Her jaw sagged as she searched for the words. It didn't take her long to find them.

"You look positively dreadful," she said.

"Thanks for those few kind words," I replied. "Nice to receive a bit of sympathy when one's feeling like death!"

She looked at me reproachfully. "Self-inflicted or natural causes?" she enquired, placing her paper on the bedside locker.

"A bit of both," I answered, with a sorrowful look.

"Looks like a *lot* of both from where I'm lying."

"I was missing you so much last night," I started.

"That's it. Blame me," she interrupted, smiling as her solitary act of sympathy. "Trouble is, I think there's a bit of your sister in you. You simply cannot bear someone near you being ill and upstaging you," she said, with a reproving finger pointed in my direction.

"You know that's not true," I said, trying to look hurt. "I agree that the *old* me didn't need much excuse getting to look like this. But I like to think that you've had a wonderfully calming influence on me."

"Looks like it slipped a little last night," she said, with a disapproving frown.

"That's what I mean," I continued. "You weren't there. And that's why I was feeling so down. It had been a long day and I really needed your support at the end of it." Boy, I really was feeling sorry for myself.

"Poor old Andrew. Why don't you sit on my bed and tell mother all about it," she purred.

I dutifully sat on the edge of the bed as we chatted away for the next forty minutes. A nurse appeared and handed Victoria some pills. As she did so, she took one look at me and kindly offered to fetch a cup of strong coffee. Following the coffee I rallied and could feel the colour returning to my cheeks.

"You're looking a bit better now," Victoria said, taking hold of my hand and giving it a big squeeze. Despite her recent problems she still looked absolutely radiant, lying there in her blue negligee, her hair neatly brushed and with the minimum of make-up to highlight her beautiful features.

"I suppose a bonk's out of the question?" I enquired, with true optimism in my voice, and a crafty wink in her direction.

"Why, I do believe Dr Ryan's feeling a little better already," she whispered in her sexy voice, leaning forward and kissing me lightly on the cheek. "I'm afraid that's all my little friend's going to get for the moment," she said, in her teasing way.

"He could be your big friend, if you treat him right," I winked again, now at my smuttiest.

"Why Dr Ryan, I do declare. I'm afraid that's off the menu for the time being. The kiss will simply have to do." She had acquired the accent of Scarlet O'Hara in *'Gone With The Wind,'* but I was certainly no Rhett Butler at this particular moment in time.

"In that case, as you say, it'll have to do," I responded, resigned to the situation. "But when you're recovered and I come to take you home, you'd better watch out for me in the lift. They can be very sexy places you know! Especially if they break down."

"Why, Dr Ryan. You're positively depraved," she said, returning my wink as she coyly patted the sheets down.

"Ope so! "

* * *

I was at my desk by eight thirty, having collected my mail from Anne on the way. On catching sight of my appearance she too had offered me coffee. An offer I gladly accepted without waiting long enough for one of her well meant lectures. I really would not have been able to have survived such an ordeal on this particular occasion.

I sat at the desk sipping the welcome coffee, while I shuffled slowly through the various envelopes in front of me. Half way through the pile I suddenly stopped, my attention attracted to a white envelope bearing my name and hospital address written carefully in black ink. It bore a local post-mark and had been posted the morning before. I sat there, frozen to my chair for a moment, staring blankly at the writing in front of me. Written at an angle across the top left corner in capital letters were the words *STRICTLY CONFIDENTIAL.*

A cool shiver ran the length of my spine as I reached for my desk keys and clumsily unlocked the bottom drawer, removing the envelope I had placed there the previous week. On comparison there was no doubt that they had been written by the same person.

I took another long sip of coffee as I slowly opened the letter. It contained a single foolscap sheet that had been folded in three. As I unfolded it I could see that it contained ten typewritten numbers and nothing else. There was no writing, date or name. Only the ten numbers. They consisted of ten different five figure numbers, all followed by a dash and the number *97.* All the numbers were prefixed with the same letter, *'P'*. I turned the sheet over, but there was nothing written on the reverse. That was all that could be seen, the ten numbers typed on the front of the sheet and nothing else.

I stared at the sheet for a full five minutes, unsure what to make of it. It meant nothing to me. Yet it had to have a meaning, and some anonymous person was trying to tell me something. Eventually I folded the sheet, placed it back in the envelope and locked it with its fellow in the bottom drawer.

I called through the open door to Anne, asking for a badly needed coffee refill, before turning back to deal with the rest of the mail.

* * *

The sneezing started midway through the morning and succeeded in resurrecting my, by now, quiescent headache. I grabbed a box of tissues from the ward, where I had been discussing the patients with Hugh, and then headed back to the laboratory to tackle the pile of blood and bone marrow slides waiting by my microscope for my scrutiny and comments.

I couldn't help thinking, as I peered carefully down the eye pieces that, on this occasion, it was probably the bravest thing I had done in a long time. With my head still pounding I had slowly worked my way through half of the trays, writing any relevant comments on the accompanying forms, when there was a gentle tap on my door and in walked Alan Makepiece. In his hands he carried two more trays of slides that he carefully placed on the bench beside the microscope.

"I'm sorry Dr Ryan, but Dr Kennedy had to leave in a hurry. He asked me to remind you that he was going off early to look at houses with his wife. He said you had agreed to finish his slides for him." He stepped back rather sheepishly on catching sight of my pained expression.

"Yes I did, didn't I," I sighed, looking forlornly at the trays.

"I'm sorry, Dr Ryan," he repeated.

"It's not your fault Alan," I tried to say, reassuringly. "By the way, how are things in the lab these days? I feel I've been neglecting you a bit, what with all the work we've had on the wards recently."

"Not too bad, considering the pressure we've been under to comply with the new CPA regulations," he said, backing away slowly.

"I've been meaning to have a word with you about the other day," I said, looking back at him as he slowly edged his way toward the door.

"Oh! That's alright," he said, looking acutely embarrassed and beginning to blush.

"No, it's not alright," I continued. "In the first place, upon reflection, I don't think I had any right to approach you on a matter that was pure speculation. I exceeded my responsibilities and I would like to apologise to you."

"You don't need to do that, Dr Ryan, really. It's true I was attracted to Julie. Who wouldn't be? I'd be a fool to deny it. But when I had a chance to sit down and consider it all and what with her situation and everything.... Well, I mean, there was no mileage in it. It was an accident waiting to happen. A recipe for disaster.

"You'll be pleased to hear we've sorted it all out now. We won't be any more trouble to you. Anyway, there's someone else in my life now." He looked immensely relieved to have got it all off his chest.

"It's good of you to put it in those terms Alan," I said, smiling back at him. "I appreciate your honesty."

"Will that be all," he asked, looking toward the door and obviously wanting to get out of the room as quickly as possible.

"Yes Alan. Thanks for your help."

He left the room with an expression of abject relief on his face as I returned to the microscope and the misery of my *viral* hangover. No instant relief for me!

* * *

By twelve thirty I had had enough and was ready for a slow, medicinal brandy. My nose was streaming and every joint was aching. To top it all, peering down the microscope for an hour had not helped matters. I returned the slides and reports I had completed to the lab and headed off in the direction of the Blue Boar.

I found Johnny in his usual place, a magazine in one hand and, in the other, a fork with which he was delicately stabbing at a plate on the table in front of him. I carefully carried my glass of Remy Martin over to his table, taking the seat beside him.

"Hitting the hard stuff a little early in the day aren't you?" he said, staring at the double brandy as he put his magazine down.

"Purely medicinal," I snuffled in his direction, slowly sniffing the fumes and taking my first sip, before placing the glass on the table in front of me.

"What's the problem?" he asked.

"Bloody cold. What do you think," I retorted, as I reached for my handkerchief, only just in time for the next sneeze.

"Oh! You poor dear." He certainly wasn't in his sympathetic mood. "Got your usual clever quote then? Or are we too sick."

I didn't like him in this mood. Or, more accurately, I didn't like him in my current mood. Whatever, never wishing to be beaten on the field of quotations I trawled the depths.

"'*Medicinal discovery, It moves in mighty leaps, It leapt right past the common cold, And gave it us for keeps,*'" I blurted out. "Pam Ayres."

"O.K. So you're not feeling too good. But it's hardly my fault," he pleaded.

"I'm sorry, Johnny. I didn't mean to be such a complainer. I suppose it didn't help having that extra glass of wine I didn't need last night."

"Only *'one'* you didn't need! It must be love," he concluded. "The first time the little lady's in trouble you take to the bottle. It's a fascinating new side of you, never before witnessed. My God, if only your adversaries in the Trust Board office could see you now. They might even take pity on you, though I doubt they would actually allow themselves to go that far in your particular case," he grinned, as he poked the tuna salad in front of him with his fork, half expecting it to bite back.

"Here, Johnny. Do these numbers mean anything to you," I asked, thrusting a card, on which I'd copied the numbers from the letter, under his nose.

He grasped the paper and glanced down at the numbers for a few seconds before looking back at me.

"They look like histology numbers to me, Why?" he answered, shrugging his shoulders as if to say *'so what,'* before returning his gaze to the salad.

"What?" I asked.

"Histology report numbers. I think the *'P'* stands for *'pathology.'* Anyway, I'd say they are most likely to be histology numbers, in which case you should be able to look them up on the pathology computer," he said, placing the card on the table in front of me, and getting back to his tussle with the salad.

"Of course they are," I stammered, looking down at the numbers. "It's funny, but I never remember having looked at the numbers at the top of their reports before. I'm sure I must have done so often enough but I don't ever remember taking in the fact."

"Why? What's it all about?" Johnny asked, trying to make up his mind, which part of his meal to attack next. His appetite had obviously returned with a vengeance.

"Oh! Nothing really," I lied. "I was browsing through some old notes and papers when I came across these numbers and wondered what they all related to." I quickly returned the piece of paper to my top pocked and reached for my brandy.

Johnny paid no attention as he pressed on with the battle in hand.

* * *

Back in my office after lunch, my headache a distant memory, I frantically waited for the pathology computer to log me on. Eventually I got into the system, following which I slowly found my way to the histology module. Once on line, I carefully tapped in the first of the numbers on the sheet I had received that morning and sat there staring at the figures for a full minute before finally pressing *return.*

There was a few seconds wait, and then the screen burst into life, throwing up all sorts of information. This included the name of the patient from whom the histological sample had been taken, their hospital unit number, the date the sample was taken and the consultant the patient had been under for the procedure. It also recorded the hospital where the procedure had been carried out.

Following the patient and hospital information came the text relating to the actual histology report on the sample. At the end of the text came the name of the consultant who had been responsible for the report, typed in bold capitals.

I stared at the screen, refusing to believe what was set out before me. For, the name at the bottom of this histology report was that of Dr Tony Knowles, our consultant in cytopathology. I quickly retrieved all the numbers I had been sent. All the reports bore the same name, *'Tony Knowles.'*

I sat there in total disbelief. There in front of me on the screen was the very evidence that proved what I had been told in the first of the confidential letters and that had later been corroborated by Nick Forsyth.

I may well have started the day with a viral infection and a hangover but I had no memory of it now. My mind was buzzing, as I slowly locked the letter bearing the numbers back in the drawer and turned to finish the slides beside my microscope.

CHAPTER TWENTY

When men die of disease they are said to die from natural causes. Whenever they recover (and they mostly do) the doctor gets the credit of curing them.
– George Bernard Shaw

"And finally, the p value clearly shows a statistically significant advantage for this particular drug regimen in relapsed, advanced, poor prognosis Hodgkin's disease, compared with the other chemotherapy regimens used in this controlled study. Thank you." Pausing a few seconds for effect, the speaker finally replaced the infra-red pointer on the podium, collected up his papers and slowly stepped down to the applause of the audience.

It was eleven thirty on Wednesday morning, and I was in London attending a symposium on the treatment of Hodgkin's disease at the Royal College of Pathologists in Carlton House Terrace. The morning had dragged on rather slowly although, in fairness, my mind really wasn't focused on the meeting. Many of the speakers had been good and, under normal circumstances, I would have been more involved, but somehow my thoughts kept straying to other problems.

One of the talks had managed to catch my attention though. It had been on the investigation and staging procedures currently used in the pre-treatment work up of Hodgkin's disease. The speaker had been meticulous in his approach to the subject, and had included all the current approaches employed in this most important aspect of the management of the condition.

He had even concluded his talk with a section on the newer, more experimental and, in some cases, more risky techniques currently being researched. This had included a summary of the possible risks associated with a number of the procedures and he had stressed to his audience the importance of our continuing awareness of these complications. He had concluded that we must never forget these potential problems when deciding upon a line of investigation in these patients.

The presentation had taken my thoughts back to the tragedy of Lynn Harris' death; a memory I knew was destined to haunt me for a very long time to come. That had made it very difficult to concentrate fully on the rest of the meeting, as I still suffered a significant amount of guilt over the whole business.

I glanced at my watch and decided that there was little to be gained by staying for the last talk. I carefully threaded my way along the row towards the aisle, and ambled through the exit into the lobby.

The daylight momentarily blinded me and, in a daze, I knocked into another delegate also seeking a break from the proceedings. As I looked up to apologise I saw that it was Lawrence Peters, a consultant haematologist I knew and who worked in Nottingham.

Lawrence and I had been trainee registrars together in London. We had always got on well and had both played tennis for the hospital. I hadn't seen him for some years and tried to hide my surprise at noticing how much weight he had put on since our last meeting.

"Lawrence, nice to see you. How have you been keeping?" I asked, offering my hand.

"Andrew," he replied, shaking my hand briskly. "Good to see you. It must be three or four years since we last met. Seattle, wasn't it? At the ASH meeting in December."

"Yes, The American Society of Haematology. That's right," I answered.

"That was some meeting." He continued, gazing into the distance as he recalled the event. "Boy, do you remember that last night, when that gorgeous Cytotec rep took us all out for that hugely expensive meal and we all got pissed out of our brains? I seem to remember falling down the stairs on the way out. Most embarrassing." He winced at the memory of the incident, rubbing his right hip as he did so.

"Yes. I don't remember having had so much myself. If memory serves me right I had to carry you to the coach, where you promptly threw up all over my shoes," I reminded him, with a reproving finger wagged in his direction.

"Yes. I did seem to lose control that night. Must have been a combination of all that expensive wine and that gorgeous rep. Don't think I've had the pleasure of seeing her since. Suppose she must be working another patch. What was her name now? I can't seem to recall it."

"You mean Victoria. You were obviously so embarrassed with your actions that night that you've shut it out of your memory. The psychiatrists have some sort of phrase for it, I'm sure."

"Yes, Victoria. That's it. Lovely girl," he winked at me. "Have you seen anything of her since?"

"Yes. She's covering our area in the south. I see her from time to time," I said, not wishing to go any further with this particular line of conversation. Changing the subject, I continued, "What do you think of the meeting?"

"Quite good. Not a lot of new stuff though," he said, looking down at his watch and rubbing his brow. "Tell you what. Why don't we get out of here and find us a quiet little pub where we can catch up on events over a pint?"

I didn't really feel like a drink so early, but I wasn't too keen on going back into the conference either. The last presentation had certainly stirred the demons and right now I wanted to bury them. I decided on the lesser of the evils and we made our way out of the College into the light drizzle where we hailed a taxi. We made for a little place near Charring Cross Road that I knew well and tended to frequent whenever I was in town.

It was small, relatively quiet and still retained a lot of it's original old world charm, not having been 'plasticated', as I call it, and modernised like so many of my favourite London pubs. Added to this, the staff were in the habit of treating you like a customer, with politeness and respect, a quality sadly lacking in so many of our watering holes these days.

As we arrived at the bar the epitome of buxom barmaids swaggered up, placing her large hands firmly on the counter in front of her and stared me straight in the face.

"Why, It's Dr Ryan isn't it?" she said, a warm smile creeping slowly over her countenance.

Daisy was part of the establishment. No one knew her exact age, but she must have been approaching at least sixty, most probably from the wrong side. Whatever it was, it was carefully hidden behind several layers of thick rouge and the brightest of red lipsticks. Her voluminous, sagging breasts positively fought to escape the tightest of brightly flower-printed cotton blouses. Her black skirt was easily two sizes too small must have taken an hour to fasten in the mornings. It finished two inches above her knees that were covered with a pair of black tights containing one or two small holes.

All this was balanced precariously on the tallest pair of black, shiny high heels I'd ever seen, that must have been at least four inches over the legal safety limit. Consequently, whenever she moved she listed dangerously from side to side, threatening to flatten anyone unfortunate enough to be positioned on her flank.

"That's right, Daisy. My you've got a good memory. It must have been at least a year since I was last in." I said patting her hand as it lay on the counter. "How have you been keeping?"

"Oh! You know. Not too bad. Bloody cough's still playing me up though. All that money they pay you and you doctors still can't cure that can you?" she said, with a mischievous smile.

"But we can Daisy. Trouble is, you'll listen very nicely to what we have to say then, once you're on your own again, you'll simply go out and buy yourself more cigarettes to replace those over there, once I've thrown them away," I replied, pointing to the pack beside the lighter at the other end of the counter and grinning back at her.

"You doctors have an answer for everything."

"Sometimes, Daisy. Anyway, on this occasion you're outnumbered," I said, gesturing to Lawrence, "Because this is another doctor. My old friend Dr Peters, who I ran into at a meeting earlier and who I haven't seen for over three years."

"Pleased to meet you I'm sure," she said, making a bad attempt at a curtsy and almost falling backwards into the row of bottles on the shelf behind her.

"Likewise," Lawrence contributed, smiling at me with a look that said, *'she should be put away!'*

"What'll it be then, Doctors?"

"A pint and a half of the best bitter," I said, with enormous pride in my voice.

"You ill or something?" Lawrence enquired, looking quizzically at me.

"No. Only exercising my new found strength of character," I replied, with an obvious note of pride in my voice. "Thing is,

I've got a few things to do this afternoon before getting back to Eastwich, and boozing in the middle of the day slows me down."

We collected our drinks and headed for a small table in the corner. The bar was fairly empty and, joy of joys, it was quiet. The publican, in his infinite wisdom, had refused to allow the installation of a piped music system or juke-box into his establishment arguing, quite rightly, that it only stifled natural conversation.

Lawrence and I chatted away for half an hour, catching up on the events of the past few years, filling in on the gaps since we had been registrars together. It was really good to see him again after all these years.

Eventually we got back to discussing the meeting and I mentioned the tragic case of Lynn Harris. When I had finished, Lawrence slowly placed his mug on the table and leant back in his chair.

"Funny, we had a similar case last year. A young woman, early thirties, admitted in status epilepticus. She was very ill on admission but responded brilliantly to the intravenous diazepam. Then, bang! Later that evening she was found dead. None of the other patients remember anything strange. No evidence of further fits. Nothing. The post-mortem failed to elicit any obvious cause.

"All very strange. But then we know these things can happen. I read somewhere that up to five percent of post-mortems fail to demonstrate any obvious cause of death. It doesn't seem to stop the pathologist slapping down some woolly cause for the coroner though."

"It must be so disturbing for the relatives," I commented. "I mean, somehow you can learn to come to terms with a road accident, or even a fatal asthma attack, sad though it may be. But, no demonstrable cause leaves it all so up in the air, with everyone saying *"what if?"* I mean you can't really blame the relatives for getting angry sometimes."

"Well, they certainly did in our case. They're in the process of suing the health authority."

"Of course. I heard about it on the early morning news a few days ago, driving to work. Do you think they'll win?" I asked.

"My guess is it won't get that far. The Authority's bound to settle out of court. Can't afford the adverse publicity. There's far too much of it concerning our hospitals already."

"I suppose you're right," I agreed. "Hey, let's get off this morbid subject. Fancy another pint? I feel another half coming on."

* * *

After promising to keep in touch, I eventually bade farewell to Lawrence and made my way to Foyle's bookshop. A few weeks before I had ordered a copy of a book on the life of Elgar, and they had promised to get hold of it in time for my trip to London.

Browsing through book shops is always a dangerous preoccupation for me. Somehow I always manage to find something I persuade myself I really have to buy. And, of course, this was no exception.

Tucked away in a small recess, half-hidden on the second floor, I came upon an obscure tome on *'The Philosophy of Chess.'* Flipping through the pages I was fascinated with some of the articles I found. On impulse I decided to buy it and, together with the book on Elgar, I duly headed for the 'Pay Here' desk.

After Foyle's I headed for Oxford Street where I had intended to pick up a few small gifts for Victoria. I spent a long time at the perfumery counters in John Lewis , before finally deciding on the *'Panthere'* by Cartier. By now it was extremely crowded in the store but, after much shoving, I eventually managed to acquire the *'River Café Cook Book'* she had been unable to find on her recent shopping excursions Flushed with success, I moved on to HMV where I wanted to get hold of the latest Julio Iglesias CD.

I had just passed through the doors when I caught sight of Alan Makepeace paying for his purchase at the cash desk. It was obviously his day off, following a night on call and he was making the most of it.

As I changed direction to say hello, I could see that he was accompanied by one of the young secretaries from the histology department. At that moment Alan looked up from the slip of paper he had finished signing and caught sight of me. His jaw sank as our eyes met, but his expression remained frozen as he instantly looked the other way and, grabbing his companion's hand, pushed his way through the crowds entering by the end door and disappeared out into the street.

What had that all been about? I wondered, as I made my way into the store. There was no reason that I was aware of for him to want to avoid me. Then again, he had acted a little strangely yesterday when he was in my room. All he had seemed to want to do was to get out as quickly as possible. I put it all from my mind as I concentrated on finding the CD I was after and then getting back home as soon as possible.

CHAPTER TWENTY ONE

As for consulting a dentist regularly, my punctuality practically amounted to a fetish. Every twelve years I would drop whatever I was doing and allow wild Caucasian ponies to drag me to a reputable orthodontist
– S. J. Perelman

Perched precariously on the edge of Victoria's bed the following morning, I was handing over the few gifts I had acquired in London.

"This is to make you smell even lovelier than ever," I said, handing her the gift-wrapped bottle of *Panthere,* "while you are cooking me one of your culinary delights from this," I continued, handing over the cookery book. "And, whilst all this is going on we'll be listening to the latest offering from old Joe Church here," I said, dropping the CD in her lap.

"Joe who?" she asked.

"Joe Church," I repeated. "That is the correct translation of Julio Iglesias, isn't it?" I asked, looking innocently into her smiling eyes.

"You complete fool," she said, leaning forward and gently squeezing my hand before unwrapping the disc. She carefully read through the list of titles on the back, before laying it on the bed and picking up the *River Café Cook Book.* "You really shouldn't have gone to all that bother," she said, opening the book. "I can't wait to try some of these recipes, though," she continued, thumbing through the pages, with their colourful pictures of sumptuous dishes laid out so beautifully.

"When's old Matthew letting you out?" I asked, glancing over her charts, where I found a pleasing set of horizontal, parallel lines.

"He said probably tomorrow, provided he gets a reassurance from you that I'll not be doing any of the work around the house for the time being."

"Only *work*? He didn't mention anything else?" My eyes gave it away, as I looked wantonly for her response.

"He didn't have to, you sex maniac. I don't need him to tell me when that's allowed. And I certainly don't need your advice on that matter at this time. I fear it's liable to be a little biased."

"Whatever you say my little cherub. You're in charge. Well then, I suppose I'd better tidy the place up this evening in preparation for the royal visit." I bent over to kiss her, before getting to my feet and heading for the door.

"I probably won't be back before tomorrow evening as there's a lot on at the moment. Better be packed and ready when I arrive, or it's walking home time for you my girl." I blew her a kiss.

"Yes, oh masterful one."

* * *

Back in my department, later that morning, I was slowly going through the mail and messages that had been left on my desk the day before. Beside the pile of papers I had a large cup of strong coffee and a plate of digestive biscuits. I hadn't eaten much the night before, and I was feeling ravenous.

I munched away slowly as I waded through the mail. It contained the usual rubbish consultants have to read regarding the implementation of yet more new NHS innovations. Items such as *'waiting list strategies'* and *'clinical governance'*, whatever that means. All very boring stuff and designed, no doubt, as a permanent cure for a consultant's insomnia.

I had been at it about an hour when finally I came to a badly typewritten message Carol Donnelly, the senior technician, had left me. It was concerning her proposal for a more structured training schedule of the junior technicians.

She had apologised for the state of the article but apparently her computer printer was broken. Since she was the first to admit that even she had great difficulty deciphering her own handwriting on occasions, she had had to drag the dilapidated old laboratory typewriter back into service, in order to put her thoughts and suggestions down on paper.

I perused the proposals, which seemed quite reasonable and made a written note to myself to discuss it further with Carol later in the day.

I then turned my attention to the final draft of the drug protocol for the acute leukaemia trial that was now ready for my proof reading. As I slowly read down the first page something niggled away at the back of my weary brain. Something wasn't quite right, but I couldn't put my finger on it.

Was it something I had seen? I racked my brain, but found it difficult to focus on what it might have been. I put the trial document down and picked up Carol's letter again. I stared blankly at the words for a few minutes. Then it struck me.

I sat there transfixed for a few moments. Finally, I searched for my keys, opened the bottom drawer of the desk and retrieved the *Strictly Confidential* letters. I placed Carol's letter beside these and glared at the text. I looked first at one page, then at the other, and then back at the first.

That's when I saw it. It wasn't all that obvious at first, but it was there nevertheless. The letter '*P*' on both documents had an identical small fault. There was a tiny break in the loop of the letter at about two o'clock. It must have been due to a fault on the type-face on the typewriter, as it was consistent throughout the document. What's more the two sheets bore the identical abnormality and must, therefore, have been typed on the same machine, namely the one in the haematology laboratory.

I sat back in my chair, smugly content with the success of my detective work. As I stared at the wall in front of me I took a heavy, congratulatory bite on the biscuit currently occupying my mouth.

It was, with hindsight, a singularly foolhardy thing to have done. For, in an instant, I felt something give in my upper jaw on the right side. A fraction of a second later the pain started and quickly built to the most severe form of dental agony that it had ever been my misfortune to experience. I yelled a profound obscenity at the top of my voice, but fortunately the door was closed. Stunned, I fell back clutching my jaw, completely transfixed with pain, the success of my clever sleuthing far from my mind.

* * *

"It's absolute bloody murder," I said, in my most theatrical tone, as I sat quivering in my dentist's chair.

Mike Collins was bent over me, peering into my gaping mouth at the scene of carnage and destruction before him. He was a fine dentist and I had been seeing him on and off, but mainly off, for over twelve years. Stupidly, I had managed to miss most of my regular dental checks over the past few years. Somehow I had always contrived to mislay those irritating little cards one receives from time to time, informing you of your next appointment.

"It's an absolute mess," Mike began. Over the years he had become used to my wanton dental neglect. But he never gave up trying to instil in me a sense of responsibility for my own canines. He had tried every angle he knew. He had tried being nice to me, and then treating me like a ten year old. When that hadn't worked he had gone on to, what I had termed, *'the headmaster approach,'* threatening me with expulsion from his books unless I conformed to his advice.

After that he had even tried that most common of dentist's ploys, namely, increasing his fees. But that had only served to delay even more my attendances at his surgery. Eventually he had given up and attended to me as and when I decided to favour him with a visit.

I knew from the expression of deep satisfaction on his face, as he peered into my buccal cavity and probed the offending tooth, that he had been waiting for some time for this inevitable moment.

"Well, Andrew, I'm afraid there's a fair bit of damage to your upper right six," he continued. He didn't look all that *'afraid'* to me, from where I was sitting. At least, not nearly as afraid as the owner of the *'broken upper right six.'*

He continued with his probing and then announced, "It would seem that not only did you break the filling with that biscuit you were chewing on so voraciously, but you've produced an A/P fracture of the palatal cusp of the tooth. That's why the inner wall is *'wobbling,'* as you so aptly put it."

"What does all that mean in plain English, Mike? You can tell me. I'm brave, I can take it," I said, lying through my rotten teeth.

"It means, my brave doctor, that once again the good Mike Collins is going to have to come along and save the day with some pretty extensive, which happens to rhyme with expensive, and nifty dental salvage work."

"Like what," I enquired.

"Like almost certainly a root canal treatment, followed by yet another crown. This will need a further three visits to complete the work. Do you think you could summon up the character to complete three visits in the same month? A feat never before known in your case!" He had been waiting years for that exchange, and he was savouring every minute of it.

"Another crown! That makes it four in the last five and a half years. I've got more bloody crowns than the queen. It's going to cost me an absolute fortune. Why is it that my teeth seem to be conspiring to bankrupt me?"

"They're no different from any self-respecting woman. If you will insist on neglecting them, then you can hardly act surprised when they start letting you down." My, he was enjoying this. I think he must have been practising this speech for years and now he was word perfect.

Having finished his soliloquy he turned to his serious looking nurse and asked, "When did Dr Ryan last have X-rays?"

"A little over two years ago," she said, even more straight-faced, "on his *last* visit!" Now she was putting the knife in. I was surrounded, with no way out.

"We'd better repeat them now, before he does a runner," he said, I thought a little unkindly. Then, looking back at me, he continued, "Andrew, in all fairness your mouth's a complete mess. Not just the broken tooth that could probably have been prevented with regular checks and repair, but your whole dentition that has suffered from years of dedicated neglect. It's no exaggeration to say that I've seen gorillas with better teeth."

"I didn't know old Boris Baldwin came to you as well!" I said, clutching my aching jaw.

"Who?"

"Oh! Nothing."

"After the X-ray I'll put a temporary filling in the damaged tooth. Then you can book the other appointments with the receptionist on your way out. It looks like you're going to need a whole week with the hygienist. It's almost worth your while considering camping out here for the duration."

Like Queen Victoria, he was not amused.

* * *

I ran into James when I got back to the department a little after five. He had been good enough to cover for me in my afternoon clinic, whilst I was being lectured to in the dentist's chair.

After thanking him for his help I wandered into the microscopy section, where I found Carol sitting at the bench signing out the day's reports. There was a massive pile of forms beside her still requiring her scrutiny, and she looked a little weary.

I began by discussing her suggestions for the juniors' training, and within twenty minutes we had agreed upon a suitable programme. I moved the subject on to her computer and the problems she had had with the printer. She was pleased to recount that it had been remedied and was now working properly.

We then talked about the typewriter I told her I had never seen. She said that it was a throwback to the old days before computers but somehow had never been discarded when we had gone electronic.

Apparently it had come in handy from time to time when some of our technicians had had projects to complete. Some of them did not possess a computer or word processor, so she had been in the habit of lending them the typewriter that was not too cumbersome to take home for the duration of their project. When they had worked on it and got their ideas into shape with a rough draught they would then transfer the text to the laboratory computer in their own time.

When I asked her who had been the last person to borrow it she told me it had been Alan Makepiece. He had finished his work earlier in the week and had returned the machine yesterday morning.

I asked her if I could see this antique as I was quite interested in old typewriters and she had taken me into her office where it was kept locked up in her locker. A quick inspection of the machine confirmed my suspicions. I thanked Carol for her time and returned to my office.

CHAPTER TWENTY TWO

I can't stand whispering. Every time a doctor whispers in the hospital, next day there's a funeral
– Neil Simon

Friday was destined to be a pig of a day. My morning out-patient clinic was grossly overbooked and I had an Oncology/Clinical Haematology Directorate meeting to make by noon. There was a special meeting of the Pathology Management Group scheduled for two following which there was the end of week ward round to conduct. Once I'd got through with all that there would be a mountain of work in the lab to be finished before the week-end.

Oversleeping by half an hour had not helped my overall strategy. Frantically trying to make up for the slippage, I completed the *shaving by a thousand cuts* routine in record time. Rushing into in the kitchen I collided with a chair I could have sworn I had never seen before and finally managed to complete my disastrous start to the day by spilling my scolding coffee down the front of my new tie.

The roads were awash with drivers competing for the Eastwich *who can drive the slowest without stalling the engine* award and, to cap it all, I managed to miss every green traffic light. The last straw came when I pulled into the car park just in time to find Boris parking in my space. Glaring ferociously at him as I passed, I only just missed colliding with the side of a badly parked, gleaming, new, top-of-the-range Mercedes belonging to one of our more successful gynaecologists, and bearing the sickening number plate *GYN 1*.

I couldn't help wondering why it was that so many of our surgeons had felt the need to have personalised car number plates and concluded that perhaps it had something to do with not even being capable of remembering their own bloody names! Glancing back at the number, as I climbed out of the car, I thought to myself that perhaps GIN 1 would have been more acceptable, albeit a bit of a give-away!

As I stumbled into the department I all but collided with Anne, as she appeared round the corner carrying a pile of patient notes.

"Thought you'd decided to take the day off," she said, raising one eyebrow that was her way of telling you, *"you're late!"*.

"Changed my mind at the last moment," I said, ignoring her rebuke. "Where's my mail?" I gasped, rushing into my office to drop my brief case and jacket and grab the white coat and stethoscope. She held it out for me to snatch as I dashed back past her on my way out.

Although she had seen it all before, I made a mental note that this was positively the last time she would have the pleasure of witnessing this middle-aged twit attempting the land speed record.

Down in the out-patient department I could hear the mumbling of seething discontent running down the rows of waiting patients as I approached.

"It's a bloody disgrace," one old dragon in a moth-eaten, knitted woolly hat whispered loudly to her neighbour as I passed. Then, even louder, in case I hadn't heard, "You'd think, with all that money we pay them from our taxes, they'd have the decency to be on time."

"Awfully sorry I'm late ladies," I smiled, in passing, "Been up all night with a terribly ill leukaemic patient on the ward. Poor little mite. And, only twelve years old, you know! Pretty close run thing but we won through in the end, I'm sure you'll be only too pleased to hear!"

"Bloody liar," she continued behind me, as I disappeared into my room. Oh! The joys of medicine, I thought to myself as I greeted the nurse and pulled on the white coat.

"I don't know who that old bat out there wearing the vomit-coloured woolly tea-cosy is nurse, but be a good girl and put her notes to the bottom of the pile will you," I said, easing myself into the chair behind the desk.

* * *

The clinic had been murderous, with alternate patients either complaining about the long wait, or actually being unwell, which I felt was most inconsiderate. I was put in mind of something one of my colleagues had once said about medicine. He had quipped that, "Medicine would be fine if it wasn't for the patients, and their relatives!" A little cruel perhaps, but there are certain days in a doctor's life when it approaches the truth and this was definitely one of them.

I managed the Oncology meeting a mere twenty minutes late. By now I had calmed down and had been able to collect my thoughts on the issues before us. The most important one we had to discuss was the proposed extension to Manvers ward.

For some time now we had been experiencing problems over the insufficient number of beds available on our ward to accommodate our ever-increasing workload. We were all experiencing a significant increase in our number of patients. Coupled with this, we were undertaking more complicated forms of treatment, often requiring longer stays for our patients in hospital.

On the haematology side I had certainly noticed an increasing number of leukaemic patients, each of whom would require a bed for upwards of four weeks or longer. The net result was that the ward at present simply could no longer cope with the pressure of work, and many of our patients were placed on other wards. These *'outliers,'* as they're known, had been growing in number over the past two years and were proving a major problem.

One obvious cause for concern was that these patients were often placed on wards whose nursing staff had little experience of our patients' particular problems. They were not specialist-trained in this nursing field and couldn't be expected to possess the skills now required in nursing this particular group of patients.

Another problem with this arrangement was that it was becoming increasingly more difficult for our junior doctors to keep a close eye on all their patients, with them scattered to all corners of the hospital. The only positive feature regarding this arrangement was that the ward rounds often provided me with an opportunity to catch up on my exercise schedule!

The discussion had been quite productive and John Lindsey had agreed to prepare a business case regarding the necessary ward extension for us all to review, before presenting it to the Hospital Trust Board next month.

The meeting had gone well and I had a spare quarter of an hour to grab a sandwich before the afternoon session. I snatched up my folder, arranged with John to meet early next week regarding the stem cell fund, which I felt possibly could be woven into the plans for the extension and made for the door.

Halfway down the main corridor I caught sight of Boris in the distance, huddled in a corner whispering with Patrick Skinner, the histopathologist. I quickened my pace a little, hoping to catch a bit of their conversation but as I approached it became obvious that I had been spotted. The two immediately straightened, nodded sullen-faced in my direction, bade each other farewell and set off at a brisk pace in opposite directions.

It hadn't done much for my paranoia rating, which was already at a rather high level. Whatever could they have been talking about that had made them cut of so abruptly at the sight of me? It all looked very suspicious.

It was still playing on my mind as I bought myself a sandwich in the hospital shop and wandered back to my department. Anne stopped me as I entered to tell me that Nick had called in for a word with me but had had to go back to his department. I phoned him once I had settled at my desk and unwrapped the sandwich.

"You were looking for me," I said.

"Yes. I was wondering whether the golf's still on tomorrow."

What with all the problems of the past few days I had completely forgotten that we had agreed to play late Saturday morning.

"I'm glad you phoned," I said, snatching a quick bite from the sandwich. "I'm afraid it wont be possible this week, Nick. I'm sorry I forgot to contact you but Victoria is being discharged this evening and I don't really want to leave her alone at the moment."

"That's O.K. I've got plenty to do anyway. The ruddy mower's packed up and I've got to get it repaired. Funny how it never happens at the end of the summer but waits for the spring. Sod's law I suppose."

Whilst he was on the phone I mentioned seeing Boris and Patrick in the corridor and their suspicious actions. What Nick told me helped lay my paranoia to rest. Apparently Boris had lost a patient unexpectedly six weeks ago and despite his normally cold outlook on life he had been quite cut up about this particular case.

It would seem that this woman, in her late forties, had been admitted with Addison's disease in adrenal crisis. She had appeared moribund on admission but had responded well to the immediate treatment she had received with intravenous fluids and hydrocortisone.

Within forty eight hours she was sitting up and back to her normal self. Within another forty eight hours she was dead, having collapsed suddenly at night. All attempts at resuscitation had failed and the medical team were at a loss to explain the cause for her sudden deterioration.

The post-mortem hadn't helped much either. Patrick had carried it out and had failed to identify any obvious mechanism for her death. He had sent a lot of material off to specialist units for further analysis, including toxicology to exclude possible poisoning with any drugs she may have been taking.

Apparently he'd only that day received the final reports back and once again there were no answers to explain the sudden death. That's probably what they were discussing in the corridor and why they had been wearing such morose expressions.

I threw the rest of the sandwich down, and headed off to the conference room for the Pathology Management meeting, delivering a loud hiccup as I passed Anne on my way out. She looked at me like Queen Victoria. Another one not amused. I was having a good week!

* * *

The afternoon meeting had also gone well with no adverse events. In fact the whole business had become quite boring, with everyone agreeing on the major issues and not a sign of any infighting or petty jealousy over funding or staffing problems. The sort of thing that, on most occasions, would take up at least twice the time and usually served to add a bit of entertainment to the proceedings. All very boring really and I caught myself nodding off more than once.

The ward round also went smoothly, apart from David who had spiked a temperature once again and wasn't feeling so well. He had developed a bit of a cough and wasn't responding any more to the battery of antibiotics we had him on. He was producing some pretty murky looking sputum and the urgent chest X-ray showed some ominous shadowing in the right lower zone.

In addition to this, the renal function tests demonstrated some degree of kidney failure. The whole picture looked suspiciously like a possible systemic fungal infection with pneumonic involvement. The relevant blood and microbiology tests were sent to the labs and he was started on the expensive intravenous antifungal drug *ambisome,* together with an I/V rehydration programme.

The difference in poor David's appearance over the past forty eight hours was striking and epitomised the problems encountered with these patients, whose blood counts remain very low for such a long period. When an infection of this nature takes hold it can progress extremely rapidly if unchecked and can prove fatal within a matter of a day or two. It can become a multi-system problem overnight and requires prompt and decisive action from the medical team.

By now David was at his lowest ebb and was receiving a blood transfusion of red blood cells for his anaemia, in addition to daily transfusions of platelet cells to prevent problems with bleeding.

This was one time when he was in no mood for his work and I felt great compassion for him as he lay there, obviously very ill with tubes and I/V drips attached to both arms. He was not the complaining sort, asked very few questions of me and seemed to accept his fate with a grim sense of determination. I sat by his side explaining our suspicions and what measures we were taking to combat the situation.

When I had finished though he did ask me one question, "Tell me, Andrew. What are my chances of dying from this?" he looked me straight in the eye and was fully expecting the worst.

"That's not an option," I countered. "Although you've achieved a lot at Eastwich since you arrived, you still have a lot more to do to complete the job. And I don't know of anyone, not even administrators, being capable of achieving that from the grave."

"Nicely put, my expensive haematological friend But I subscribe more to the Woody Allen philosophy," he said, raising a smile.

"You've lost me there," I said.

"Wasn't it him who once said, 'I don't want to achieve immortality through my work...I want to achieve it through not dying'?"

"One up to the administration," I announced in defeat, gripping his arm and promising to look back in the morning.

* * *

"Tell them to fuck off!"

"I beg your pardon?"

"Tell them to fuck off," I duly repeated, as Boris began to fidget nervously behind his desk.

I had been summoned urgently by Dr Baldwin to answer a complaint that had been levelled against me by 'MAC Laboratories'. This is the private laboratory in Killikrankie, Scotland, that had derived its ingenious name from the two senior partners; a Mr MacMurdoch and a Mr MacCallum. In my opinion, it is a scurrilous private laboratory, which happened to be used by the infamous Lansdowne surgery for their pathology tests, in preference to our own local service.

It transpired that my outspoken feelings of disgust at what I believed to be an inferior service offered to the patients of our district had been fed back to their illustrious managing director. He, in turn, had written to me a few weeks before, to say how concerned he was at my comments. In a bullying attempt to embarrass me, he had copied his letter to the senior partners of the four local practices that chose to use his service.

His letter had been most explicit and had gone to great lengths to explain that their laboratory was fully accredited by the relevant official, national body as an efficient organisation. It had also outlined the quality issues involved. The letter had concluded by stating that, despite these issues, Mr MacMurdoch was deeply concerned that I had reservations regarding the quality of the service they were offering to the patients of our district.

Finally, he had said that since we were all in this business for the ultimate benefit of the patients, his laboratory would value any advice I could offer that would result in an improvement in their already highly efficient service; an invitation obviously inviting me to libel myself and an invitation I had not readily accepted at the time.

However, one week ago I had been referred by Dr Pauling an unfortunate eighty one year old lady. She had presented eight weeks before with severe crippling pain in the region of her right hip and was finding it increasingly more difficult to get about.

At the surgery she had been seen by an orthopaedic surgeon, brought in on a contract from another district. Presumably, our orthopaedic surgeons were not good enough! After examining her he had ordered a series of special X-ray scans that had revealed a massive bone-destroying tumour in her pelvis.

As a result the surgeon had arranged for the patient to be admitted to his own hospital, a mere twenty five miles away, for an investigative biopsy under general anaesthetic. In the meantime he had ordered a series of blood tests and the necessary samples had been taken from the patient before she had left the clinic.

The patient had eventually been admitted to the other hospital for the biopsy, five weeks after her original visit to the Lansdowne surgery. The result of the biopsy had shown that she had a bone marrow malignancy not unlike leukaemia, which required referral to the haematology department for further investigation and subsequent treatment.

The patient referral letter had included copies of the test results from the Scottish laboratory. These had shown that although the blood had been obtained from the patient on the third of the month, it had not actually been analysed in Scotland until the tenth, seven days later. To make matters worse, the results had not been reported for release until the sixteenth of the month. It was clear to me that this long delay in analysing the samples had led to a number of seriously erroneous and misleading results.

Furthermore, and what is even more significant in this particular case is that, the reports had failed to highlight one highly significant abnormal finding, which was a spectacularly high level of a specific protein in the blood. Since there are very few possible causes of this finding it gave an obvious clue to the diagnosis, which would therefore have prevented the unnecessary anaesthetic and operation that this poor old lady had undergone.

In other words, had these findings been acted upon immediately and the necessary confirmatory tests instituted, as would have been the case with our biochemistry laboratory, the patient's condition would have been diagnosed within two days of her first visit; we're talking here of a whole six weeks and much unnecessary suffering could have been prevented.

Following this scandalous catalogue of clinical and laboratory mistakes and ineptitude, let alone the unnecessary delay in treatment for the patient, the bloody practice now wanted me to sort her out. This I willingly did, after firstly admitting her to the ward for immediate medical assessment and pain control.

After organising her management, I turned my attention to the private laboratory. Some weeks before they had written asking for my advice and now I felt I was in a position to offer it, completely free of charge!

I took the patient's private laboratory results and blanked out her name, the laboratory test reference number and the name of the requesting surgery. I then enclosed a copy of this with my letter to the managing director of the private laboratory. Lastly, I copied the letter and enclosure to all twenty five GP's involved in the four practices whose senior partners had received copies of the managing director's letter to me.

My letter was brief and basically stated that the report from the private laboratory was typical of the type of service that, on occasions, I had witnessed. It went on to explain that this was exactly the point I had made when expressing concern for the quality of service they were offering the patients of my district.

I have highlighted the gross errors in this case and how if avoided, as in my opinion they should have been by any officially accredited laboratory, this patient's diagnosis would have been reached seven weeks earlier.

I concluded that, as this was such a serious matter, I felt the laboratory would welcome my opinion, especially since in their letter they had requested any positive advice I could offer to improve their service.

Somehow, I got the distinct impression that the private laboratory had taken great exception to my letter, because I had now been summoned before the Deputy Chief Executive to answer their complaint.

"On what possible grounds do you think I could tell them to 'fuck off', as you sso abruptly pput it?" Boris stammered, reaching for a glass of water to help steady his nerves.

"Boris, my old darling. You called me here to tell me that you've had complaints about my letter from both the Scottish private laboratory, and Dr Appaling. Sorry I meant Dr Pauling. When I asked to read the complaints, you told me that these are not written complaints but complaints that had been made to you on the telephone. Well, as I see it, two significant issues come to mind here.

"Firstly, why, and on what grounds, would someone to whom I merely copied a letter, namely Dr Pauling, have to make a complaint?"

"I hadn't thought of that," Boris whispered quietly, as he pondered that question.

"Well I have. Would you like me to point this out to Dr Pauling, or will you?"

"I think that had better be left to me." Boris was now on the defensive.

"The second point I would make is that if this wretched laboratory or infernal GP really felt that they had a leg to stand on regarding this issue they wouldn't be wasting any of our time with verbal complaints. They would be sending you an official, legal, letter demanding, at the very least, a written apology.

"The obvious reason they haven't proceeded down that particular line of action is that they greatly fear everything that would come to light if this issue ever got as far as the courts. This is because, over the years, I have made them well aware of the fact that I have collected a large dossier of all the crap results from this laboratory that have come to my notice." And with that I threw a large folder, brimming with results, onto his desk, as he drew his chair back in surprise.

"And you can rest assured that I would make quite sure that every one of these results would be noted and discussed at great length by my lawyer in court. I am quite certain that this is the very *last* thing that this laboratory or Dr Pauling would want.

"No, they don't see any legal mileage for themselves in all this. However, being the selfish bullies they undoubtedly are and sore losers to boot they want you, the headmaster, to slap the wrists of this unruly, upstart pupil. And I have to tell you, Boris, that I have no intention of holding my wrists out to be slapped, by you or anybody else!"

Boris moved forward, and made to interrupt my tirade. "One of their complaints," he began, "was about the widespread distribution of your letter, when apparently their one was only sent to three GP's."

"Boris, do I have to point out to you that we are living in the adult world now, not Noddyland. They sent their letter to the senior partners of these practices. By the laws of partnership they involved all twenty five GP's and whether they like it or not, by the laws of partnership, they are all involved. I merely saved them the photocopying!

"Besides, the other GP's are basically nice guys, even if they are inherently inept sheep, opting for the quiet life by taking the easy money and avoiding confrontation. Well, this way they simply have to be involved. There really is no way for them to avoid the issue any more.

"You never know, as a result, one day in the near future one of these Davids may well find the courage to stand up against their Goliath, and effectively point out just how close to medico-legal danger they have been sailing all these years. And, by so doing, they may also manage to steer them back to using their vastly superior local service, which can only mean better standards of care for our patients.

"I understand that it may well seem to you and that infernal practice somewhat decadent putting our patients' interests first but being old-fashioned I still find it the most important part of my job. No doubt though, as a result, I may soon be removed from my position on the grounds of economy....sorry, I meant insanity!"

By now Boris had virtually given up but he still had one more card to play. "Their other gripe was that the results you sent with the letter weren't, to quote them, 'suitably anonymised.' They pointed out that the combination of the date and these particular results were sufficient to enable anyone with access to their computer to obtain the other information, including the patient's name."

"I can see someone frantically breaking into this pathetic, god-forsaken, poxy excuse for a laboratory, somewhere in the nether regions of Scotland, hell-bent on obtaining this patient's name, like some coveted top secret in Whitehall!"

"Well, Dr Ryan, need I remind you that there are certain very serious issues concerning patient confidentiality that we all have to bear in mind?" He was back on the attack and once more sporting a smug expression, as he pointed his finger at me.

"In that case, you might like to read this," I said, thrusting a sheet of paper under his bulbous nose.

"What's this," he asked, taking the sheet and peering intently at it.

"That, my old darling, is the patient's signed permission for me to divulge any information about her medical condition to whosoever I wish, whenever I wish," I replied, in triumph, as I headed for the door.

Before moving out of the office, I turned and added, "Boris, if I hear of any form of apology relating to this matter being sent to either of the complaining parties I will go straight to the *News of the World* with this collection of MAC reports and will spread the gospel according to certain Fund Holding Practices as I see it!"

He gave a deep sigh, as he stared at me in disbelief, knowing full well that I meant every word.

I added, as I made to leave, "Do you want to know what the saddest thing about this whole episode is, Boris?"

"What?" he stared blankly at me.

"I'm actually enjoying every bloody minute of it! So, tell them to fuck off!"

* * *

There was surprisingly little work left in the labs on my return, as James had been good enough to clear most of my trays in my absence. He knew I wanted to get away as soon as possible, in order to get Victoria settled back home early and had kept up with the slides as they had come in from the microscopy room. I took the remainder back to my room and sat by the microscope.

As I selected the first blood film to view together with the request form bearing the patient information the phone rang. It was Dr Gibson, the medical registrar, who wanted to discuss the treatment policy on one of my patients, as he was on call for the night and hadn't been able to get hold of Hugh to discuss our patients before he left for the weekend.

It took only a couple of minutes to brief him and, as I replaced the receiver, I couldn't help thinking what a most capable and conscientious doctor he was proving to be. In fact there was no doubt that we were most fortunate at Eastwich when it came to the quality of our trainee specialist registrars, most of whom were destined to become very competent consultants on completion of their intensive specialist training programme.

As I slowly worked my way through the slides I recalled why it was that I had been late that morning. It had all been due to the fact that I had sat up the night before, reading for much longer than I had intended. Sometimes I get so enmeshed in a book I lose all sense of the time and such had been the case on this occasion. The book in question had been the one I had picked up by chance in London on Wednesday, *The Philosophy of Chess.*

I had found it fascinating and impossible to put down. There had been a particular chapter on the psychology of the player that, among other things, dealt with the varying psychological approaches employed by some players in their bid to outwit their opponent.

In one scenario it described how, sometimes, the harder one tries actively to defeat the opponent the more it produces a stronger and often superior, defensive response from that opponent, thus making the victory even more difficult to achieve. The tendency here was to attack even harder, thereby stretching your own defences even thinner and leaving yourself more vulnerable to counter-attack and possible ultimate defeat.

What it suggested you do in this scenario is to resist the temptation to attack so openly and to appear to go on the defensive, thereby tempting the opponent himself onto the attack, so that he becomes the one stretching his defences and revealing his underbelly ripe for the coup de gras. In other words, drawing-out tactics are required!

It seemed to me that, although the book was aimed at the game of chess, it could also be applied with minimal adaptation to the game of life. As I finished up and set off to collect Victoria, I couldn't help thinking to myself how glad I was I'd found that book.

CHAPTER TWENTY THREE

The desire to take medicine is perhaps the greatest feature which distinguishes man from animals
– William Osler

"How dare you read at the table?" Victoria glared across the breakfast table at me, feigning disgust.

"But I always read the *Times* at breakfast. It's a habit I picked up quite young. Besides, it helps the digestion," I pleaded.

"Well, it's rude. Didn't your mother ever tell you? What are you reading about that's so enthralling, anyway?" she asked, desperate to get in on the act.

"If you must know, miss bossy boots, I'm taking a gander at the matches, hatches, and dispatches column."

"The what?" she looked at me with a puzzled expression.

"To the uninitiated it's the Marriages, Births, and Deaths page."

"Why ever would you waste your time with that?" She continued the inquisition.

"Because as Noel Coward was once thought to have said, 'I read the Times, and if my name is not in the obits I proceed to enjoy the day.'"

"And is it?"

"What?"

"In the obits. Your name?" She said, pointing her knife at the paper and dropping a large glob of marmalade onto the tablecloth.

"Oh! No. I'm pleased to say it's not to be found within these pages." I said, with a note of triumph in my voice.

"That's good. You should be able to wash up then," she said, with even more triumph in her voice.

"I usually do," I bitched. "Unless it had escaped your notice there is no wife, ex-wife, maid or even slave in this establishment and I have been accustomed to cleaning up after myself for some years now."

"Who's getting shirty then?" she teased, scraping the marmalade off the tablecloth with a clean knife.

"I'm not getting shirty," I replied irritably, folding the paper and laying it on the table, resigned to the fact that I wasn't going to be allowed to finish it.

"Whoops! This is one aspect of the usually cool Dr Ryan I've not seen before! Could it possibly be that we got out of bed the wrong side this morning then?" she continued to prod, enjoying every moment of the cross-examination of this hostile witness. "Or was it the lack of sex that's brought the bear out in you today?"

"I'm quite used to the latter by now, and as to the former, there is no wrong side," I proceeded to inform her. "If you really want to know, they're all the wrong side when you've only managed one hour's sleep."

Now she began to feel bad, as she slowly got to her feet and waddled round to the back of my chair, where she placed her hands on my shoulders and began to massage gently. "I'm sorry Andrew. I didn't know, or I wouldn't have teased you like that. Why ever couldn't you sleep?"

"I've got quite a lot on my mind at the moment. Finding it virtually impossible to relax. All I could do was to lay there looking at the sleeping beauty most of the night."

"You should have woken me."

"What for? A round of poker," I said, engaging my mouth before my brain, failing to realise the unintentional double entendre.

"Your mind always comes back to the same thing." It was her turn to feel hurt.

"I'm sorry, Victoria," I said, swivelling on the chair and hugging her close to me. "I didn't realise what I was saying. I certainly didn't mean what it sounded like. Forgive me." And I laid my head very gently against her sore midriff.

"I know you didn't. You're duly forgiven," she pronounced, placing her hand on my head and fondling my hair, sending a shiver down my spine. "Hey. I've forgotten my tablets. I should have taken them when we got up. I'm usually very good about those things and never miss."

"I wouldn't worry too much. Surgeons haven't a clue when it comes to antibiotics. They only know one sort, and that's usually the wrong one."

"No, seriously Andrew. I've never missed a dose yet, and I don't intend to start now. I'd better go and get them," she said, leaving go of my head just when I was beginning to relax, and disappearing upstairs to retrieve the pills.

With a sigh, I picked up the paper and turned to the sports page. Having caught up with the latest results of the test match currently being played in Trinidad, I had just started to read an article on the Davis Cup when the back door flew open, and Mark and Emma appeared over the threshold.

"Surprise!" they shouted, in unison.

"I eventually found them, Andrew. Would you believe it, they had rolled right under the bed. Can't imagine how they managed to get there." Victoria appeared from the other direction.

Mark's jaw dropped halfway to his feet, as Emma stood riveted to the floor staring blank-faced at Victoria, who herself remained frozen in space like one of the victims trapped when Vesuvius erupted near Pompeii.

I glanced across at Emma and Mark, then at Victoria, then back at the other two. They all remained completely motionless, staring at each other. After what seemed an eternity, I managed to stammer, "I think it's time for me to do the washing up!"

* * *

It had not proved quite as embarrassing as I had thought it would, under the circumstances. For me, the most surprising thing had been seeing my son in vertical mode at such an unearthly hour. I racked my brain, but couldn't remember which particular year this achievement had last been recorded. Emma, as usual the quickest to suss the situation, had dropped her things and wandered over to introduce herself, as if it was the sort of thing she did every other week.

Mark's jaw was eventually scraped from the floor, and replaced in its natural setting. Within minutes they were both settled at the kitchen table firing questions wildly at Victoria who, bless her, took everything in her stride, and handled the situation impeccably.

I couldn't get a word in edgeways, as they carried on as if they had known each other for years. I might as well not have existed. In the end, after nearly an hour of this excited banter back and forth, I decided to count my losses and retire back upstairs to get ready. They were still at it, with all those nervous giggles, when I bade them farewell on my way out to see how my patients were doing. I don't believe they even noticed me leave.

* * *

The tour of the wards was completed relatively quickly, considering how many patients I had, scattered all over the hospital. The majority were doing quite well, and it had proved more of a social visit for most of them. It was gratifying to see David sitting up and looking considerably improved since starting the ambisome only the day before. His temperature was nearly back to normal and, if I had any doubts about his well-being, these were rapidly dispelled by the sight of him surrounded by his folders and paperwork once again.

I returned home, having been away only two hours, to find the place empty. On the kitchen table I found a frantically scribbled note informing me that Emma and Mark had effectively kidnapped Victoria and taken her into town *'to get a few things.'* It also said that if I wished I could meet them at *The Anchor* pub for lunch at one thirty.

I was not at all pleased that they had taken Victoria off in her condition but I quickly decided to control my feelings, as I didn't want to make a scene at this stage. In truth I was more annoyed at the fact that, of all the pubs, they had chosen *The Anchor*. That was one of the pubs that had recently been expensively modernised, and turned into a pathetic excuse of a noisy, plasticated drinking house, where the beer was warm and mediocre, and the juke box was fixed on full volume.

Putting all this to the back of my mind and psychoanalysing myself into a state of unusual calm, I changed into my casual clothes, grabbed the paper and mobile phone and set off for town.

Coming off the ring road and heading for the town centre, I stopped to post two letters I had composed and addressed whilst in the hospital earlier. Hovering by the post box I hesitated for a few seconds, giving considerable thought to my actions and was barely able to suppress the grin slowly creeping over my face, before finally dropping the envelopes into the box and proceeding on my way.

* * *

It wasn't difficult to spot them in the overcrowded, smoky bar. They were the ones making most of the noise, seated at a small table in the far corner. As I approached them Victoria burst into laughter at something Mark had said and Emma rocked forward on her chair giggling to herself. They all suddenly fell totally silent at the sight of me and started to look at each other a little guiltily, Victoria with her hand over her mouth.

"You've been talking about me," I said, my paranoia surfacing, and heading straight for the stratosphere.

"Whatever makes you think that?" Victoria asked, breaking into a fit of uncontrolled laughter once again as Emma resumed her giggling.

"You were. I can tell from your expression. What were you saying?" I asked Mark, eyeing him with my droopy expression.

"If you must know dad, I was just telling Victoria about your tendency to little temper tantrums when you're losing at tennis."

"I'm sure I don't know what you mean," I lied.

"Apparently, Andrew, it's not only in the hospital that you have to win," Victoria managed between guffaws. "But I was trying to imagine the scene at that snobby tennis club when this highly respected hospital consultant suddenly loses his cool at the end of a long rally, bouncing his poor, innocent racket off the court whilst letting loose a few well chosen epithets."

"The whole place goes decidedly silent," Mark chimed in, "and I don't know where to put my face, while dad of course looks about him somewhat awkwardly, searching for his wayward racket. Inwardly he's secretly hoping against hope that the wretched thing hasn't broken. You wouldn't believe the total look of innocence on his face as he retrieves the offending article and resumes his position as if nothing had happened."

"Oh! I believe I would," Victoria volunteered, brushing my shoulder affectionately with the back of her hand.

"I don't know why you make such a big deal of it," I said, playing it all down. "I'm only trying to get a bit of anger into my game. I need to get the adrenaline flowing before I can get into top gear. Not unlike that other great player, John McEnroe!"

"More like Dick Dastardley," Mark contributed with a shrug,

as Victoria and Emma broke down once more.

I bought them a round of drinks and had just settled at the table, pint in hand, when the phone burst into life. Colin Sampson, the haemophiliac, was back in the A&E department complaining of further problems with his knee. As the on-call registrar was not experienced in this field I agreed to pop in and sort it out.

Bidding farewell to the others, I told them I'd see them back at the house later. I also asked Mark to book a restaurant for us all for eight o'clock.

* * *

It had been a very enjoyable weekend, with Emma and Mark staying the night and generally taking control of events. Apparently, Jane had been hoping to get over later on Saturday but in the end she phoned to apologise as, at the last moment, she had been invited to a party and would be staying with a friend afterwards.

Emma had spent an excited thirty minutes on the phone telling her all about Victoria. No details were omitted and a complete and thorough picture was drawn, almost down to the shoe size. There had been a lot of nervous giggling, but in the end the consensus was that it could only be a good thing for *'Aged P.'*, and of course in the long run for them.

The others had eventually left at around midday, as Mark had a local football match that afternoon and Emma had promised to help her mother with some project around the house. There had been much idle chatter with Victoria before they left, the main topic concerning how best to handle me.

Victoria and I had spent the rest of the day generally lazing about reading, chatting about nothing in particular and watching the television. We had retired to bed quite early, where we had continued our reading, eventually falling asleep with our books open in front of us.

It was about four o'clock in the morning when Victoria awoke feeling unwell and complaining of lower abdominal pains. She felt clammy with a high temperature and her abdomen was extremely tender. I was convinced she had developed an infection related to her recent surgery and immediately had her readmitted to the hospital for further investigations and intravenous antibiotics.

CHAPTER TWENTY FOUR

'Night starvation' was the classic thirties disease. It was invented by the makers of Horlicks, who, having thought up an illness that didn't exist, claimed to cure it by guaranteeing deep sleep ('ordinary sleep is not enough')
– Michael Green

"Wakey, wakey, Andrew."

"What!" I opened my eyes with a start. Temporarily blinded by the bright sunlight streaming over his shoulder, I stared into Johnny's eyes as he bent over my chair in the medical library.

"It seemed a shame to disturb you, you looked so comfortable. How long you been asleep then?"

Slowly sitting upright in my chair and staring through sleepy eyes at my watch I replied, "Must have been about ten or fifteen minutes."

Following yet another disturbed night the morning had gone relatively smoothly, with only a small clinic for a change. After having Victoria admitted to the ward, I had only returned home to shave and dress for work. I was back in the department by seven fifteen where I got up to date with my paperwork.

Following the clinic I had checked on Victoria, before seeking refuge in the medical library. I had hoped to catch up on the current medical journals but, no doubt due to my recent cumulative sleep deficit, I had soon slipped off into a deep and peaceful slumber.

"Having a pleasant dream were you?"

"If you really want to know it was a bloody nightmare," I said, scratching my head and rubbing my eyes.

"About what?"

"Well, I dreamt that I had murdered Boris and was on the run. Eventually I'm cornered by the police in *The Anchor* car park. There's no way out, so I do the honourable thing and commit hara-kiri by falling on a beer bottle....an empty beer bottle, of course! Anyway, I end up in heaven where I meet Marilyn Monroe, and we're having a great time. Then, of course, along comes my ex-wife and they start fighting over me."

"So. Where's the nightmare there?" he asked.

"My Ex was winning!"

"Very funny. How's Victoria, by the way? I gather she was readmitted."

"Not too bad this morning. Still a bit sore though. Probably a post-op infection. You'd think those bloody surgeons would wash their hands, especially when considering the over inflated salaries some of them take home when compared with us humble physicians!"

"I'm glad to hear she's feeling a bit better. I thought I'd wander along and introduce myself later, if that's alright with you."

"O.K. by me. I'm sure she will be only too pleased to meet you. Even if she's not, she can hardly run away," I commented, giving my eyes a further rub and making them sore.

"Andrew. I was looking to have a word with you, and Anne told me I'd find you down here," he said, looking a little concerned.

"Well, I do declare, the good Dr Frobisher is sporting a concerned frown upon his countenance. What have I done this time? Parked my car in Boris' space?"

"I fear it might be a little more serious than that." He momentarily looked away as I stared at him, searching for some inkling of what it was all about.

"Like what?" I enquired.

"Boris has written to me in confidence, in my capacity as a member of the *Three Wise Men,* about a matter concerning you. He wants to convene a meeting of the group as soon as possible to discuss the possible implications and, if indicated, what further action should be taken. There's no doubt he's really gunning for you this time, Andrew." I thought poor Johnny was about to burst into tears.

"Did he mention what this heinous crime might be?" I asked.

"No. Only that he had reason to believe that there had been a breach of the rules and that it needed to be looked into at the earliest possible moment."

The *Three Wise Men* is a group of senior consultants that exists in every NHS hospital. The name given to this group is now quite inappropriate, since it no longer consists of only three members and rarely are they all that wise. In addition, the composition of the group is no longer limited to only men. The overall wisdom of the group will depend on the particular composition of the body, and in the case of Eastwich, with the exception of Johnny, this did not amount to much.

Their sole function was to meet as and when required to discuss possible breaches of a professional or ethical nature in relation to a consultant's activity. This would include matters relating to a particular consultant's health, with specific reference to their mental health

For some time now it had been considered important that the consultant-body take responsibility for policing themselves with respect to their professional performance and for making the necessary recommendations to the administration for any action it deemed necessary.

Our particular *Three Wise Men* included Boris and Patrick Skinner, which did not bode well for my chances in any fight with them.

"And you haven't been given any clue as to what sort of a breach of rules this might be?" I asked.

"None whatsoever."

"'*It's a riddle wrapped in a mystery inside an enigma: but perhaps there is a key,*'" I whispered quietly to Johnny.

"What are you going on about? If that bunch could hear you now they would probably feel they have every right to bring you before them," Johnny hissed back at me.

"It was something Churchill once said, but it seems somehow strangely appropriate to this situation right now. Thanks for telling me about it, I do appreciate your support. Seriously, Johnny it's good of you to keep me informed. Now, if that's all, I have some serious sleep to catch up on," I said, getting back to the journal lying open on the table in front of me.

"Sometimes I'm at a loss to understand you, Andrew," Johnny said, shrugging his shoulders and turning to leave. "If I were in your shoes I'd show a little more concern. But then, I'm not in your shoes I suppose, and we each have to handle these things in our own way. I'll let you know if I hear any more," he said heading for the door.

I'm not sure I caught the last part, as my eyelids were already half closed, staring incomprehensibly at the long medical words dancing before them.

* * *

I ran into James at lunch, when we were able to discuss the final on-call arrangements. The main problem was that, until he was able to move locally, it was not going to be feasible for him to be on at night. I didn't mind doing the cover until he was settled, and since he and Joanne had now found the house they wanted I was confident I wouldn't have to cover for too long.

James had also taken over the ward responsibilities, as we had previously agreed to alternate one month on the wards followed by one month on laboratory duties. We would continue to see our own patients in our separate out-patient clinics, thereby offering the patients continuity of care.

I took this opportunity of familiarising him with the current group of ward patients and filled him in with their progress. He asked after Victoria and said he would like to call in and introduce himself to her on the ward round that afternoon, provided I had no objection. I pointed out that she would probably be feeling a bit like a politician, after all the handshaking she was in for today.

On my way back from lunch I wandered over to the ward to pay a social visit to a few of my patients. David was continuing to improve, twelve days after completion of his chemotherapy, and we were all now eagerly awaiting the recovery of his blood count. He made no mention of Boris or the *Three Wise Men* and I was sure that as yet he knew nothing about the business involving me. I would have thought that Boris would want to be sure of his ground first, before making any move involving the administration.

After seeing David I moved on to Colin Sampson who I had admitted at the weekend. He was sitting out of bed in his easy chair, reading the sports section of the *Daily Mail.*

"How's it going, Colin?" I asked, almost tripping over the crutches propped precariously against the end of the bed.

"Not so bad, thanks Dr Ryan. I can actually walk a few steps without it giving way," he replied, lowering his paper.

"How about the pain-killers. Are you still requiring them regularly?"

"Not nearly so often now," he answered, with a note of triumph in his voice.

"Decided to stay with us this time, and see it through then," I said, a little sarcastically but with a grin that he knew implied I didn't really mean it.

"Well, Dr Ryan," he said, with a smirk on his face, "You're running a better hotel this time. Sort of makes it a pleasure to stay."

I perched on the edge of the bed and craned my neck a little to get a look at the headline on the paper in his lap. "What was wrong with our hotel last time then that made it necessary for you do a bunk before you were fully ready to leave? And, incidentally, probably resulted in the recurrence of the bleeding into that knee and your subsequent readmission," I enquired, pointing at the offending joint.

"It was so bloody noisy Dr Ryan. I mean you'd need a week off in a rest home to get over this place sometimes," he said, climbing onto his soap-box. "You must admit I'm a pretty good patient normally but on this occasion I'd really had enough."

"Well, Colin, it was a fairly traumatic night for the ward as you well know. We lost that poor young lady after her operation, and everyone would have been running around like crazy trying to resuscitate her. Sometimes you cannot avoid noise, especially in an emergency."

"But it wasn't only then doc. It had been quite noisy earlier in the evening, when the young doctor came in to change her drip."

"Even you can make a noise having a drip sited, Colin. I've heard you," I answered, wagging my finger at him.

"In actual fact she had been very good about it. Although I was in my side room, the door was open and I could see everything clearly across the ward. He'd finished getting the drip to work and I was nodding off again when he let out an almighty shout. It frightened me at first. He'd been so quiet up to then. When I looked over I could see he had cut his hand opening a glass vial that had fragmented at the last moment. You know, the way they do sometimes. Well, he seemed quite flustered by now because he had to open another one, and he seemed to be in a great hurry looking nervously over his shoulder all the time. Mind you he was very careful but I could hear him swearing away quietly to himself until he had done it."

"I know the problem only too well. I nearly severed a tendon on one a few years ago. There was absolutely no warning, the vial simply collapsed in my hand. It needed five stitches, and took simply ages to heal. I'm not surprised he let out a yell. I'd probably have thrown the whole damn tray down the ward."

"Well, after that it took me over two hours to get back to sleep. Then, as soon as I had got to sleep again, the other commotion started and there was no hope after that. That was the end for me."

"Well, I'm glad it's been a little quieter this time, Colin. Your knee obviously needs a lot of peace and quiet. It's a sensitive knee, I can see that," I joked, borrowing his paper to check Saturday's lottery numbers.

"You'll never win on that, Doctor Ryan. I mean it's fourteen million to one against your line winning. Did you know that? You've got more chance on the *gee gees*. I've got a dead cert for the two thirty at Kempton tomorrow if you want it," he said, reaching for his notepad.

"No thanks, Colin. It's too late for anything less that three million for me now. See you tomorrow."

* * *

The afternoon had proved almost as uneventful as the morning, much to my relief. Anne, noting my sagging energy levels, had been her super efficient self in keeping all hawkers, peddlers and tinkers from my door. She had even broken with tradition, and actually brought me coffee and biscuits, just as I was about to fall fast asleep at the microscope.

The only patient I had seen was one of Johnny's, from whom I had had to obtain a bone marrow sample in an attempt to explain his curious anaemia. On returning from the renal dialysis unit there was a message on my desk to phone my brother-in-law.

Adam had answered the phone himself. He was obviously feeling a little low and asked if we could meet for a drink the following evening. Since it was his turn to come to me we agreed to meet up at The Dog and Parrot at eight o'clock.

Before leaving for the day, Matthew put his head round the door to tell me about Victoria. The scans had been normal with no evidence of any abscess. He felt the episode was probably a straight forward case of post operative infection, and certainly she seemed to be responding well to the intravenous antibiotics. I thanked him and took him over to the Blue Boar for a quick drink to finish the day.

I can't remember the last time I had seen Boris and Patrick Skinner in a pub, but there they were, large as life, huddled over their orange juices in deep conversation at the other end of the bar. I grinned at them, as I raised my glass in their direction.

CHAPTER TWENTY FIVE

A psychiatrist is a man who goes to the Folies-Bergere and looks at the audience
– Mervyn Stockwood

"I fully realise you're only doing all this and faking your symptoms because you just have to be near me," I said, poking my head round Victoria's door next morning. I had a break between seeing a couple of patients in the department, so I thought I'd pop up and find out how she was doing.

"At the risk of deflating your ego, I have to tell you, Dr Ryan, that my symptoms were genuine. But then, of course, it would take a surgeon to realise that. Couldn't possibly expect a lowly physician to be that astute."

"You're just an old crock," I continued, plumping myself in the chair beside her, and placing my feet on the bed. "I suppose I really should be looking around for a younger model. You know, one with a bit less mileage and a new paint job!"

"You do have the knack of saying the nicest things, lover boy. You really know how to charm a girl, don't you! Phew! I feel I've been swept off my feet....straight into the gutter," she said, pulling the sheet over her face.

I leant forward, pulling the sheet down, and gave her a warm kiss. "Well my cherub, it was Oscar Wilde who wrote that immortal line, *'I may be in he gutter, but I'm looking at the stars'*........ I suppose...."

"*No*! You depraved pervert. That's all you haematologists ever want. A bone marrow, and a bonk a day keeps the haematologist at bay. Well, I'll have you know I'm a good girl from a decent background. So you're jolly well going to have to earn your spurs the honourable way, Dr "Randy" Ryan," she whispered in my ear, following which she gave it the sexiest kiss it had ever received in its forty eight year existence.

"Whatever you say, if you put it that way my dwarling," I said coyly, blinking my eyes at her with my sheepish, innocent, but hungry look.

"By the way, I finally got to meet Johnny yesterday. He's a sweetie isn't he? Full of charm, and brimming with kindness. Whatever does such a wonderful person see in the likes of you, I wonder?"

"Do I know this chap you're talking about?" I asked, a look of total bewilderment on my face.

"Probably not. He's far too nice to associate with riffraff like you," she retaliated, pushing me back into the chair.

"What did he have to say for himself, this charming doctor, then?"

"For one thing, he told me of his fears for you. He's obviously genuinely concerned about your welfare, even if you are not. He told me about this Dr Baldwin, and the long running feud between the two of you. He also mentioned the business of the *Three Wise Men*. You must be careful, Andrew, I really do care for you, you know." She swung her feet round and plopped them over the side of the bed, leaning forward and took hold of my hands.

"Boris is a complete prat. He couldn't tie his own shoes without a diagram in front of him. Besides, I can't think of one thing he could possibly have on me that's so bad it needs to go before the *Three Wise Men*."

"Well, apparently Johnny ran into Dr Baldwin in the corridor when he was on his way up to see me. And this Boris told him that he was concerned about your drinking habits."

"My drinking habits are as normal as the next man. I tend to swallow, a second or two after putting the glass to my lips. But he is right about one thing. I do indeed have a drinking problem," I said, raising my voice a little for effect.

"You see, you even admit it now!"

"Yes, it's a real problem alright....they close the pubs at eleven!"

"It's all very well you being flippant but Johnny did say that

Boris was a very serious type, who was a known teetotaller and was in the habit of preaching abstinence."

"You don't say. '*He came to see me this morning positively reeking of Horlicks!*'"

"He what?"

"Oh! Only joking. Something amusing Thomas Beecham once said about Sir Adrian Boult. Seems to sum old *Boring* up perfectly. I wouldn't take any notice of him. He growls a lot, but he hasn't got any teeth to speak of. He constantly annoys me. You know, like a bull terrier forever snapping away at your heels, but he's relatively harmless really," I said, getting to my feet and making for the big kiss.

Victoria placed her hands on my chest, holding me back as she said, "I'm not convinced he's that harmless, Andrew. Not from what Johnny was saying. By all accounts he has certainly had enough of you and your actions and he wants more than anything to get rid of you.

"Johnny was saying that, in his considered opinion, you've succeeded in pushing him too far, and now he's got you firmly in his sights, and won't rest till he's got rid of you, once and for all." She leaned forward and kissed me again before adding, "You really must be careful, Andrew. I am now genuinely worried about you."

"I'm walking on bottle tops as it is now."

"Shouldn't that be egg shells?"

"In my case it's bottle tops. Anyway, what more could I possibly do?" I asked, my palms upturned to the ceiling.

"For one thing, you could try exercising a little more restraint in Dr Baldwin's presence. You know, hold back a bit more. Don't keep flying off the handle at the very sight of him," Victoria pleaded.

"Your wish is my command, my gorgeous little drug peddler. Must rush, I've got another of those beautiful young reps coming to see me and I really need to tart myself up a bit! Do you think this tie's O.K., or should I change it for that lovely new, bright-coloured, silk one I keep in my locker for special occasions like the retirement of some administrator? "

I just made it out of the room in time to hear the dull thud of her paperback hitting the back of the door.

* * *

Alan Makepiece came to see me in the afternoon to go over the written project he had only recently completed as part of his final exams. The work was very good, as I had expected it would be in his case. He was an excellent technician in every sense and I had no doubt that he would reach the top if he decided to stay in the laboratory sciences.

On the other hand, I wouldn't have been too surprised if he eventually left the Health Service for the relatively rich pickings of the commercial world. So many of our good trainees had chosen this route in the past, and who could blame them? I didn't want to lose him but under the circumstances, one had to be philosophical about our chances of keeping him.

I glanced back at his manuscript to confirm that I was right before speaking. Sure enough, there was the proof. Every capital letter *P* had a tiny break in the loop at about two o'clock. It was all I needed.

"Tell me, Alan," I said after we had finished and he got up to leave, "it was you who sent me those confidential letters the other day, wasn't it?" I continued to stare him straight in the eye after I had finished speaking.

His inability to return my look, coupled with his tendency to fidget from one foot to the other, gave me my answer.

"I'm sorry, I don't understand you Dr Ryan," he said, still refusing to look me in the face.

"I think you do, Alan. Now, come on, you can be honest with me. This is strictly between the two of us. You have my word." I tried to convince him that I was sincere in my intention to retain a sense of confidentially over this matter.

"Alright," he said, after a long pause, and with a hint of relief in his voice. "Yes, it was me." He still found it difficult to look directly at me.

"Why me?" I asked.

"I'm not sure I know what you mean."

"Of all people, why did you choose to send me this information? And where did you get it in the first place?"

"You have a reputation for being fair and you're known for your tendency to fight these causes," he said, once more able to look in my direction. "As for where I came by this information, I'm sure you'll remember seeing me the other day in London. Well, at the time I was with Rosemary, one of the secretaries from the histology department. We're quite close and she confides a lot in me these days. She was aware of what was going on and felt compromised, since she was being involved, much against her will, in this matter by the actions of her boss.

"At first she tried ignoring it all, but since she was responsible for typing up the reports she found this impossible and started to feel very angry about being unfairly implicated in the matter. In the end she couldn't stand it any more and decided to tell me. The rest you know."

"But what did you possibly expect me to do with this information? And, bearing in mind that even if it were true, proving this sort of thing would never be an easy matter. Especially with the closing-of-ranks manoeuvre that my profession has become more expert at than the British Army."

I was having to be very cautious in this matter, as poor Alan was obviously feeling quite ill at ease, standing there in front of me nervously fiddling with the lapel of his white coat, as he shifted uneasily from one foot to the other.

"I don't really know. I only wanted to help poor Rosemary, because she was getting a bit panicky over the whole business. In reality, I don't suppose there was a lot you could have done about it." He seemed to settle a little and the nervousness had gone from his voice.

"Well, let's forget the whole matter and put it out of the window. I don't think you would like to get caught up in the sort of fight this thing could produce. It would undoubtedly get very messy, believe me. I think we'd be well advised to leave these particular consultants alone with their petty little scam," I said, getting to my feet and grabbing his manuscript from the desk.

"I don't think they're very happy this morning, according to what Rosemary told me at lunch," he chipped in.

"What do you mean?" I asked, trying hard to suppress the grin by now beginning to cover my face.

"Well, apparently they were happy enough earlier on and their usual sneaky, smiling selves when she took them each their mail. But a quarter of an hour later there was all hell let loose in the department.

Dr Skinner's door was suddenly thrown wide open, and he stormed out fuming with rage, and disappeared down the corridor to Dr Knowles's room clutching a letter in his hand. Before he had reached his office, Dr Knowles himself appeared in the doorway in a similar state, also holding a letter in his hand.

They disappeared into his room, where they remained for over an hour in conference, and no one was allowed to disturb them. Rosemary was given strict instructions not to put any calls through. Eventually they both reappeared, still in a filthy mood, and left the building together. And, what is more, they haven't been seen since." Alan appeared quite exhausted after relating this little tale.

"Probably a lover's tiff," I whispered to myself but loud enough to be heard.

"What was that, Dr Ryan?" Alan asked, grinning from ear to ear, certain that he had heard it correctly.

"Probably a departmental rift," I said, not that convincingly. "I wonder what could possibly have been in their mail to have triggered such behavior?"

Alan stared blankly in my direction, fully realising that only I knew the answer to that question.

"Whatever it was, it sure as hell produced an explosive reaction!"

"Anyway, Alan, as far as the other matter's concerned, I think we'd both better forget it. I don't see a lot of mileage in it myself. What do you say?" I looked him square in the face, as I handed him back his project.

"Whatever you say, Dr Ryan. I'll be guided by you. I'm sure you're right."

"That's excellent work," I added, niftily changing the subject, and pointing to the folder. "In my opinion, you deserve a very high mark for that work."

"Thanks very much," he smiled as he turned to go.

"Oh! And by the way," I added, as he paused for a moment, looking back at me from the door. "I want to tell you that I really do rate you, not only as a first class technician, but also as a true scientist. If you are prepared to put the work in, I see a bright future ahead of you and I very much hope it will be here at Eastwich. I'd hate to think we might lose you to someone else."

"Why, thanks very much, Dr Ryan. I really appreciate that." He gave me a warm smile as he tugged at the door and disappeared back to the laboratory.

* * *

I was able to leave work early that evening and had plenty of time to get home and change before going on to the Dog and Parrot to meet Adam. I arrived at ten to eight, but he had beaten me to it and was sitting at a table near the bar. He had his paper in front of him and was busily at work on the crossword.

The bar was unusually quiet and to my surprise I was served straight away. Carrying the two pints of best bitter in one hand, I made my way over to Adam and took the seat opposite him.

"Did you read about that crossword expert who died last week?" I asked, plonking his pint on the table in front of him.

"No, I didn't Andrew. What happened?" he asked, putting his paper down and grabbing hold of his pint.

"Well, apparently he was buried six down and two across!" I answered, taking a welcome slurp of my beer.

"Highly amusing, I'm sure! How have you been then? It seems ages since I last saw you."

"Not too bad, my poor long-suffering brother-in-law. I have been very busy though at the old factory," I said, guzzling the beer and managing to spill a little down the front of my favourite jacket.

"Glad to hear they've got you overpaid doctors under control at that overrated infirmary of yours," he quipped, leaning slowly back in his chair and stretching his feet out in front of him.

"That's two overs in succession, Adam. You must be a cricketer and I never knew it!"

"You're certainly on form today Andrew. You must have had a very stimulating day, I can always tell." He was in his patronising mood, which I knew of old. It usually meant that he was having a bad time with all the *sickness* he was experiencing at home.

"How's Jill, or need I ask?" I knew the answer before it hit me.

"Dreadful. I think she's getting worse if anything. I never cease to be amazed at the sheer variation of her continuing ailments. One minute it's TB, the next it's coal miner's lung. God knows how she thinks she contracted that!" Adam was obviously at the end of his tether and badly needed the company of his one and only true ally.

"I suppose we could give her something real to worry about. You know, sort of take her mind off her imaginary illnesses," I suggested.

"Like what, for instance?" He looked at me with hope in his eyes.

"Like anthrax!"

"Be serious, Andrew," he sighed, taking a long gulp of his drink. "I need genuine help with this. It's beginning to drag me right down. There must be an answer. I mean last night she was lying on the settee, right in the middle of the film I've been waiting weeks to see, clutching her stomach, moaning loudly and shouting *'It's murder, it's murder I tell you.'* It didn't stop her eating every bit of the spaghetti bolognese I had prepared and coming back for more!"

"I have been wondering for some time now whether a spot of hypnosis might not do the trick," I said, smiling at Adam as I managed to spill even more of my beer down my jacket.

Wiping it away with the back of my hand, I continued, "You know, I've been reading a bit about it lately, and it's quite amazing what uses it's being put to these days. It might be worth a go. That is, if her highness agrees to it. After all, she has steered well clear of psychiatric illnesses so far, and she may believe we're intonating that she's nuts. Which, of course, she bloody well *is.* Pardon me, Adam, but you see I've suffered her hypochondria for even longer than you."

"Be my guest," he said, swatting at a lazy fly on the table with his folded paper. Missing it by a mile, he replaced the paper in his lap and continued, as he idly watched the fly disappear in the direction of the bar, "Why should I be the only one to suffer? I always feel blood relatives should shoulder some of the burden. But do you really believe it could work this hypnosis thing?"

"I really don't know Adam. But it's got to be worth a try. I don't see we have anything to lose. I know of a relatively sane psychiatrist who dabbles in hypnosis. I could have a word with him if you like."

"Would you really, Andrew? I'd be eternally grateful to you. Anything that gives me some relief from this bloody nightmare. I swear, I don't think I could go on with it much longer." He drained his pint and looked across at me. "Let's have the other to celebrate this action-plan," he said, grabbing my empty mug and heading for the bar with renewed vigour.

"Now you're talking, my good friend!"

CHAPTER TWENTY SIX

CECIL GRAHAM: What is a cynic?
LORD DARLINGTON: A man who knows the price of everything and the value of nothing
– Oscar Wilde

It had been good seeing Adam again, although I was a little worried at how unsettled he had become over Jill's obsession with illness. I decided to pursue the psychiatrist idea as soon as possible, as much for his sake as hers. Although I had had to put up with a lot of her raving over the years, poor Adam had been stuck right in the centre of it all with no place to run. And it was now obviously catching up with him in a big way.

We left fairly early and I was back home parking the car in the garage at five to ten. I knew this since the BBC news was starting by the time I turned on the television on entering the study. The familiar introduction theme for the news programme was all I needed to reach forward and turn the set back off.

It seemed a little early for bed, so I settled in the lounge with a glass of wine and turned the radio on while I browsed through the paper. As part of a season of Shakespeare the BBC was running a version of *Othello* that had been recorded a few years ago. As I tuned in Othello was in the process of murdering Desdemona.

Somehow I wasn't quite in the mood for this heavy stuff and immediately switched the radio off and concentrated on the paper as I began to unwind from a heavy day. It was all pretty uninteresting stuff with the usual doom and gloom spread over most of the pages. By the time I had got to an article on the senseless, unsolved, and apparently motiveless murder of a young woman in London I had had enough for the evening.

I decided to call it a day and grabbed the wine as I headed upstairs for bed. As I approached the top of the stairs I noticed I had left the bathroom light on when I had gone out earlier. Staring across the landing at the bathroom floor I recalled the vision of Victoria lying there so helpless when she had first collapsed not that long ago. I suddenly felt a strong pang of loneliness descending upon me as I continued to the bedroom.

Whilst I was preparing for bed I could not help thinking that if only Jill could have witnessed this picture of someone being genuinely ill, perhaps she would learn to take a more rational approach to her problems, instead of crying *'It's murder, it's murder'* whenever she experienced the slightest twinge of pain.

I climbed into the cold bed and took a long gulp of the wine, before reaching for my book. As I turned the pages, searching for my place, I thought to myself how it had been nothing but *'murder'* all night. Perhaps I should have been a police inspector rather than a doctor.

I settled back into a comfortable position and began to read. Somehow I was finding it hard going, often having to go back and read a passage a second time. Although my eyelids were beginning to droop I was in no way tired. My mind was wandering in and out of reality as I stared at the lines in front of me.

After a few minutes I was forced to give up, as I found it impossible to sustain the concentration. My thoughts were buzzing with the events of the past few days, and I found it difficult to focus on the plot. As had so often been the case over the past two weeks, whenever I was alone and unable to get to sleep my thoughts would wander to the tragic cases in my clinics, such as that of Lynn Harris.

Once again, I found myself dwelling on the events of that night, and then on the other sad unexplained deaths that had occurred over the past few months. Our hospital certainly seemed to have experienced more of these tragic cases recently than the national statistics would have led us to expect.

Life could certainly be unkind at times and there didn't seem any rhyme or reason to the whole business. I finished off the wine, put the book down, and turned off the light before settling down on the pillow. I lay there, tossing and turning for ten minutes before finally slipping into a light, restless sleep.

MURDER! MURDER! I sat bolt upright in bed, a cold sweat running down my forehead. My heart was pounding, and at first I wasn't sure where I was, or indeed whether I was still dreaming. That panicky feeling of disorientation can be so unnerving, especially when you are alone in the dark.

I frantically reached for the light and glanced over at the clock. It was a little after eleven thirty and I'd been asleep for only about ten minutes. Still feeling a bit shaky, I swung my feet out of bed and threw on my dressing gown, before rushing downstairs to the study.

I quickly found Johnny's number and dialled it whilst I settled at the desk, doodling on the pad in front of me. It was answered by Johnny after five rings, and I was pleased that he hadn't yet gone to bed. I kept the conversation as brief as possible, and hung up within five minutes. He couldn't give me the information I wanted, but promised to look it up first thing in the morning and leave it with Anne while I was in clinic.

I glanced down at the pad in front of me, on which I had inadvertently written the word *'murder'* four times. I stared at the words for a few seconds before returning to bed and a more peaceful sleep.

* * *

Anne had already arrived when I entered the department at around eight the following morning. She had only just sat down at the computer and was busy arranging her work on the desk beside her, whilst waiting for the screen to burst into life

"Morning, my little angel of mercy," I greeted her with a smile.

"And what is it you want me to do, Dr Ryan?" she enquired, without looking up from her screen.

"What is there about you, Anne that immediately jumps to the conclusion that I want something, merely because I greet you in a pleasant manner? Can't a chap be polite these days without it being misconstrued as an act of deception?" I responded, pleading my defence.

"After all the years I've known you, Dr Ryan, the answer is probably *no*!" She still hadn't looked in my direction and by now was tapping furiously on the keyboard in front of her.

"Well, thank you for those few kind words my little cynical one. As chance would have it there is a little something I will need of you," I continued, in defeat.

"Now, however did I guess? And what might that be, oh wise and sober one?" she asked, this time looking directly at me with her inquisitive expression.

"When I'm in clinic later, Dr Frobisher will be in touch with the names of two recently deceased patients. Would you be an absolute dear and get me the notes, together with the notes of Lynn Harris whose unit number I'll give you before I go to clinic?"

"Is that all? I thought it was going to be some major project, the way you build it up," she said, returning her gaze to the screen in front of her and completely dismissing me.

"Thank you for your deep concern my little icon," I whispered, as I moved on to my office to deal with the mail and prepare for the clinic.

A little before nine I picked up the phone and dialled the number of the hospital in Nottingham where Lawrence Peters worked. After two minutes I was put through to him on the ward, where he was preparing to start his ward round. We chatted for a couple of minutes and he agreed to get back to me later in the day with the information I required. I was a little late for the clinic as I dashed past Anne leaving her the hospital unit number of the notes I required.

* * *

The clinic was running late, which was becoming par for the course these days, and always seems to be the case when you have so much else to do back in the department. It wasn't helped by my last patient, a gregarious old cockney who simply refused to be placated by anything I said in answer to his problems.

Having pointed out to him that the lump on his arm was a lipoma, a simple harmless collection of fat that did not require major surgery, he moved on to the problem with his hearing. By now he had been in the chair for fifteen minutes, during which time he had taken me on a Cook's tour of half his anatomy and was proceeding to start on the other half.

"It's probably a spot of wax Mr Deacon," I tried to reassure him, closing his notes and offering him the forms for his blood check.

Usually this manoeuvre produces a corresponding reaction from the patient, in the form of him getting to his feet to leave. But, alas, not so in Mr Deacon's case. He remained glued to his seat, his gaze fixed on me, seeking yet another answer. It was obvious that some outflanking manoeuvre was required if this battle was ever to be won.

"I suppose we'd better have a look at it," I said, getting to my feet and ushering him into the examination room next door, where I placed him in the upright chair.

"It's not often yer te-takes me into the te-torture chamber Doc," he stammered, as he settled in the chair.

"Drastic times require drastic measures," I whispered.

"Sorry Doc, I couldn't catch that. Bit mutton yer see," he said, pointing to the offending ear. He was obviously enjoying every moment and was settling in for a long stay. Not a healthy attitude in the out-patient clinic as far as I was concerned.

"Well, let's have a look see," I said, placing the instrument carefully into his external auditory meatus, and bending forward to take a look.

"Cor, what yer doing, Doc. Lookin' at me brains?" he asked, grinning from ear to ear.

"My good man, this is an auroscope........not a microscope!"

* * *

I had decided to forego lunch as I was running late, and I desperately wanted to have a look at the sets of notes that Anne had retrieved for me whilst I'd been in clinic.

As I sat at the desk thumbing my way through the thick pile of pages in front of me, I slowly munched a rather stale ham sandwich I'd picked up from the shop in out-patients on my way back to the department.

In every case, all the legal documentation was there including the coroner's post-mortem report and official findings. Everything seemed so neat and conclusive when, in fact, it was all a complete muddle. No specific cause of death had been found in any of the cases.

But, since there was nothing to suggest anything but natural causes as the reason for the sudden deaths, the standard statements for these situations were applied to the death certificates. It was simply a tidy way of concluding an untidy business. Everything dated, timed, categorised and signed before finally being lost forever in the vaults.

I painstakingly went through every page and entry from their admission to their deaths, frantically looking for any clue as to why they might so suddenly have been taken ill. But if there was any answer there I couldn't see it. Everything seemed so correct; all the procedures had been properly carried out and described in detail in the notes. It had all been a wild goose chase, and whatever it was that I was expecting to find wasn't there.

With a deep sigh I closed the last of the notes, leaving them stacked on the edge of my desk, and set off for the wards to catch up on how David was doing.

* * *

"They tell me your white cell count has eventually started to climb at last," I said, entering the inner sanctum of his isolation suite.

"Yes, at long last," he repeated." James told me this morning that I'll be out of here by the weekend if this trend continues." He looked decidedly pleased with himself, as he relayed this fact.

"Plenty of time for more expensive complications," I mentioned.

"Don't even suggest it," he winced at the thought of it.

"Here," I said, handing him a slip of paper as I took a seat beside the bed.

"What's this," he asked, unfolding the paper and staring at the figures set out on it.

"That," I began, "is what this Chief Executive will have cost the tax-payer by the time he leaves the ward at the weekend, hopefully in complete remission from his disease."

"£19,360!" he exclaimed, placing his hand on his brow and glancing up at the ceiling, before looking back at the row of itemised figures in front of him.

"Give or take an oz," I replied. "Taking into account the hotel breakdown costs per day, and the cost of all the blood products. Not to mention the prohibitively expensive growth factor injections, the antibiotics, and that long course of the anti-fungal drug *Ambisome.* Then of course there's the chemotherapy drugs themselves." I think I had made my point.

"I always knew that haematologists were an expensive bunch. Now I can see why," he said, laying the paper on the bed and looking across at me. "I don't suppose there's any particular point you're trying to make here is there?" he asked, fully knowing the answer.

"Me? No, not particularly," I lied, unconvincingly. "It's only that I was thinking, now you're obviously feeling a bit better, you'd be interested in the facts and figures behind the sorts of things we get up to here. After all, what price can one possibly put on fitness and health, let alone actual life, in this modern day and age?

"And to think, I have two other patients with acute leukaemia going through the same treatment at this very moment." I was enjoying this. "I mean, your remission has only cost the country the equivalent of a year's worth of lease-lend cars for a few national health executives, or probably the cost of sending a couple of administrators to New York on a course on *Clinical Governance!* And, whilst we're on the subject, why it's got to be New York I've never understood!"

"I think the point has been taken Andrew." David had heard this sort of tirade from me before, and was fully aware that if he failed to stop me at this point he was in for the full ten minute session.

"Well, good to see you looking so much better David. I mean that. Sorry about the lecture, but I do think it hasn't done you any harm to have witnessed why it costs what it does to achieve our results. I promise not to mention the subject again," I said, raising my outstretched palm in his direction.

"I wish I could believe that, Andrew," he responded, shrugging his shoulders, as if to say *'I've heard it all a thousand times before.'* "I think when you stop mentioning it, they'll probably be seeking a special place for you on the funny farm."

"Why, I do believe you're becoming as cynical as me David," I said, getting up to leave while I was still winning. "Remember, it's never too late to consider a career change. We can always do with more haematologists in our crusade for *might and right.*"

"I may have been very sick but, as far as I'm aware, it hasn't got to my brain yet!"

CHAPTER TWENTY SEVEN

My aunt died of influenza: so they said. But it's my belief they done the old woman in
– George Bernard Shaw

"Andrew?"

"Yes. Who's that?"

"It's me, Lawrence."

By now it was early evening, and I was back at my desk working on some reports. After seeing David I had looked in on Victoria and spent some time chatting away, generally avoiding the work that was piling up on my desk. She was now well and truly on the mend and I had eventually dragged myself away to face the music down in the department.

"Lawrence. I didn't recognise your voice for a moment," I said, reaching for the notepad and clearing a space in front of me. "What have you managed to find out?" I asked.

"Well, I've got the notes, but I'm not sure I'm going to be of much help," he began. "In fact I can't see that the relatives have much of a case for compensation, if the truth be known."

"But, is it?" I asked.

"What?"

"The *'truth.'* Is it really known? These cases always leave an element of doubt. By the very nature of the suddenness of everything it's difficult to be really confident something didn't go wrong," I said.

"Well, anyway, she was brought in early morning in status epilepticus. She was fitting non stop and was obviously very ill and in extreme danger for a while. But she soon responded to the i/v valium and settled quite quickly. Once she was safely out of danger she was moved to the ward for observation.

Throughout the rest of the day she was constantly monitored; the usual parameters, pulse, temperature, respiration, i/v drips, the lot. It's all in the notes and seems straight forward enough to me. Everything that was done has been properly documented, dated, timed and duly signed."

"But, how did she die?" I asked.

"It was after midnight. One of the night staff found her. She was lying stretched across the bed deeply unconscious, drips still attached. By the time the resuscitation team arrived she was gone. They tried for thirty minutes to revive her, but it was obviously too late. It was concluded that, despite the medication, she had suffered another bout of *'status'* and succumbed.

"Obviously, the relatives were not satisfied with this explanation, and have taken legal action. My bet is that the Authority will eventually settle out of court for the sake of peace even though, as I've said, they would probably come out of it O.K. if they stuck in there and stood their ground. But they can't stand the adverse publicity these cases can generate and they usually calculate it's a lot easier to settle out of court. Is there anything else you want to know?"

"No. Thanks for your trouble, Lawrence. You've been a big help." He hadn't, but I didn't want to hurt his feelings as he'd gone to a lot trouble on my behalf.

"Well, if there's anything else you want don't hesitate to give me a ring. I gave you my home number didn't I?"

"Yes. Thanks once again. I appreciate your help." And with that I replaced the receiver.

I sat back in my chair and stared at the photograph of my children. I had got nowhere. When I had set out that morning I was sure I would uncover something. Perhaps some little fact that linked these cases together. But there was nothing. Not a single clue. They were suffering from different conditions, none of which were related in any way. They had occurred at different times, and had come in under different physicians. Why, Lynn Harris had even come in under the surgeons.

There simply was no common denominator, as far as I could make out. At least, nothing obvious that connected these cases. Initially, it had seemed to me that there must be some connection.

But now it was all too plain to see that there simply wasn't any such link.

For some reason I'd got this crazy notion in my head that all these sudden deaths were related in some way, but I had got it all wrong. There plainly was no connection and I had been wasting my time all along.

I turned to the notes, picked them up and placed them on the table beside the desk, ready to be returned the next day. As I was doing this James put his head round the door and asked if I fancied a quick drink before he set off for home. He didn't need to enquire twice.

"That's the best thing I've heard all day," I said, grabbing my jacket from the back of the chair and heading for the door.

* * *

I have always found music a must when I need to relax. But, for the most important acts of relaxation, like those occasions when I need to clear my head of a heavy week at the hospital, it simply *has* to be Beethoven.

Such was the case on this particular evening, after returning home from my drink with James. I had not been that hungry, and had made do with soup and a sandwich for my dinner. Fate had decided to throw temptation my way in the shape of my monthly delivery from *Wine Without Tears.* On arriving home I had found the case, containing twelve assorted bottles of an Australian selection, sitting on the front door step.

So there I was, sprawled out on the sofa, staring peacefully at the ceiling as I listened to a particularly good recording of Vladimir Ashkenazy playing Beethoven's fifth piano concerto. In my right hand I carefully balanced on my chest a glass of *Yarruga Field, Special Reserve, 1998,* from New South Wales. It was so good that I was glad I'd had the foresight to bring the bottle and place it on the coffee table beside me, as I was feeling very relaxed by now and would definitely need another glass later.

This was oblivion, and it only needed Victoria to complete the picture. At least, with luck, it would only be a couple of days, and then she would be back home. Funny how in such a short time it had become as if it didn't seem like home without her presence. How things had changed. There was no doubt about it, I was completely smitten, and what's more I didn't mind admitting it.

The music weaved its brilliant message and flowed gently, as my mind wandered slowly over the events of the previous few days. This was indeed an unusual piano concerto, in that the slow, second movement, or *adagio un poco mosso,* merges directly with the faster third movement, *rondo allegro,* in one of the most beautiful examples of a perfect union in music that I have ever experienced.

I was in my seventh heaven waiting for Victoria. And it wouldn't be long. Not long at all, until she was eventually discharged from that surgical ward and back home with me. Only a few days and she would be out, and well away from the world of surgery and surgical complications.

I lay back and let the music do its work. My mind wandered to and fro, enjoying the vision of Victoria at last by my side. Then the vision of her in that surgical bed once again, being so brave. Much braver than I ever could be. Surgery had never appealed to me, not even as a student. I don't know why, but to me it held no fascination whatsoever.

I poured myself another glass and settled back once more, staring at the ceiling. *Surgery.* Huh!

Surgery! That's it. SURGERY! I sat up with a start, spilling half a glass of wine over the sofa in the process. That was it. *Surgery!* All the patients had had medical problems and were admitted under physicians. But Lynn Harris had come in for an operation under the surgeons. She may have gone into a bed on our ward, but officially she was under the surgeons, and not the medical side.

I leapt from the sofa, spilling the rest of the wine in the process, and rushed from the room. In an instant I had my shoes on and my keys in my hand, as I fled the house in a mad rush to get to the hospital.

The roads were thankfully empty, as I hurled the car round the country bends at speeds I didn't know the car was capable of achieving. I eventually screeched to a halt by the front entrance, in what turned out to be half the time I usually take getting to the hospital.

Within a couple of minutes I was in my office and seated at my desk. In front of me I had Lynn Harris' notes, as I frantically searched for the last entries to be made before her death. At last I found the page and scanned my way down the entries. Everything was as I had expected.

Then I picked up the other sets of notes and did the same. When I had finished I was even more certain I was right. But I had to be sure that my theory fitted. I picked up the phone and asked for the number of Lawrence Peters' hospital. Their switchboard was very helpful and agreed to contact him at home and get him to phone me.

He was on the line within five minutes. I apologised for the lateness of the call and explained my problem. When I had finished he agreed to help me and promised to get back to me within twenty minutes.

Whilst I was waiting I got back to the switchboard. The telephonist informed me that Fiona Green, the night sister who had been on duty the night Lynn had died, was currently doing nights again. I bleeped her and asked if she could spare me a few minutes. She was in my room within a quarter of an hour.

"Thank you for coming, Fiona. I know you're busy, so I won't keep you long." I said, gesturing for her to take a seat.

"That's alright, Dr Ryan. How can I help?"

"I'm sure you will remember that night when Mrs Harris died," I began.

"Of course. Who could forget it. Tragic case. Those cases live with you for ever."

"Well," I continued. "As far as I can remember she was a surgical case under Mr Bryant wasn't she?"

"Yes, that's right. I remember my handover session that evening when I came on duty. Because it was noted that, although she was on a medical ward, she was still under the surgeons. The staff nurse in charge of the handover made a particular point of mentioning it," she said, looking back at me as if to say *'so what's the problem?'*

"Exactly Fiona. That's my point. But late in the evening Mrs Harris' drip tissued, and needed to be re-sited," I said, fixing her gaze.

"So," she said.

"So why, if she was a surgical patient, did you call a *medical* registrar to come to re-site it?" I stared at her, waiting for the reply.

"Because Paul had met me earlier on Manvers ward, and we were talking by the sister's desk about the patients. I had mentioned we had a surgical patient on the ward who had been referred by you for a biopsy, and whose drip had been playing up. He said that, since he was on the ward anyway, he didn't mind having a look and went to check it over. After that he said he didn't mind me calling him if she had any more problems, as he was likely to be up most of the night anyway."

"So, he attended to Mrs Harris *before* he came back later in the evening to re-site the drip?" I asked, my brain buzzing with thoughts as I looked at Fiona.

"Yes. He was really very helpful, and saved me calling the on-call surgical house officer who I knew had already gone to bed," she answered.

"Thank you Fiona, you've been very helpful," I said, getting up to escort her to the door.

"Is there a problem then, Dr Ryan," she asked me, looking a little worried.

"No Fiona. It's only that it's all been playing on my mind a lot lately. Since I was in anyway, and I knew you were on duty, I thought I'd clear a few things up. That's all. Thanks very much for your time." I opened the door for her and smiled as she went out.

As I closed the door the phone rang. I hurtled across the room and snatched up the receiver. It was Lawrence.

"That you, Andrew?"

"Yes Lawrence. You were quick," I said, taking my seat at the desk once more.

"Yes, well. It doesn't take long to get in at this time." I detected a note of sarcasm in his voice.

"It's really good of you to do this," I said, feeling the complete creep.

"Anyway, I've got the notes in front of me," he said. "What do you want me to tell you?"

"Can you look at the last entry before she died, and tell me the name of the doctor who attended her?" I asked.

"No problem," he answered, as I heard him place the receiver on the desk. Then there was the sound of pages being flipped over. It seemed to go on for an age. At last everything went silent. After what felt like an hour there was the noise of the receiver being scraped across the surface of the desk.

"Here, I have it," he said triumphantly. "She was seen about a quarter of an hour before the night sister found her collapsed. Apparently her drip had tissued, and the registrar was called to re-site it. It seems he was called earlier in the evening as well, for a similar problem with the drip not working too well."

"Lawrence, can you tell me who that registrar was," I asked, holding my breath and closing my eyes.

"Yes. Here it is. The writing's not all that easy to read, but it looks like Dr...Gibson. Yes, that's it. Dr Paul Gibson. Is that all you want?" he asked.

"Yes Lawrence. That's terrific. You've been a great help. I can't thank you enough, especially for agreeing to come out at this hour. I'll be in touch very soon and fill you in on what's happening," I promised, as I slammed the phone down.

Without giving the receiver time to settle in the cradle I snatched it back up again and dialled the switchboard.

"Yes?" the gruff voice at the other end enquired.

"This is Dr Ryan here. Can you tell me when Dr Paul Gibson is next on night duty?" I asked.

There was a brief pause, during which I could hear the tapping of a computer keyboard in the background. "Oh! Dr Ryan. You're in luck. He's on call tonight. Would you like me to bleep him for you?"

"No. Err, no thank you," I replied, slowly replacing the receiver.

I sat there, not really knowing what to do next. I suddenly felt helpless without Victoria to talk to, and to confide in regarding what I'd only recently learnt. Victoria, with the cool head, would know exactly what to do next in this situation. Oh, how I needed Victoria at this difficult time. Suddenly she had become a vital part of my strength. I found it impossible to concentrate on the problem I had just unearthed. I so needed to speak to Victoria, but she was inaccessible. Stuck on a ward as a patient, when I needed her so much. A surgical patient getting over a severe infection, with drips stuck in her arm...........*a surgical patient...........with drips in her arm!*

VICTORIA! VICTORIA!

My brain raced as I began to panic like I'd never panicked before. My legs turned to jelly, as my mind fought with the idea that had completely taken it over and refused to let go. I had to get to her. At all costs, I had to get to her.

I rushed for the door, tripping over the notes stacked on the floor as I did so. Frantically I got to my feet and threw myself out of the door in the direction of the lift, sheer panic driving me forward.

CHAPTER TWENTY EIGHT

Death has got something to be said for it:
There's no need to get out of bed for it;
Wherever you may be,
They bring it to you, free.
– Kingsley Amis

I stood in front of the lifts staring at the indicator lights, with my finger stabbing furiously at the call button. *Why is it that the lifts are always stuck at the top when you're in a hurry?* I couldn't wait. With a giant leap I made the third stair and hurtled upwards, two at a time.

On the first floor I collided with a nurse carrying a tray of surgical instruments, smashing her heavily against the wall as I continued on upwards. The noise was deafening and I could hear her screaming loudly as I caught the top of a step near the second floor level and sprawled flat on my face, winding myself badly in the process. I picked myself up and threw myself at the stairs once again, in a monstrous effort to get to the fourth floor.

I eventually reached the ward and nearly collapsed at the nurses' station, the duty staff nurse staring in bewilderment at me. At first she thought I was a drunk who had found his way up from the Casualty Department. However, she eventually recognised me, once I had pulled myself together and tucked my shirt in.

Moving from beside the drug trolley, and positioning herself in front of me she asked, "Dr Ryan. What are you doing here so late?"

"I've come to see Miss Hall. I'm worried about her." I answered, trying very hard to compose myself, my heart pounding away at a rapid rate.

"Oh! You shouldn't have bothered. She's fine, really. There was a small problem with her drip earlier on that was all. But Dr Gibson kindly came up and adjusted it."

"A problem with the drip," I repeated, a feeling of absolute doom descending upon me, as I clung on to the side of the desk for support.

"Yes. It went alright after that for a while, but it eventually tissued about half an hour ago," she said, turning back to the trolley and busying herself with a drug chart.

"Do you want me to re-site it?" I asked, willing her to reply, *'Yes.'*

"Oh! That wont be necessary, Dr Ryan," she replied, without looking up from the chart. "Dr Gibson came up as soon as I told him and he's doing it right now."

I stood frozen to the spot. Part of me hadn't heard what she had said. It had been blocked out because I really couldn't believe this was happening. The whole scenario had to be one colossal bad dream. A nightmare. The sort one experiences perhaps once in a lifetime.

Yes, that was it. The whole thing was a nightmare; an extremely bad and frightening dream. Soon I'd wake up, and there would be Victoria, lying there beside me. Sleeping peacefully, her head resting lightly on the pillow, her lips poised ready for my kiss. That was it, just a very bad dream. These things don't happen to people like us in real life. Soon I'd wake up and everything would be back to normal.

"Are you all right, Dr Ryan?" The staff nurse was staring at me with a look of genuine concern on her face, as she slowly patted my hand.

"Call security," I shouted as I suddenly leapt into action, lunging at the door to Victoria's room.

The door smashed against the wall with such force that it sent a shower of paint and plaster to the floor. Paul Gibson was standing by the side of the bed, a 30ml syringe in his right hand. It was filled with a colourless fluid, and in front of him, lying on the edge of the bed was a metal tray containing swabs, needles and a number of open, empty glass vials. His hand was outstretched with the syringe poised, about to insert the needle into the rubber bung of Victoria's intravenous drip.

His eyes had a cold, mad glaze to them as he looked across at me, startled by my sudden entrance. Victoria was lying there, talking softly to Paul as I entered, but the sudden noise had caused her to start, knocking the tray off the bed and sending it crashing to the floor. She began to call my name, but got no further than, "And...", when I launched myself across the bed with all the force my weary body could muster.

Momentarily paralysed by the commotion, Paul regained his composure, and took a quick step backwards thrusting the syringe out in front of him in my direction. The needle penetrated the skin of my right arm and entered my biceps muscle, finally coming to rest against the humerus bone. I continued forward, screaming with pain, as Victoria fell to the right and slipped to the floor convulsed in hysterics.

By now Paul and I were locked together, rolling about the floor, frantically trying to get a grip on each other. He was threshing about in a complete frenzy, acting like a cornered wild animal fighting for his very survival.

Eventually he ended up on top of me, pinning me to the floor as he wildly looked about for something to help him in his struggle. All the time Victoria lay there on the floor, screaming at the top of her voice, completely dazed by the events unfolding before her.

At last Paul managed to grab hold of the metal tray in his left hand, whilst I struggled in vain to escape his hold on me. The last thing I remember was the cold thud of steel on my forehead as I lashed out wildly at his throat. I sank back half conscious, with the sound of Victoria whimpering in the background. The back of my head hit the floor with a crunch and, with a feeling of immense hopelessness, the world slowly caved in on me.

* * *

"Andrew."

"Um!"

"Andrew!"

There were a million thoughts racing through my scrambled brain, not one of them pertinent to reality. Somewhere there was a sensation of pain, but I couldn't be sure in which particular area.

"Andrew!"

I slowly opened one eye and caught a very blurred vision of Victoria in her dressing gown, sitting beside the bed. Her hands were clasped over mine and her head was bent forward in my direction.

"Ah! Back in the land of the living are we?" She smiled, as she leaned forward and gave me a gentle peck on the cheek.

"I know it's a well worn cliché, but *where the hell am I*?" I asked, by now placing the pain firmly at the back of my skull on the right side.

"You're in Manvers ward. Where else for a haematologist! You were transferred here last night," she answered, giving my hand a squeeze.

"Transferred?"

"Yes, you spent the first twelve hours on the High Dependency Unit."

"On HDU," I repeated, like a dutiful parrot.

"Yes. You were badly concussed when you took the full force of the metal tray on that thick skull of yours. And the subsequent impact of the back of your head on the floor didn't exactly help matters. You've been out for over thirty six hours now, catching up on your sleep. And the hospital has never been so peaceful!

"The scans didn't show any sign of internal bleeding, but you were so deeply unconscious they had to put you on the HDU for close observation at first. Then your signs improved, so they moved you here, to David's old room."

"David's room. I thought it looked familiar. But where's he?" I asked, my head pounding.

"A lot's happened while you've been *away* Andrew," she said. "To start with Boris Baldwin has been suspended sick. Apparently he completely flipped with paranoid delusions or something. The new Medical Director was involved, and invoked the *Three Wise Men.* The result is that he's been suspended on full pay pending a psychiatric report."

"He's malignant, not psychiatric," I interrupted.

"Feeling a little better already, I see!"

"But where's David?" I repeated.

"He was feeling fine and, as you know, his blood was improving. Well, once all this blew up he decided to discharge himself, so that he could take over the helm of the ship once again."

"I trust he signed the bloody discharge forms and they stuck them in his notes. All I need now is the administration suing me! That would be the last straw," I said, trying unsuccessfully to turn on my side and, in doing so, producing an acute, stabbing pain in the nether regions. "What the bloody hell's that?" I shouted, placing my hand under the sheet to explore the cause of the discomfort.

"No doubt that's your catheter you've been trying to pull out for the past hour or so," she answered, placing her hand over her mouth and wincing.

"My what?"

"Your catheter, Dr Ryan. Surely you know what that is. You *have* been unconscious for thirty six hours you know. Didn't they teach you about those things in medical school? Think on the bright side, you're going to have to get used to one eventually. After all senility *is* just around the corner in your case!"

"Alright. But now I'm conscious the bloody thing can come out. Where's the nurse?" I bellowed, lightening striking the back of my head yet again.

"Calm down you great coward, I'll get her in a minute," she said, standing to help get me into a more comfortable position.

"Tell me, what happened to Dr Gibson?" I asked.

"As you were hitting the floor unconscious the staff nurse, having heard the commotion, rushed in and surprised him. He immediately dropped everything and fled the room in panic.

The police were alerted immediately and were swiftly on the scene. They arrived in time to spot him fleeing the grounds of the hospital in his MG sports. They eventually apprehended him on the outskirts of town, following a high speed chase, and a dramatic crash involving two other cars."

There was a gentle knock on the door, and I glanced up to see David put his head round, grinning from ear to ear.

"Is this a private party or can anyone join in?" he enquired, pulling up a chair beside Victoria. "How do you like my room?"

"How are you feeling?" I asked, completely ignoring his question.

"Shouldn't it be *me* asking you that question?" he smiled.

"I asked first," I raised my voice a little and immediately felt the pain return.

"I'm fine. Never better in fact. According to James my white blood count's fast approaching normal," he answered, with a look of pride on his face.

"That's good," I said, gently feeling the lump at the back of my skull.

"What's more, he gave me the good news about my younger brother," he continued.

"And?"

"And, his tissue type matches mine sufficiently for a bone marrow transplant. So you may be stuck with me for longer than you thought."

"Better the devil you know!" I whispered, eyeing the cracks on the ceiling. "Now, will someone tell me about Boris?" I asked, looking back at David.

"There's not a lot to tell," he started, brushing some fluff off the front of his trousers. "Pressure of work, presumably. A number of his colleagues had begun to notice a change in him recently. One or two of them had actually started to comment on his strange behaviour and were obviously becoming increasingly worried about his welfare.

"Then, Dr Skinner decided he had to report him to the Medical Director. Apparently, Boris had button-holed him the other day in the pub. He had been trying to drum up support for his crusade against you. It would appear that Boris became quite manic and uncontrollable when he realised that Dr Skinner wasn't having any part of it. It would seem that he eventually broke down in a big way. He was becoming acutely paranoid and Dr Skinner didn't want any part of it. Especially now he's going."

"Who's going?" I asked, by now completely confused and wondering if I was still dreaming.

"Dr Skinner. He's resigned. Decided to take early retirement. Just like that, out of the blue. No one had any idea until he wrote to me this morning. And he's not alone. It seems there's an epidemic of it at the moment, especially in that department. I mean, Dr Knowles has also decided to go early. 'Making way for younger blood', he says. It all seems very strange if you ask me."

"Couldn't happen to a nicer couple," I hissed, under my breath. Then a sly grin crept slowly across my face as I recalled my stop-off at the post box on my way to meet the others at the *Anchor* pub on Saturday.

"I don't suppose it had anything to do with what they got in their post bag the other day, could it? That's it; they retired on account of the *mail* menopause!"

"What are you going on about?" David asked, looking strangely at me.

"Oh! Nothing really, David. It's only something to do with the *numbers racket*. But I don't expect you'd understand," I said, grinning at Victoria, who appeared as bewildered as David.

"Well, I must be going," he said, getting to his feet. He reached into his pocked and produced a piece of paper, which he nonchalantly dropped onto the bed in front of me.

"What's this?" I said, picking it up and beginning to unfold it.

"That is what this haematologist will have cost the tax payer by the time he leaves the ward at the weekend!" he replied, grinning at Victoria.

I glanced down at the sheet. "£921! It's a bloody pittance!" I yelled, bringing the ceiling down on my head.

"Well, you are only a haematologist! I mean, you're not exactly a Chief Executive, are you, now!" And with that he was out of the door before I could give him the benefit of my rhetoric.

"Bloody cheek! After all I've done for him. Some people are never grateful."

"Tell me, Andrew," Victoria asked, taking hold of my hand once again, "Whatever made you suspect Dr Gibson in the first place?"

"It was staring me in the face, but I didn't see it for a long time. Something was decidedly not right but, try as I did, I couldn't put my finger on what exactly it was it.

"Then it struck me. When Lynn Harris died she was a surgical patient in the hospital. But it was a *medical* registrar who last saw her alive, for a routine procedure; re-siting her drip. Well, she *was* on a medical ward, so it could easily be accepted that the medical registrar might help the night staff out in this case, since they were on the ward anyway.

"Then, when I was speaking to a haemophiliac patient who was in the ward at the same time, he described to me how the doctor concerned had got very flustered and angry when he had crushed a glass vial in his hand and cut himself. *That* was it. Why did he need anything in a glass vial? He was merely re-siting a needle in a vein and connecting back the drip. In other words, the 500ml bag of saline. What had he taken from the vial and injected into the patient's vein so soon before she died?" I looked at Victoria.

"What could it have been?" she asked.

"My guess is probably something like potassium chloride." I answered.

"What would that do?" She looked at me quizzically.

"In sufficient quantities it causes irreversible cardiac arrest. That's what they use in America for judicial executions by lethal injection. And in this case it wouldn't leave any obvious trace as to what the cause of death had been. It would all look like a tragic case of unexplained sudden death, a not unknown occurrence in every hospital from time to time. Although I did think three such cases in a short space of time was a bit suspicious. It took me a while to find the link, " I said, scratching the back of my head carefully.

I continued, "Then, when I went back to the notes of the other two unfortunate women, I saw that on both occasions it had been Paul Gibson who had attended them just before they died, and always late in the evening. What is more, he had seen them an hour or two before his last visit to adjust their drips, which had been playing up. Or, he may well have just made sure he was in the patient's vicinity so he could have "noticed" a problem with their drip. Whatever, it was easy enough to effect and in each case seems to have been accepted by the other staff as a "normal" procedure.

"I'm sure now that, on the first visit, what he actually did was to make certain that the drips would finally have tissued within a few of hours. That way he would be called back to re-site them, at a time when everything was a lot quieter on the ward. For this to work he would have needed to sedate the patient first with an i/v shot then, because high doses of potassium would cause uncontrollable muscle spasm, he would need to infuse a muscle block. Just a few minutes then the lethal dose of potassium chloride, and he walks quietly away, leaving the patient 'sleeping comfortably', and no one any the wiser."

"But wouldn't the police have been suspicious? These sudden deaths so close together and the same doctor attending them," Victoria asked.

"Why? Who was going to involve the police at this stage? No one's suspicion had been aroused. The patients were under different consultants, on different wards, and at different times. You know what it can be like in a busy hospital like this. I can go many weeks without bumping into some of my colleagues.

"Thank God! I know as much about their problems as I do of nuclear physics. The only common denominator was Paul Gibson, and he wasn't going to do anything to throw suspicion on himself. He continued in his usual way. A most plausible, bright, seemingly conscientious, and very helpful doctor. It had been niggling away at me for some time, but I just couldn't see it. Then eventually it struck me."

"Left it to the last moment though, didn't you?" Victoria said, giving me another much-deserved kiss on the cheek.

"Well, I had to finish my wine, didn't I," I retaliated. Then, taking stock of the events of the past few weeks I continued, "I wonder what possessed Paul Gibson to commit those horrible murders. Obviously a psychopath, but what triggers them in the first place? I suppose we'll never know." I leaned back contemplating the wall in front of me.

"According to the police, he started spilling the beans as soon as he was arrested. It seems that, once he was nicked with no way out, he was only too pleased to admit to the crimes. Isn't that true of all psychopaths, eventually? I was once told that it was part of their makeup. A driven need to be known eventually to have been the one responsible for these *clever* crimes."

Victoria was holding on to my hands tightly, and staring into my eyes as she continued, "According to his girlfriend, a staff nurse on one of the surgical wards, he had once when fairly drunk poured his heart out to her regarding his upbringing.

"Apparently, Paul's father left home when he was only one, and following this he had been badly abused by his mother for some years. Eventually he had been abandoned and spent two years in an orphanage before being adopted. I suppose the seeds could very well have been planted in those early years."

"My, quite the psychiatrist ain't you?" I prodded.

"Anyone who sees a psychiatrist should have his head examined!" she countered.

"Touché! A nice little quote from Sam Goldwyn. You've now, at long last, qualified to join the team!"

* * *

It was the loud cough, followed by an equally loud wheeze outside the door that gave it away.

"Come in, Johnny," I shouted, immediately wishing I hadn't, as the back of my head caved in with yet another crescendo of pain.

"How did you know it was me?" he asked, as he almost fell into the room, his bow tie on the slant. "Finished playing at boy scouts now, have we?" He looked at me with his fierce expression, a reproving finger pointed straight at my bruised torso.

"You've been at those cigars again you naughty boy. Just you wait till I tell Jean Drummond. She'll make your life hell." I wagged my finger at him, as if shaping up for a fencing bout.

"Leave it off Andrew. I've come to see how you are and all you can do is to attack me. That's the thanks I get," he said, flicking an envelope onto the bed.

"What's that?" I asked, picking it up and scrutinising the handwriting.

"Why don't you open it and see?" he wheezed.

It had not been sealed and I slowly pulled the flap back and removed the contents. There was a brief letter explaining that the cheque was for *The Eastwich Stem Cell Transplant Fund*, and that the donor wished to remain anonymous as far as any publicity was concerned. I glanced at the cheque and read the signature, *Mavis Heggerty*. I then looked across at the amount.

"One hundred thousand pounds!" I shouted, at the top of my voice, frightening Victoria who nearly fell out of her chair. "Wherever did she get that sort of money? She didn't exactly give me the impression she was rich when I saw her."

"Apparently she inherited a considerable sum from a distant relative recently and was most embarrassed by the whole thing. She told me that her needs have never been that great and she's never been a one for lots of luxuries.

"She had made sure that she will be comfortable for the rest of her life and decided to donate the rest to charity. She chose your fund as one of the causes she intends to support as a mark of her immense gratitude for the way you had treated her. She obviously got you on one of your rare, good days!"

"Blimey!" I exclaimed. "But I only saw her a couple of times."

"Well, it was obviously enough to impress her that your cause was worthy of her support. Besides, if she had seen any more of you she would probably have got to know what you're really like and your fund wouldn't have stood a chance then!"

"Blimey!" I repeated. "We're on the way. What a start." I gave Victoria's hand a big squeeze as I nearly burst into tears with emotion.

Johnny took one look at us and started to fidget. "I don't think I could bear to watch you get emotional. It would ruin my image of you for ever."

He got slowly to his feet, coughed loudly and added, "If you two love birds will excuse me I feel the need for a cigar coming on." He opened the door and, looking back over his shoulder, uttered, "And by the way, Andrew, just in case you were thinking of trying it, as a waterworks specialist, I can definitely advise you that it is not possible with that tube still in your willy!" The door slammed behind him and he was gone.

"What a dirty old consultant he is," I exclaimed, staring blankly at the cheque in front of me.

Victoria got up from the chair and seated herself on the edge of the bed, placing her arm round my shoulder as she peered at the cheque. "Well, I think he's gorgeous," she said, craning her neck and giving the lobe of my ear an affectionate nibble. Then she placed her lips against the ear and gently whispered, "I don't suppose......"

"Very funny!" I giggled. "You've been waiting for that, haven't you?"

"What's up, can't the clever consultant accept a dose of his own medicine?" She laughed, slowly sitting back as she nonchalantly dropped yet another envelope on the bed.

"What is this, a rubbish tip or something?" I blurted out, fishing up the envelope and slitting it open. I removed the contents and surveyed them as I asked, "What's all this about then?"

"That, my darling, is a couple of tickets for Paris. Flying out next Saturday morning. Plus the reservations for a week at the George V Hotel. Courtesy of *moi*. As my way of saying a big, 'thank you' for saving my life. In more ways than one." She leant forward and gave me a huge kiss. The sort that always gets me interested. As the pain started to return I pulled back.

"Victoria, it's getting very painful!" I protested, nodding in the direction of my nether regions.

"That's the way I like it. I want you to remember me till you see me again tomorrow. And what better way than through pain? And, in your case, in what better area than you know where?" she grinned, as she got up to leave.

"Well, if you're not playing I'm going." She brushed the hair from her face in her most seductive manner, causing me considerable pain in the process!

On reaching the door she turned to blow me a kiss.

"On your way out, send that bloody nurse in to take this frigging catheter out, will you? There's a good drug rep!"

"You know, I've changed my mind. I think it would be more appropriate if I took you to Frinton to recuperate rather than Paris."

"What the hell are you talking about?"

"Well, I would have thought that you of all people would have been familiar with that famous saying."

"What bloody saying? Whatever are you going on about?" I asked, laying my defences wide open

"Oh, you know! The one about travelling, *Harwich for the continent: Frinton for the incontinent!*"

"Get out!"

"Yes, oh wise and wonderful one............ Cheerio for now"

THE END

Michael Mills studied medicine at St Mary's Hospital Medical School, London in the 1960's. Following qualification he spent 5 years as a Medical Officer in the RAF including 2 years in Hong Kong. On leaving the service he specialized in haematology, ultimately being appointed a Consultant in a busy General Hospital close to London where he was responsible for establishing a successful clinical haematology division with particular interest in the treatment of haematological malignancies (eg leukemia). He has now retired and is pursuing his interests in writing, playing jazz and golf.

www.ingramcontent.com/pod-product-compliance
Ingram Content Group UK Ltd.
Pitfield, Milton Keynes, MK11 3LW, UK
UKHW020132250726
13967UKWH00002B/609